Also by Sylvia Halliday

Summer Darkness, Winter Light
Gold as the Morning Sun
The Ring
Dreams So Fleeting

The French Maiden Series
Marielle
Lysette
Delphine

Diversion Books
A Division of Diversion Publishing Corp.
443 Park Avenue South, Suite 1008
New York, New York 10016
www.DiversionBooks.com

For more information, email info@diversionbooks.com

First Diversion Books edition November 2015.
Print ISBN: 978-1-62681-876-7
eBook ISBN: 978-1-62681-875-0

MY LADY GLORIANA

Sylvia HALLIDAY

DIVERSIONBOOKS

Chapter One

London—1725

"Gads! This pantomime is tedious. And it's stifling in here." John Havilland, Duke of Thorneleigh, scowled at the players on the stage. He brushed impatiently at the sleeve of his brocaded coat and turned to his companion. "Let's go get a drink, Felix. Someplace common and vulgar, so I can take off this damn periwig."

Lord Felix DeWitt inhaled a pinch of snuff, sneezed delicately, and shook his head. "There's no pleasing you these days, friend Thorne. What's happened to you?"

Thorne shrugged, unwilling to probe the festering sore inside of him that was growing more difficult to ignore. "God knows. I find life boring, that's all. The same old pleasures, the artificial women, the carousing that produces nothing but a headache the next morning. Even my gambling gives me no joy. I always win."

DeWitt's laughter held the edge of envy. "Yes, damn you. You've got a bloody fortune, even without your winnings, while I just scrape by."

"Faugh! You're comfortably fixed. You're just tight-fisted. I pity the woman who marries you, forced to come begging for every petticoat and ribbon."

Just then, the actor on the stage turned his back, bent over, lifted the skirts of his coat and pretended to pass wind. The audience roared.

Thorne felt his stomach lurch with disgust. How had he come to this—a rakehell existence, a life without meaning or direction? Shallow friends, empty days and nights, a mad pursuit of pleasure that left him increasingly dissatisfied. But what else was there for a man of his station and social class? He couldn't very well disgrace the family honor by going off to be a ditch-digger! Besides, he'd never worked a day in his privileged life; he wouldn't even know how to begin. "Damn it, let's go," he muttered.

DeWitt grinned and tapped the side of his nose. "I have the perfect cure for your boredom. A gambling spectacle so exciting that even you will be stirred. And perhaps my bad luck with you will change tonight, and I'll clean out your purse, damn my liver!" He gave a tug to Thorne's coat. "Follow me."

He led Thorne out of the main theatre at Lincoln's Inn Field and into a long corridor studded with closed doors, behind which Thorne could hear the sounds of shouts and raucous laughter. He sighed tiredly. "Not cock fighting again, Felix. Or a round of cards. And the thought of whores dancing naked on a table doesn't stir me one whit tonight."

DeWitt uttered a braying laugh. "Oh, ye of little faith. There's something here that I've never told you about. You won't be disappointed." He led a reluctant Thorne down a staircase and through a rabbit-warren of passages beneath the theatre. Coming to a small door, he opened it with a flourish.

To his surprise, Thorne found himself in a gallery overlooking a round stage below. The gallery seats were already crowded with spectators, idle gentlemen like himself, placing bets on some unknown outcome. Several of the men turned to greet Thorne as a companion in riotous living. He suddenly felt disgusted to be of their number.

As he and DeWitt found chairs, two women appeared on the stage below. They were short and squat and ugly. One of them, clearly the favorite of the crowd, raised her arm in salute to the gallery, and was showered with applause and a handful of copper coins.

The two women were nearly naked, dressed only in small, tight bodices that accented their bosoms, and short linen petticoats that scarcely hid their thighs. Bunches of ribbons decorated their heads, waists and right arms; one woman sported red ribbons, the other blue.

When the cheering had died down, they bowed to the spectators, then launched into boastful tirades, extolling their own courage and vigor. One woman, a blond whose thick brogue identified her as Irish, announced that she should have been a man, so great was her prowess. The other, the favorite, interrupted her to declare that she herself beat her husband regularly to keep up her strength. The spectators roared with laughter and she pranced around the stage, reveling in their approval.

"Christ's blood," muttered Thorne. "If we're to be treated to another performance, with bickering women no less, I'd rather watch the pantomime. At least the actors are silent."

DeWitt held up an admonishing finger. "Only wait a moment."

Several servants appeared on the stage, bearing short swords, some three inches wide and three feet in length, which they handed to the women.

"My God!" exclaimed Thorne. "Do they mean to fight with those weapons? And are they as sharp as they look?"

DeWitt laughed. "Fight? Of course. They don't call those creatures 'gladiators' for nothing! And only the last six inches of the blades are honed. As sharp as a razor." He pointed to the Irish woman. "Keep your eye on Dirty Meg, there. She's not favored to win, but I've seen her last two bouts. She has heart and spirit enough to endure."

Thorne eyed the other woman. Her greasy black hair was piled into a knot on top of her head. She seemed small next to her robust Irish opponent, but there was a fiery agility in the way she danced around the stage, brandishing her sword. "I'd put my money on that one."

"Cheapside Grace? Fair enough. Five hundred pounds?"

"Done."

"I knew I could persuade you. I've never known you to pass up a wager."

At a signal from a man bearing a large staff, the two women faced each other, grasping their swords in both hands, and began to circle warily. Their faces were twisted into fierce scowls. To DeWitt's delight, Dirty Meg suddenly lunged and struck the first blow with the flat of her heavy blade, catching Grace on the side of her ribs. Grace staggered back, gasping for breath. Seeing the advantage, Meg pummeled her with a series of savage blows, which drove the other woman to her knees. Grace's bare arms and legs were covered with reddening welts.

Thorne turned his head aside. He thought he had seen all the depravity that London had to offer, but the sight before him sickened him. "I'm leaving, Felix," he growled.

Oblivious to Thorne's mood, Felix cackled. "Afraid to lose your wager, and so soon? I didn't think you'd turn tail and run as soon as a bet was going against you." He indicated the two women. "Don't leave. Your champion seems to have rallied."

Never one to dodge a bet, or even appear to, Thorne reluctantly turned his gaze back to the gladiators. Grace had struggled to her feet and was now beating back Meg, attacking the Irishwoman with vigor. They fought for interminable minutes, bashing one another with flat-bladed strokes, until the sweat poured from their bodies and their flesh was livid.

With a sudden shout of triumph, Grace leaped forward and slashed at Meg with the point of her sword. Blood gushed from a great cut on Meg's forehead and she gasped and grimaced in pain. At once, the man with the staff separated the two women. The spectators cheered or hissed, according to their preferences.

DeWitt swore in disappointment and tossed a sack of jangling coins into Thorne's lap.

While several handlers appeared with needle and thread to stitch up Meg's gaping wound, and handed her a small bottle of gin to fortify her, Grace enjoyed her triumph. She scooped up the shillings and half-crowns that rained down on the stage and blew a kiss to a particularly noisy admirer.

DeWitt's face had turned red with anger. He leaped to his feet and shook his fist at Dirty Meg. "Stupid Irish slut!"

SYLVIA HALLIDAY

he screamed. "You can't fight worth a damn!"

Dirty Meg jerked her head upward to the gallery, catching Thorne's gaze. Her eyes—beneath her bloodied forehead—were large and luminous, and filled with all the pain and naked anguish of her hard life.

"Sweet Jesus," muttered Thorne, ashamed to be a witness to her degradation. He clenched DeWitt's purse in his fist, tossed it to the stage at Meg's feet and dashed for the door.

"Don't go!" cried DeWitt. "They'll fight again, as soon as Meg is patched up. We'll make another wager."

But Thorne was already out the door, racing through the twisting corridors until he had found the sanctuary of the open street. He leaned against the wall of the theater, his heart pounding, and gulped in great breaths of clean night air. He needed time to think, time to wonder what would become of his soul if he didn't stop his mad descent into Hell.

"Egads! Why did you vanish like that?" DeWitt suddenly appeared beside him.

"I want to get out of London now," he growled. "Spend some time in the country."

DeWitt reached up under his periwig and scratched his head. "But Lady Penelope's assembly ball... the races next week..."

"Now!" exclaimed Thorne hoarsely, aware of the note of desperation in his own voice.

"Well," grumbled DeWitt, "Lord Gilbert *has* invited us to Shrewsbury. I suppose it could be arranged."

"I'll go with you, or without you," said Thorne. "But I must get away."

Or go mad, he thought.

• • •

"I've won again. That's four hundred quid you owe me, Felix." Thorne tossed down his cards and yawned in boredom. "Gads. There's no joy in besting you anymore. You play like a fool."

DeWitt took a deep draught of his wine and grimaced. "This tastes like pig slop. Do they know nothing of storing a keg properly outside of London?" He scowled once more at his cards, then brushed his carefully-manicured hand across the rustic table, sweeping the entire deck to the floor. "Damme, but I hate to lose to you."

"Then don't play with me."

"How else are we to pass the weary time until we get to Shrewsbury? Besides, I can beat every other buck in London but you, Thorne. Strike me, but I think Dame Fortune smiled upon you the very day you were born. Cards, dice, horses. Is there a game where you don't triumph? A wager you don't win?"

Thorne twisted his finely-carved lips into a cynical smirk. He was already beginning to regret that he'd invited DeWitt on this country escape. How could he hope to be free of his current life if he brought a part of it with him? "Lucky at gaming, unlucky at love," he said. "Isn't that what they say?"

Dewitt snorted. "You? The reigning rake of London? How many hearts have you broken this past year?"

Thorne felt oddly flattered by his friend's words, yet sickened at the same time. What kind of a society measured a man by his romantic conquests?

"How many?" Thorne repeated in a drawl, feigning

a satisfaction that he didn't feel. "Let me see." He shook his hands to toss back the delicate ruffles of his cuffs and began to tick off the numbers on his fingers. "There was Lady Barbara in March, I remember. Then Cecily. Then Elizabeth—she of the large breasts. And those two agreeable viscountesses, bored with their husbands. I can't recall their names. That's five." He paused in his count. "Do you want them all? Even the wenches?"

DeWitt shook his head. "No, damn you. Only the gentlewomen you led on, until they were panting for your kisses."

Thorne smoothed the crown of his black hair and gave his friend what he hoped was a smug grin. "A great many of them wanted more than kisses. And I was happy to oblige."

"And then, having ensnared them, you threw them away without remorse. Jilted them while they were still falling at your feet."

Thorne shrugged. Faceless, useless women. "I'm not about to wait for a woman's inevitable duplicity," he growled. "I prefer to strike first. And remorse doesn't enter into it. I pleasure them. They pleasure me. I have nothing with which to reproach myself." He ground his teeth together. "But I'll not be made a fool of by a woman. *Ever.*"

He suppressed a sigh. Poets through the ages had written of true love. Were they all pretending? Or was there a woman out there for him—a creature full of love and trust? Someone who would want him for himself alone, not for his money or title. Someone who wasn't easily seduced by the careless charm he had perfected. A woman who didn't have betrayal knitted into the very fiber of her being.

DeWitt snickered. "Pride goeth before a fall."

"What the devil do you mean by that?"

"Have you forgotten that Lady Penelope refuses to stay jilted?"

Thorne stirred uncomfortably in his chair. Lady Penelope Crawford was a current thorn in his side. "Balderdash!" he said with an air of bravado. "I haven't truly jilted her yet."

"Is that why we're here?" With a mocking wave of his arm, DeWitt indicated the simple bedchamber of the country inn. "By the horn of Satan, I think that's why you fled London like a frightened rabbit. Because of the wager she offered."

Thorne took a moment to thank the gods that DeWitt hadn't guessed his real reason for leaving London. He forced his next words from his mouth in an indignant sputter. "What the devil would you have me do? It was an absurd bet!"

DeWitt roared with laughter. "Damme if I've seen you so rattled in a long time. As for absurd wagers, I've seen you gamble a fortune on the number of beetles to emerge from a pile of dung. You'd bet on a man's capacity for honest labor—if you believed in it."

"But to wager a marriage proposal on the toss of the dice! The lady may be beautiful, but she's mad to think she can trap me."

"And so you ran away here. To a backwater like Shropshire." DeWitt took another sip of his wine and made a face. "And forced me to accompany you and endure these primitive conditions."

Thorne bristled, feeling the challenge to his pride, to his common sense. What the devil *was* he doing here? "Damn it, I didn't run away! I thought it would be pleasant to visit Lord Gilbert in Shrewsbury. The countryside is charming in May."

DeWitt gave a braying laugh. "Make your excuses to someone who believes them. Lord Gilbert is a bore—as we both know. We shall spend a tedious fortnight. And the gardens of Kensington outshine every unkempt field of wildflowers."

"Well," Thorne said sourly, "we'll be back in London soon enough."

"And then what? What do you intend to do about your lady?"

Thorne sighed and closed his eyes. This trip had been a mistake. He couldn't run from himself. A man was what he was. It was far too late for him to change. He opened his eyes and shrugged in resignation. "Perhaps I'll marry her after all. What does it matter? I'm twenty-eight, not getting any younger. I ought to have an heir."

"And love?"

He raised a sardonic eyebrow. "Love doesn't exist." *And if it does*, he thought bitterly, *it only brings a man grief.*

DeWitt stood up, stretched, and scratched his groin. His handsome face—puffy from too much self-indulgence—twisted into a leer. "But the *act* of love is another matter. And I'm becoming horn-mad in this country isolation. Three days without a doxy! Fortunately, the chamber wench made calf-eyes at me when she brought up our supper. I think I persuaded her—for a price." He indicated the door. "I regret to throw you out, my friend, but..." he cupped his groin in a suggestive manner, "...nature calls."

Thorne rose in his turn. "I leave you to your pleasures." He ambled to the door, moved down the dimly-lit passageway, and opened the door to his own bedchamber.

The innkeeper's wife turned in alarm as he entered the

room. "Oh, Your Grace!" She gave a little curtsy.

"What the devil are you doing here, woman?"

Two bright spots of crimson appeared on her rounded cheeks. "I… I were just turnin' down your sheets, Your Grace." She nervously twisted her fleshy fingers together, staring down at the buckles of his shoes.

Thorne noted that she was young and comely, in the manner of a buxom country milkmaid who has dined too often on her own cream and cheeses. An ample bosom and wide, accommodating hips. Time was, his body would have responded to such a lusty wench. But tonight, he couldn't shake off the restlessness. "You may go," he muttered.

Her glance slid to the bed, golden in the glow of a single candle, then returned to contemplate his footwear. "But sir… Your Grace… 'tis a sweet, pleasant night. And you so alone, and all." She raised her head and looked boldly into his eyes, a sly smile curving her lips. "My husband be a fine man, you understand. But there ain't been many fine gentlemen stoppin' at the inn. Leastwise, none as well-favored as Your Grace. You're a hell-fired prince o' the night, or I miss my guess. With them steely gray eyes, what looks right through a body."

She was beginning to disgust him. "And your husband?" he asked coldly.

She had clearly not noticed the icy tone in his voice. She grinned and gave him a suggestive wink, her hands going to the bodice of her gown. "Sleepin' like a babe. He'll not disturb us. What do you want me to do?"

Did country women cuckold their husbands as easily as city ladies did? "Do?" he repeated, his mouth curling in scorn around the word. "I want you to get your bloody carcass out of here and take to your husband's bed. And think long and hard on the loyalty a woman owes her man!"

"B-but, Your Grace," she blubbered. "I only meant to…"

"Begone, woman!" he roared. "Lest I tell your husband you deserve a beating at his hands!"

Though she was clearly shaken, she managed to collect herself. She thrust out her chin and shot him a look of disdain. "I'll wager you ain't no angel, for all your fine talk. Not when your cock be needy!" She tossed her head and sailed from the room, slamming the door behind her.

Thorne sank onto the bed and groaned. She was right, of course. Who was he to lecture her on chastity and fidelity? He peeled off his velvet coat and waistcoat, threw down his silken neck cloth, and tore off the ribbon that tied back his shoulder-length black hair. Maybe a good night's sleep would rid him of his nagging discontent.

He bent to blow out the candle, then paused. He could hear sounds coming from DeWitt's chamber next door—soft giggles and murmurs, obscene grunts. He felt the warmth of the spring night crowding in on him, making it impossible to breathe. By the cross of St. George, he'd suffocate if he had to spend another moment in this room!

He glanced toward the window. The moon was full and bright, casting a brilliant patch of silver across the floor of his bedchamber. It seemed to be calling him, beckoning him into the freedom of the soft night.

Why not? he thought. If he went for a midnight walk, the pathways would be well-illuminated by the moon's glow. No chance to get lost, even in an unfamiliar region. At the very least, he wouldn't be forced to listen to the disgusting noises of DeWitt's conquest.

He left his coat behind—it was uncommonly warm for the beginning of May—tiptoed down the stairs and eased himself out the door of the inn.

The night was more glorious than he would have imagined. The sweet scents of new grass and spring flowers filled the air with their delicate perfume, soothing his troubled soul. He heard the soft rustle of nocturnal creatures, the distant chirp of a bird disturbed in its rest. A soft breeze burrowed in the open neckline of his shirt, reminding him of a childhood that had seemed to be eternal May, pristine and innocent. How long ago!

Impulsively, he rolled up his sleeves, then laughed and pulled off his shirt completely. He half-expected to hear the voice of his long-ago nursemaid, chiding him for common behavior that didn't suit the heir to an ancient dukedom. *Gentlemen* didn't go around half-clothed.

"Rest in peace, Nurse," he murmured, recalling her with tenderness. He'd stripped naked many a time since those days—and for far less innocent reasons.

He tossed his shirt over one shoulder, enjoying the gentle breezes on his bare torso, and looked around for a path. The moon showed him a well-beaten track that meandered toward a stand of trees. He remembered seeing the chambermaid this evening, hauling a bucket of water from that direction. Perhaps there was a pond or stream. He chuckled softly. It was a mild night. Maybe he'd further scandalize Nurse's memory by going for a swim.

As he entered the grove, he picked his way carefully along the path. The moon shone in patches through the young leaves of the overhanging trees, making vision more difficult. He trod softly, reluctant to disturb the sweet tranquility of the night.

He heard the gurgle of a stream close by and saw the sparkle of moonbeams on running water. He knelt, cupped his hand, and drank deeply. Perhaps it was the magic of the night, but he couldn't recall anything he had drunk for weeks—not the finest Madeira or good French wine—that had tasted so delicious.

He rose to his feet. He felt young, adventurous, free— yet strangely sad and melancholy. What had happened to the carefree lad he once had been? What had turned him into this idle dissolute? Surely there was a moment he had missed—a turning point that might have taken him in a different, more satisfying direction. When had it happened? How had it happened?

But of course he knew. Damn womankind. Damn... his mother.

He shook off the black thoughts. No! Tonight, with the earth wrapped in silvery moonlight, was for magic. He felt as though something extraordinary was about to happen. Something that would change his life, lead him to a path more splendid and glittering than the moon-dappled one he now followed.

Then he laughed, low and sardonic. "You must be an addlepated fool, Thorne, old man," he muttered. Perhaps the innkeeper had put fairy dust into the wine to disguise its vile flavor. Surely that must be what was putting such ridiculous thoughts into his head.

Something extraordinary? Nonsense! His life and his future were set: The despairing boredom of marriage with Penelope or some other woman hungry for his title and his money. He sighed. He could see no other alternatives.

He reached a large tree at the edge of the path and paused to lean against its thick trunk. Beyond its spreading branches was a small clearing, an unexpected strip of sand that led to a pond of water. The rest of the pond was ringed with trees and brush sweeping down to its edges, dim and mysterious.

But the moon shone full upon the sand, as bright as day, and its reflection danced on the glassy stillness of the water. He was enchanted anew. Fairy dust or not, he wanted to feel the water embracing his naked body, bask in the radiance of that brilliant moon.

He pulled off his shoes and stockings and stripped off his breeches. The sensual night air caressed his nakedness like a harlot's hand; he felt a quivering and stirring in his groin. He suddenly ached for a woman. But not a clumsy slattern, like the innkeeper's wife. Nor even a perfumed beauty who strolled St. James's Park by day and slept on satin sheets by night. He wanted a goddess, as magical and lovely as this moon-kissed midnight.

He turned to step out into the clearing, then stopped. He heard the soft whinny of a horse, the gentle thud of hoofs upon packed earth. The sounds seemed to be coming from the far end of the clearing. He shrank back against the tree trunk, concealing his naked body, and waited.

The woman galloped onto the sand, magnificent upon her horse—a vision of perfection that took his breath away.

His longed-for goddess.

Chapter Two

She was strong and robust, yet possessed of a slender grace. And tall—perhaps even close to his own not inconsiderable height. She sat her horse with easy familiarity, riding astride as a man would. Long bare legs emerged from a white nightdress that had been pulled up to her thighs. Her flesh gleamed silver under the moon.

She reined in her panting horse and leapt lightly to the ground. Thorne was astonished to see that she had ridden without a saddle, like a wild Gypsy. And surely there was something wild and untamed about her manner, her looks. Her long hair swirled in riotous curls, nearly reaching her waist. And her features, illuminated by the bright moon, were bold and well-defined, with a striking nose and full, sensuous lips. She was splendid—surely the most beautiful creature he had ever seen. He wished he could see the color of her night-dark hair, the tint of eyes that caught the moonlight and sparkled.

Thorne frowned down at his nakedness, then scowled at

the stretch of sand that separated him from her. He wasn't ready to reveal himself, but he longed to see her more closely.

Just then, she turned toward her horse, murmuring softly and rubbing its ear. Thorne glanced up at the tree that sheltered him. One large branch stretched over the clearing, a perfect vantage point from which to watch her. He took the opportunity of her turned back to leap for the branch, then hauled himself up and crawled stealthily along its length. He grimaced as the rough bark scratched his bare skin, then grinned in the gloom. She was worth a few scratches.

He settled himself comfortably among the branches and gazed down at the woman, still half believing she was an apparition that had been conjured up by his heated thoughts. A wondrous creature summoned to his presence by the magical night and the luminous, mystical moonlight.

Suddenly, she turned and threw her arms wide. A low, throaty chuckle emerged from her mouth. Its sweet sound pierced his soul, made him shiver as he did when he heard a beautiful chord on a church organ. *Oh, speak, glorious apparition!* he thought, knowing in his heart that her soft tones would surely wash over him like a warm tide.

Instead—and to his astonishment—she began to dance. A slow, sinuous dance at first, her bare feet gliding dreamily over the sand. She dipped and bent and turned, tossing her mane of hair in time to some imagined tune. But gradually she increased the tempo, until she was spinning and whirling in a dance of wild abandon. Her nightdress fluttered in the breeze, giving him tantalizing glimpses of her limbs, and her musical laughter enchanted him.

He felt like an intruder, spying on her so shamelessly, but he couldn't help himself. Who *was* she? They were near the town of Church Stretton, in the Shropshire hills. Could she be the village madwoman? A roving Gypsy, called out by her ancient heritage to commune with nature? A poor slattern, seeking solace from a hard life by escaping for a few hours of freedom on her master's stolen horse? Or perhaps she was the enchanted sprite of his dreams. He only knew that the sight of her was spellbinding.

With a final dizzying spin, she sank to the sand. Thorne sagged against the branch, his heart pounding, his flesh tingling and alive—bathed in a sudden mist of hot sweat. *How much is a man expected to endure?* But there were more torments in store for him. She suddenly jumped to her feet, untied the strings of her garment and allowed it to slide to the ground.

He stifled an involuntary gasp. Never had he seen a more inviting body, lush and full-bosomed, pale white in the moon's glow. Her hips were wonderfully curved, springing from a narrow waist. He felt his manhood harden and stiffen; she might not be real, but God knew his body's reaction was!

He had to find out if he was dreaming. He frowned at the tree. He didn't want to alarm the bewitching creature by dropping abruptly from his perch. Not in his naked state! It would be better to make his way back to the central trunk, slide to the ground and speak to her from the shadows. He might even put on his breeches, at least. He could always take them off again if she proved to be agreeable.

She turned toward the pond and waded in. *By the cross of St. George*, he thought, captivated anew. *She's not a Gypsy. She's an Amazon!* Reluctant to take his bedazzled eyes from her for a second, he crawled backward on the branch. His bare foot caught on a twig, which crackled softly. He held his breath and peered intently at her. Had she heard the sound? She hesitated for a moment, as though she were listening, then continued into the water.

Best not to chance that again, he thought. He'd stay where he was for a while. He didn't want to break the spell too soon by coming down from the tree. He glanced at his swollen member. *Calm yourself, my friend*, he thought. *There's time yet.*

He settled himself into the crook of several branches and watched in fascination as she swam. Strong and sure, of course, as he knew she would be. Yet oddly graceful and seductive. His woodland sprite had become a Siren, a mermaid of the deep. He could watch her forever.

Suddenly, he heard shouting from the far side of the clearing, then saw a glimmer of light. The shouts became words, clear and sharp on the night air.

"Lady Gloriana! Ho, milady! Are you there?"

The creature stopped in mid-stroke, then slapped the water in an angry gesture.

Milady! Thorne thought in surprise. Not some common hoyden after all, but a highborn lady of quality, rebelling against the constraints of her aristocratic life. And not for the first time, surely, if they'd known where to look for her.

Two horses came into the clearing, bearing a man and a woman. The man was in livery and the woman wore a large white cap and a full apron over her skirts. The man carried a lantern; by its glow, Thorne could see the frown of disapproval on his face.

Thorne was equally vexed—how dare they intrude on his enjoyment of this vision? But it had its compensations, he decided after a moment. He could see clearly now that the wild head of curls was a glorious red. *And green eyes, I'll wager*, he thought, almost sorry that DeWitt wasn't here to take his bet.

Lady Gloriana waded toward the shore, her exquisite features stiff and proud. She waved an imperious hand at the man-servant; he looked abashed and turned away. She stepped onto the sand, glared at the maid and held out her arms in the regal pose of a queen waiting for her subjects to do her homage.

The maid gave a reluctant curtsy, then pulled off her apron and began to dry her mistress. "Oh, milady," she chided in a peevish tone, "why do you do this all the time? They were frantic back at the Hall, wondering where you'd got to *this* time. And at this hour, lordamercy!"

She received nothing but a cold and disdainful stare in response.

Thorne ached with burning desire. Never had he seen a more elegant, magnificent woman. He watched as the maid dried her beautiful body, helped her into her nightdress, then led her to her waiting horse. There was no need to reveal himself now. He knew her name. Surely there was not another Lady Gloriana from Shropshire among the gentry. He would seek her out and pay court to her in proper fashion, as befitted her station.

All the while, the maid had kept up a steady stream of reproaches and complaints, berating her mistress for her wild ways. Thorne was indignant. Surely a lady like that wouldn't endure such insolence much longer! He waited for the moment when she would speak her displeasure. He was hungry for the sound of the noble, cultured voice that would emerge.

Instead, she stamped her foot and glared at her maid.

The girl's tirade died in mid-sentence, squashed by her mistress's proud and haughty manner.

As Lady Gloriana was about to mount her horse, she stopped and turned toward the trees. She strode purposefully to the edge of the clearing, then stooped and picked up a large rock, the size of a child's head. Thorne held his breath as she marched toward the tree in which he was hiding.

She squinted up into the dark foliage, her exquisite mouth twisted into a sneer. "Bloody Peepin' Tom!" she shrilled. Her voice was sharp-pitched and common, blistering his ears. "Arse-lickin' fool! Damned whore-mongerin' sot! Ain't you never seen no lady till now?"

She hauled back and pitched the huge rock into the tree, dislodging Thorne from his perch. As he tumbled wildly through the branches, she stomped to her horse, leaped on its back and galloped out of the clearing.

Thorne lay at the base of the tree, winded. His body ached all over, and he could feel the sting of innumerable scratches on his bare flesh. She'd *known*, by God! The harridan had known all along that he was watching. And the sweet voice that he had expected to hear? Christ Jesus! Every foul word out of her mouth had put the lie to her beautiful, elegant exterior.

His blood boiled with anger. He felt used, outraged, humiliated at being caught like a schoolboy, spying and hiding where he had no business being. He might have broken a few bones in his fall—had the witch considered that?

But as he dressed, wincing as his clothes came in contact with his scratches, he began to laugh. What an adventure! Surely it had been an extraordinary night after all.

He hurried back to the inn, more intrigued than ever by

the Lady Gloriana. DeWitt was a font of gossip. No doubt he could shed some light on the curious creature. He dashed into the inn and raced up the stairs.

He saw the chambermaid shuffling down the hall, rubbing her bottom unhappily, and holding a small sack of coins in her palm. Felix would have finished his business, which always seemed to conclude with a few vicious slaps. Without knocking, he marched into DeWitt's room.

Felix was sitting on the bed, quite naked. He glanced up in surprise. "You really ought to knock, friend Thorne," he said. "But she was a delicate morsel, whatever her name was."

Thorne scowled. "Any port in the storm to satisfy your cock?"

DeWitt shrugged and reached for his breeches. "A woman is just a handy piece of meat."

"But a human being," he growled.

"Since when have you, the great Duke of Thorneleigh, had such concern for the lower orders?"

His own high-handed past was beginning to shame him. "Perhaps it's time I learned to show a crumb of concern," he muttered.

DeWitt fastened the buttons on his breeches, ambled to the table and poured two glasses of wine. "And to what do we owe this sudden transformation? Have you seen God?"

No, he thought. *I've seen a contradiction.* He felt his anger toward DeWitt ebbing. Why should he judge the man? He himself had chosen the world he traveled in. "Just an odd conversation I overheard tonight," he said aloud, taking the offered glass of wine. "About a Lady Gloriana. Is she the local madwoman here in Shropshire?"

DeWitt snorted. "Scarcely a madwoman. She's a harlot.

But magnificent to behold, they say."

Thorne sank into a chair, his brain reeling. "A *harlot*?" Surely DeWitt was mistaken.

"She used to be. A veritable lift-skirts, accustomed to the dregs of London's meanest streets. Oh, friend Thorne, didn't you hear the story?" He frowned in thought. "No, perhaps you didn't. It was last autumn and Christmas, when you were traveling on the Continent."

"What story?"

"The lady in question is the Lady Gloriana Baniard. Do you remember the family? Years ago. Sir William Baniard, Baronet. He and his wife and children were falsely accused of treason and transported to America. Sold into bond servitude. Their estate, of course, was confiscated. In time, one daughter, Allegra, having served out the terms of her bondage, made her way back to England and married Greyston Morgan, Viscount Ridley."

"A decent man. I've met him once or twice at Court."

"Yes. And possessed of a fortune I'd kill to own myself. He cleared the Baniard name and bought back Baniard Hall as a present for his wife. They live only a few miles from here, on Wenlock Edge. Husband and wife are quite unfashionably devoted to one another, I'm told."

"And Lady Gloriana is another Baniard daughter, forced to take to the streets in desperation?" Perhaps his vision of loveliness had only pretended to be low-bred, to confound him.

"Pshaw! Scarcely that! She's as common as dirt. Except for Lady Ridley, the original family is all dead now. But Charles, Sir William's only son, had escaped his bondage and fled back to England, where he was a hunted fugitive.

God knows what he did in the intervening years to keep body and soul together. There was even talk he'd become a highwayman. But by the time he was reinstated to his title, he had decided to marry..." DeWitt shrugged, "...the common London whore he'd been living with."

Thorne felt as if the wind had been knocked out of him. "Gloriana," he said hoarsely.

"Yes. Sir Charles was not himself, you understand. His cruel indenture seems to have affected his brain. He lived a wild life, I'm told, even after he reappeared in society. Gambling, whoring, flouting his reinstated position. On the very day of his marriage to his whore, he quarreled with the guests at Baniard Hall, got into a duel, and was killed."

"And the Lady Gloriana?"

"She lives at Baniard Hall with her sister-in-law and brother-in-law. When the Ridleys aren't in residence in London, you understand. Morgan House is a splendid place. Have you seen it?"

Thorne brushed aside the question. "But the lady, damn it!"

"They don't dare bring her to London, of course," said DeWitt with a sneer. "Think of the scandal! But they have to be nice to her. Because of the child."

Would his disappointments never end? "Sir Charles's child?"

"Yes. The new baronet. The Hall has been entailed to the child, to be held in trust until Ridley's death. But it must be awkward for His Lordship and wife. To be forced to be gracious to a lowly street doxy. Even more awkward as the child grows up with a mother like that!"

Thorne shook his head. "What a story." And to think

he'd nearly succumbed to the creature's charms. He'd look like a fool if he appeared in London society with *a common whore* on his arm. His friends would wonder if the great Duke of Thorneleigh had lost his reason!

But later, as he lay in bed and tried to sleep with the moonlight still streaming in through the window, all he could see was her bewitching face. Her tempting, womanly form dancing magically in the night.

"Begone, apparition," he whispered to the darkness. Why had he thought that she might be different from other women? If a gentlewoman practiced casual betrayal, a whore made her living at it, flitting from man to man without a twinge of conscience.

He groaned. *Oh, Gloriana*, he thought in anguish, *if only you had been what you seemed.*

• • •

"No, no, *no*, Lady Gloriana!" The tutor swirled away from Gloriana's writing desk, the skirts of his fancy coat flying, and paced her drawing room in a peevish stride. "You must form your Os with a graceful loop. Allow the pen to flow across the page. And don't pinch it as though you were afraid it would fly out of your fingers! Can you *never* get it right?"

"Bloody hell!" Gloriana scowled at the large inkblot left on the paper by the scratching quill pen. She picked up her ink bottle and hurled it across the room. It left an ugly smear on the blue damask wall covering. Barbara, her maid, gasped and ran to fetch a cloth. Gloriana shot her tutor a malevolent look. "I don't give no tinker's damn about writin' proper-like. Why do you torture me, you cross-eyed excuse for a man?"

He took a slow breath and managed a thin, condescending smile. "A *lady* should know the arts and graces of society. Lord and Lady Ridley are extraordinarily kind to take such care with your education. How else are you to get on in the world?"

"It never stopped me afore now," she muttered. She was tired of the months of lessons—reading and writing and dancing and singing and deportment—all designed to turn her into something she wasn't. Nor ever would be, however much she yearned for it. "There weren't a day in London that I didn't have somethin' to eat. And I didn't need no readin' to see a tankard hangin' over a tavern, tellin' me there were food and drink inside! I paid my way, and then some."

Barbara, sulkily blotting at the spreading ink stain on the wall, gave a soft snort under her breath.

Gloriana marched across the room, clapped her hand on the girl's shoulder and spun her about. "I weren't no whore!" she shrilled.

The girl's face dissolved into a deferential smirk, but her eyes held mocking laughter. "Of course you weren't, milady. No one ever said so."

Except behind my back, Gloriana thought bitterly. She knew what the servants in Baniard Hall thought of her. She could see it in their eyes, hear it in the quiet snickers as they passed her in the rooms. Well, damn their eyes, she'd show them! She was the widow of one baronet, the mother of another. A lady didn't tolerate insolence.

But how was she to deal with it? She didn't have the elegance of Charlie's sister, Allegra, or the imposing presence and high-flown language of Lord Ridley. She felt helpless, bested by this chit of a girl.

She did the only thing she was capable of, under the circumstances. She drew back her hand and slapped Barbara sharply across the face. "I'll have none o' your brass, you minx!" she cried. "Quit my side!"

Barbara began to wail, cradling her cheek in her hand. "But, milady…"

"Out, you foul jade!"

The girl scurried from the room.

The tutor cleared his throat and frowned, tight lips pursed in disapproval. "That was entirely uncalled-for, Lady Gloriana. A *lady*…"

If he said *lady* in that tone once more, she knew she'd scream. As though he was certain that the child of a Gypsy and a thief could never be a lady.

Her own sense of inadequacy fueled her anger. She advanced on him, her hands balled into fists. She towered over him. "A *lady* don't have to endure the likes of a priggish jackanapes, I reckon. Not if she don't want to. And I'll wager I could hoist a little squint-a-pipes like you and toss you out on your arse."

He began to quake. "Lady Ridley will hear of this," he said in a quivering voice, backing toward the door.

"*Out*, you worm!"

He fled. She slammed shut the door after him with a savage kick to the paneling.

But when he'd gone, she buried her face in her hands. She knew she treated the servants with too high a hand, shouting too often, striking occasionally, playing the proud and haughty Lady of the Manor. But how else was she to get their respect if she didn't demand it? "Oh, Charlie," she whispered. "You were a rum enough cove. Why did you do this to me?" Child or no child, she should never have agreed to the marriage.

The Lady Gloriana Baniard. She gave a laugh filled with self-mockery and sank into a deep, graceful curtsy. "How do you do, your lordship?" she said to the empty room, making a conscious effort to lower and soften her voice. "It be... it *is* my pleasure to make your acquaintance. Will you take tea?"

She went through the pantomime of pouring, handing around imaginary cups, and murmured polite small talk. "Milady, I ain't never... *have* never seen such a fine gown. Were the season... *was* the season in London pleasant this year, your lordship?"

She sighed. It was still so difficult to remember all her lessons. And the tutor—and even the servants—made her feel like a fool, treating her with a lack of respect that curdled her soul. She didn't yet have the courage to show them that she *was* learning. If she slipped, in an awkward moment or a burst of anger, she feared she would slide back to her old ways of speaking and acting. And then their mockery would bring a humiliation she wasn't prepared to endure. And though the Ridleys would be kind and understanding at her lapse, she dreaded to read pity in their eyes.

No. It was better to pretend to be unteachable—waiting for the moment when she could emerge from her coarse background and appear before them all as a perfect lady— than risk her pride.

She sighed again and glanced out the window. Evening was falling. They would expect her at supper. She dreaded it. She moved into her bedchamber and stared at herself in the large mirror. She didn't have the courage to call back Barbara to help her change her gown. The tale of her high-handed treatment of the girl would already have found its way to the servants' quarters. They would all be laughing at her by now. She couldn't bear the contempt.

Her afternoon dress would have to serve for supper. She appraised it with a critical eye. It looked so plain, so sedate, with its prim neckcloth that hid her fine bosom—stays so tight they flattened every curve. And why did she have to wear black, day in and day out? She had only been Charlie's wife for a few hours before he was killed, yet she was condemned to this unending drab color for a year. And to make matters worse, her scarlet hair—of which she was unashamedly proud, and the only bit of color on her person besides her green eyes—had been fashioned by Barbara into a knot on top of her head and covered with a large white cap, trailing black widow's weeds.

"God rot them all," she muttered. If Charlie were alive, she'd be wearing low-cut cerise or golden silk, festooned with the jewels he'd given her, her face enlivened with plenty of rouge and powder.

"But that's the way the common women dress in London," Allegra had told her, meaning to be kind. "Not fit for your station now, my dear."

She said "common women" not "whores," thought Gloriana. But that's what she had been thinking.

Gloriana stamped her foot. "I weren't never no whore," she said darkly, then corrected herself. "I was never a whore," she said in a haughty tone.

True, she'd trafficked the London streets with her Da. But only to lure men into dark alleys, where Da could relieve them of their purses. He'd wanted her to stay a virgin, and she had agreed. She'd seen too many harlots go to their deaths, riddled with disease and corruption.

But fate had made her tall and strong as she grew. Seeing a larger profit to be made, Da had trained her to be a female gladiator, fighting in the pits of theaters for the amusement of the gentry. *And I were… was the best there was*, she thought proudly. She'd never lost a match in the three years she'd been part of the sport.

"Put your guineas on Glory," the gentlemen would say. "She never loses."

But as much as she had enjoyed the ring, she'd loved the training even more. Old Diggory, the blacksmith in the squalid corner of London where they'd lived, had set her to work beside him in the forge, strengthening her arm muscles and increasing her endurance until she was a match for any other female, and a few men besides.

She had never been happier than when she was bent over the anvil, hammer in hand, sweat running down her face and arms and back. Old Diggory had even taught her to fashion glowing iron bars into graceful curlicues, turning out wrought-iron fences to grace the elegant town houses of the gentry. And then he'd let her ride the horses they had shod, galloping through the cobbled streets with reckless abandon.

No. She wasn't a whore, and never had been, though Charlie had thought it. "My sweet whore," he'd called her to his underworld companions, as though it were a term of endearment. But he'd been so drunk the first night he'd taken her, he'd never noticed her virginal flinch of pain, the spot of blood on the sheets. And the name "whore" had stuck. It hadn't bothered her—until now.

She wasn't sorry she'd gone with Charlie. Da had been

dying, and they both knew it. She would be safer with a man she could call her own. Someone to protect her. And Charlie made good money, robbing stagecoaches as a masked bandit. He had been good to her most of the time, only blacking her eye or swatting her to the ground when he was drunk, or filled with dark thoughts of his past. And faithful, except for a few lapses.

Not that he loved her, of course. Or she, him. The denizens of London's underworld couldn't afford such niceties as romantic love. But she'd found an unexpected joy in their coupling, an enthusiasm for making love that had astonished her. She'd wait impatiently for him to come rolling in from an evening at a tavern or gin shop, and tug at his breeches, eager to feel him inside her.

That's what she missed when she thought about Charlie. The wild romps, the frantic thrashing and groping in the dark. The release of pure animal passion. The few gentlemen she'd met since she'd come to Baniard Hall— friends and business acquaintances of the Ridleys—had seemed soft and pampered, scarcely the type to give a lusty woman pleasure in bed. And why would they want a woman of her sort, anyway?

She'd found some physical relief in her wild nocturnal rides. She'd bribed a stable boy to look the other way whenever she sneaked into the stable and took out a horse. She would gallop across the countryside and come back to her rooms at the Hall, tense with desire and sexual yearning. Lying in bed, she would pleasure herself until she exploded in release, then drift off into a contented sleep.

Except for last night, when that blasted Peeping Tom had disturbed her solitude. She'd come back too angry for pleasure, her blood boiling at his arrogant self-confidence. *Naked* in the tree—she'd seen that much. Was he hoping for a tussle, the wretch? She wished she could have seen the villain's face. She hoped he'd snagged his prickle on a branch on his trip down, and spent the night nursing his parts.

"Filthy rogue," she muttered. He'd got more than he bargained for, curse his prying eyes!

Chapter Three

When Gloriana finally came down the broad staircase, Charlie's sister Allegra, Lady Ridley, met her at the door to the eating parlor. A handsome woman with black hair and dark, soulful eyes, Allegra bore a striking resemblance to her brother, except that her sweet face was round and full, echoing the roundness of her pregnant belly, covered by a somber mourning gown. She moved gracefully toward Gloriana, a warm smile on her face, and held out her hands.

"Sister. Dear one," she said. "May I have a moment of your time before we go in to supper?"

Gloriana bit her lip, feeling a guilty blush color her cheeks. "If it be about the ink stain, I'll sell one o' my jewels to pay for it. Never you fear. I pays my debts." She heard the sound of her own coarse words and cringed inwardly.

Allegra gave a gentle laugh. "Don't be absurd. We all have accidents."

"It weren't no accident," she said reluctantly. She couldn't lie to this kind, trusting woman. She seemed so wise and mature that it always surprised Gloriana to remember that Allegra was only nineteen, a year younger than she herself was. "I did it a-purpose."

Allegra kissed her lightly on the cheek. "I have no doubt you did. I've just spent a most unpleasant quarter of an hour with your tutor. He would vex a saint! Of course, I dismissed him on the spot. Why didn't you tell me he was so difficult?"

Gloriana burned with remorse. "It weren't his fault," she muttered. "He were only tryin' to teach me proper ways. And I be a dolt at learnin'. As for hittin' Barbara…" Allegra would have heard that story; she might as well confess.

"Oh, pooh! Barbara is a sulky girl, given to insolence. Mrs. Carey, the housekeeper, should never have allowed her to be your maidservant. I truly wanted Verity to serve you. She's a sweet-tempered lass. But Mrs. Carey needed her elsewhere. Well, I regret to override my housekeeper, but I'll insist she make the change. As for the tutor…" She slipped her arm around Gloriana's waist and gave her a gentle hug. "Perhaps Grey and I have pushed you too fast and too hard. It must be so difficult for you, in these new surroundings. I blame myself for your unhappiness."

Gloriana gulped back her tears. How could they be so kind, when she behaved like an unruly ingrate? They were so far above her, and yet they treated her with patience and understanding, ignoring her crude speech, tolerating her outbursts, forgiving her wild nighttime rides, which surely caused them anxiety. "It aren't your fault," she said hoarsely. "I should have died with Charlie."

Allegra looked horrified. "Never! You and little William are the best legacies my brother could have left us."

"But…"

"Not another word. We're proud to call you family. As for the tutor, I think we won't hire another for a while. There will be time, when you feel more at ease here. Would that please you?"

She nodded dumbly, too filled with gratitude to utter a word.

"As for the ink stain," Allegra went on, "the wall covering can be replaced, of course. But it occurs to me that I've been remiss in doing you honor. I never even asked you if the decorations of your apartment pleased you. Perhaps you find them not to your liking? Tell me, and I shall have the joy of consulting with you to redo your suite." She laughed and patted her belly. "I have a month yet, till I'm brought to bed. Time enough to make a change in your surroundings."

Doing her honor? She couldn't bear their kindness and respect. She had been accustomed to surly words, a cuff on the ear, insolence from tradespeople, and scorn from the gentry. "I don't deserve no fancy rooms," she said, choking with emotion. She felt so unworthy in this household that she wanted to die.

"Nonsense. You're Lady Baniard. And my dear sweet sister. You deserve all that position entails." Allegra slipped her arm through Gloriana's. "Now come in to supper."

Allegra's husband, Grey Ridley, came around from his seat at the head of the table and put his hand under Gloriana's arm, guiding her to her chair. He saw to her comfort, then turned to his wife. "'Od's blood," he said with a laugh. "You've grown so large, I think I should carry you to your place."

Allegra gave him a mocking smirk, but her love shone in her eyes. "I'm not quite helpless yet."

He kissed her softly on the neck as he seated her, and whispered something in her ear that made her blush.

Gloriana swallowed a sudden rush of emotion. How she envied them! She hadn't thought about love very often—in her old life, it had been something distant and unattainable for people of her kind. When you worried about the next crust of bread to sustain your body, how could you have the time to worry about an emotion that didn't seem vital to survival? But in this household, watching the Ridleys' devotion to each other, she felt like a starving beggar.

She had an aching need to be a part of the family circle. To belong. To offer something to the conversation, if nothing more. "It be a boy," she announced confidently. "That was the way I carried my Billy. Large in the front, and with my prat stuck out behind."

She saw the look of shocked surprise in Allegra's eyes and cursed herself for speaking so impulsively. The language of the London underworld scarcely belonged in this company. She stammered out an explanation. "That is... when a woman be large in the..." she struggled for one of her tutor's fine words, "... in the *posterior*..."

"It doesn't matter," Grey said gently. "Only let your prediction come true. God knows I wish only for Allegra's safety and a healthy child. But a son..." His eyes misted with yearning.

"The creature kicks enough for two sons," Allegra said crisply, motioning to the servants to serve supper—steaming platters of delicious fare that Gloriana still couldn't get used to. As they ate, Grey and Allegra chatted amiably, discussing the news from London, the weather, the books they were reading. Gloriana listened to their conversation in silence, fearful of saying anything that would embarrass her further. Their talk was elegant and polished, with large words she could scarcely understand, and their tones were soft and cultured, reflecting generations of education, good pedigree and refinement. She longed to fit into their world.

They spoke only of trifles, or subjects that mystified her. But after enduring a particularly incomprehensible discussion about the composer Handel, the favorite of King George, she excused herself, pleading weariness.

She climbed the stairs and turned toward Billy's room. She hadn't seen him since morning, and her arms ached to hold him. After more than four months, she still marveled at the wonder of his perfection. She bit her lip in dismay as she entered the chamber—he lay cradled in his wet nurse's arms, suckling contentedly.

God had even robbed her of that joy. She had only a month to nurse him. A scant month when he had been hers alone. And then she'd fallen ill with a fever. By the time she'd recovered, the milk in her breasts had dried up.

The nurse looked up in surprise. "Oh, milady. I didn't know you were coming."

"I... I can come back," she stammered. "Tell me when I should return."

The nurse could scarcely hide her disdain. "'Tis not *my* place to give you orders," she chided. "'Tis *your* place to do as you wish."

She felt her face burning. "Of course." She lifted her head proudly and tried to sound superior. "If Billy be almost through, I'll wait. I should like to hold him for a spell."

"As you wish, milady. Little *Sir William* has begun to nod off already. I think he's quite finished his supper."

Gloriana sighed. She was even thwarted in the matter of his name. She was the only one who called him Billy.

The baby's head dropped away from the nurse's breast and his eyes closed in sleep. The woman handed him to Gloriana, rose from her chair, and covered her exposed breast. "I'll take him back from you in a moment, milady."

"No. Go away. I wish to be alone with my son."

"But, milady…"

She skewered the nurse with an angry stare. "Do you fancy a cuff on the ear, you saucebox? Do as you're told! I be all out o' patience." She jerked her chin toward the door to emphasize her words.

The nurse rolled her eyes in exasperation and left the room.

Gloriana sat in the chair she had vacated and gazed lovingly down at her child. A sweet, warm armful. "Never you mind, Billy, my lad," she crooned. "They be… they *are* naught but a bunch of sour-faced jades. You and me—we'll laugh and play from morn' till night. I'll teach you to ride bareback and swing a smithy's hammer. There won't be any folks who dare keep us apart, the stiff-necked fools."

She stroked back the pale red curls from his tiny forehead and kissed his face, filled with emotions she hadn't known since Da's death. Loyalty, a secret bonding of souls, a willingness to die for the other. *It must be a kind of love,* she thought in sudden wonder, awed by the tender emotions she felt for her child.

At last, she rose from her chair and placed him gently in his cradle, reluctant to let him go. "You and me, Billy," she whispered. "We'll be lovin' comrades to the death. I promise you." She tiptoed to the door, her face wreathed in a smile, her thoughts on a rosy future with her beloved son.

She stopped when she heard the harsh whisper of the nurse's voice, just outside the door. "Poor mite. How will he explain a mother like that, when he's grown?"

She heard Barbara's cruel chuckle in response. "If he's wise, he'll keep her locked in the larder, and only let her out to go to church of a Sunday."

"Aye. She's as wild as her unknown Gypsy mother."

"*Gypsy?*"

"Aye. I heard her telling Lady Ridley." The nurse gave a contemptuous snort. "And do you see the way she moves? She lopes like a colt, strides like a man. A disgrace to her fine name."

Barbara gave a loud sigh. "Poor mite," she agreed.

Gloriana fought back the tears. What had she been thinking of, with her foolish dreams? Billy *would* be ashamed of her as the years went by. She was uneducated, stupid, clumsy—and not likely to change enough to suit the gentry *or* the servants, even with a hundred tutors. They would always look at her with eyes that remembered what she had been—a creature not fit for refined company.

She groaned. Would she embarrass her son, watch the contempt growing in his eyes day by day? Better he had no mother at all. Grey and Allegra were the proper ones to raise him.

Better for Billy that she leave now, before she brought him grief.

She took a steadying breath, her mind made up, cast a final longing glance toward the cradle, and sailed out into the passageway, sweeping silently past the servants. She hurried to her rooms, her mind fervent with activity. "You be a fish out o' water, my girl," she said softly. "There be no place for you here." She saw the dried ink on the wall, remembered blurting out the word "prat" at the table. Ungoverned temper, crude language. This was not where she belonged, no matter how hard she tried.

But where to go? London? Jeremy Royster would take her back into the ring in a flash. She'd been his best gladiator. She'd earned a good living at it before. Why not return to the life she knew?

She shook her head. No. After her months of living like a lady, she wasn't sure she wanted to return to the sordid life of the London streets. There must be something more, she thought, anguished. A quiet life in a village somewhere, where she could pass as a decent peasant, if not as a gentlewoman.

Whitby, of course! Charlie had owned a house in the Yorkshire seacoast village. They'd lived there for a scant month last fall, lying low, while Grey worked on Charlie's pardon in London.

She remembered the charming cottage with warmth. A cozy stone house secluded in a leafy hollow just inland from the cliffs. She'd been ecstatically happy there, cooking and scrubbing like an innocent goodwife, while Charlie moped and grumped around, lost in an alcoholic stupor most of the time. She'd been heartbroken when he'd sold the place after they'd come to London.

But perhaps she could buy it, or at least rent it. She had all the jewels Charlie had given her; they were hers to do with as she wished, without being beholden to Grey or Allegra. She'd go to Whitby by way of London. Toby Swagger was the best fence in town, now that the great Jonathan Wild had been taken and condemned.

"Bloody hell!" she exclaimed, struck by a new idea. She'd have enough money from the jewels to buy a forge! Why not? Every village could use another blacksmith. And with the shipbuilding in Whitby, there might be commissions for tackle and iron fittings. There was a stable next to the little cottage—it would be perfect for her needs.

She had a sudden disquieting thought. Country folk would never accept a woman as a blacksmith. She'd have to hire a man to shoe horses, at least. She could always work in secret on the more complicated ironwork she was good at.

"That be the ticket," she muttered. "I needs me a front." Any strong young buck would do—she could always teach him to shoe horses.

Confident in her plans, she dressed simply for the long walk to Ludlow, tucking her distinctive red curls under her cap. She didn't want to be recognized in the nearby town; she meant to disappear from the Ridleys' lives for good and all.

In Ludlow, she could catch the mail stage for London; she still had a sack of guineas, the last of the king's pension that Charlie had received. There were shops aplenty in London where she could buy humble country clothes. And then the trip north to Whitby, where Glory Cook (her father's name) could live in happy obscurity.

God willing, they would never find her.

One final chore. She sat at her writing desk, pulled out pen and paper and began the difficult task of writing to Grey and Allegra. She chewed on her lower lip as she painfully formed the letters, expressed sentiments that broke her heart.

I be going, she wrote. *For goode and all. Doant look for me. This be the best way. Take cayre of my babby. Tell Billy I be dead. It were better that way. He doant need no common wench for a Ma. Gloriana*

By the time she was finished, she was weeping. She blotted at the teardrops on the page, then folded and sealed the letter, printing "A. & G." on the outside. It was done.

She slipped the bag of coins into her pocket, tied up her jewels and several pairs of stockings in a spare shift, and threw on her hooded cloak. She found her precious keepsake—a scrap of Billy's hair tied with a blue ribbon— and wrapped it in a handkerchief, tucking it into her bodice next to her heart.

"Oh, Billy," she whispered, sobbing anew. "Pray God I forget you."

• • •

Thorne swept his battered cocked hat from his head and brushed his sleeve against his damp forehead. Damme, but it was hot! He'd had a brief respite—a cooling puff of sea air—when he'd stood atop the cliffs overlooking Robin Hood's Bay, but this path through the leafy glen leading to the secluded cottage he sought seemed to exhale heat into the already humid air.

And his coat... he plucked at the coarse woolen sleeve and silently cursed his valet. Dobson had assured him that Yorkshire—and Whitby—would be much cooler than London in July. Christ Jesus! It was enough to lower himself by donning second-hand clothing that itched and chafed; to suffer in this heat made him wonder if he was mad.

No! It was worth all his discomfort. He would see her again.

He chuckled softly, remembering the faces of Felix and

the rest of his drinking companions. The gossips in London had buzzed with the news that the Lady Gloriana Baniard had vanished. The Ridleys had searched for her in vain for nearly a month.

And then, much to his own surprise, he had heard himself impulsively announce, "I shall find the lady within a four-month. And bed her." He had sealed his vow with a wager against every man crowded around the table: a thousand pounds each if he lost.

And he never lost a wager.

She was here. It had taken a score of his men, using their lowest connections, to discover that she had lived here in Whitby with Sir Charles for a few weeks. After more inquiries, they had learned that she had rented a cottage and was going by the name of Glory Cook.

And she was looking for a manservant.

He glanced down at his worn shoes, his threadbare clothes. He didn't know what she needed a servant for, but Dobson had assured him he looked common enough. He only regretted he had to walk, but a horse would have made him seem too prosperous to need such humble employment. He knew he could charm her into the job—had he ever failed to conquer a woman? And then… into her bed. That lustful thought, the memory of her magnificent body, made him warmer still.

Well, perhaps it would rain later and cool the air. The clouds over the sea had looked dark and threatening; even as he walked, he noted that the sun had begun to dim.

Yes, it was a good plan. He had a cache of gold coins hidden in the heels of his shoes, and Dobson, posing as a visiting scholar, was settled at an inn in Whitby in case he was needed. Thorne felt a sense of expectancy that was more exhilarating than anything he had experienced in months.

He reached the end of the path and saw a small stone cottage in the clearing. Off to one side was a smaller building, its wide doors open to the elements. A stable, he guessed, seeing a horse within, yet there seemed to be several tables as well. And a brick chimney—odd for a stable. Odder still were the wisps of smoke it emitted, on such a hot day.

From the deep recesses of the shed came a loud pounding sound. Someone was there. "Halloo!" he called.

She emerged from the back of the stable, a large hammer in her hand. She was as beautiful as he remembered: bright red hair tied loosely off her neck and shoulders, sleeves rolled up, exposing golden flesh, skirts tucked up into her waistband to reveal bare legs and feet. And her eyes were most assuredly green, the color of emeralds.

He gulped, feeling inexplicably shy and overwhelmed by the sight of her. Then, remembering his disguise, he swept his hat from his head and gave a tentative bow, dropping his hat to the ground. "Mistress Cook?"

She stepped closer. Small beads of sweat covered her upper lip; he fought the urge to grab her and kiss them away. "Who be wantin' me?" she said. "I be too busy to trifle with you today."

He smiled his most beguiling smile, his confidence returning. "My name is John Thorne. I hear in Whitby that you need a manservant. I thought that perhaps…"

"*You?*" She scanned him from the top of his head to the toes of his scuffed shoes, clearly finding him wanting. "Take off your coat," she ordered sharply.

He bristled. He wasn't used to being spoken to in that

tone. "Now see here..." he began, glaring at her. Then he remembered who he was supposed to be. He lowered his eyes and peeled off his coat. "Of course, mistress," he said, forcing himself to sound humble.

She threw down her hammer and reached for him, clutching and squeezing his arms with both hands as though she were kneading a lump of common dough. She grunted. "Well, some muscle there. Show me your hands."

Dutifully he held out his hands, palms up. She ran her fingers across his flesh, which gave him a thrill of anticipation. "Bloody hell!" she exclaimed. "Soft as a baby. You ain't done no work in your whole miserable life!"

"That's not so." He thought up a quick lie. "I... I was a soldier once. And I'm handy with a sword." That last part, at least, was true—he'd practiced often, and had even fought the occasional duel.

Her magnificent lips curled in a sneer. "Oh, what a bullyboy. I be in danger every day from the good folk of Whitby! Why, only yesterday, the apothecary tried to overcharge me for a powder." She snickered. "If you was my servant, you could run him through."

He ground his teeth together and swallowed his pride. This wasn't going as he had planned. "I can work hard," he said softly.

"What was you afore this?"

"A valet to a duke." That was an easier lie. A part he could play.

She laughed at that, a mocking sound that raised his hackles. "Oh, good! You can tie my garters into pretty little bows."

He ignored her sarcasm with difficulty. "I can keep your

books. I'm good at numbers."

That seemed to give her pause. "Well…" She tossed her head in the direction of the shed. "Can you do carpentry?"

"I can learn."

"Can you shoe a horse?"

Damme! He tried the charming smile again. "I can learn."

She shook her head reluctantly. "Look, my fine cove. I don't need no soft toupet-man. I be wantin' to start a blacksmith shop here. But the folks bean't takin' kindly to a woman smithy. I needs a man who can shoe a horse. I can do it myself and t'other ironwork besides, but I needs me a man who can front for me. Not a softling who ain't never done *real* man's work."

He had never felt more useless in his whole dissolute life. It stung his sense of honor that this chit of a girl could dismiss a man of his station so rudely. He grabbed for her arm and tried to still his rising anger. "Please, mistress. I need the work."

She glared at him, green eyes flashing. "Take your hand off me, caitiff! I be no country wench. I be mistress here. And you be a wretch who don't know his place!"

His *place*? The great Duke of Thorneleigh? And she dared to use a low word like "caitiff?" The anger burst forth. "Until you're Queen of Whitby, mistress, you should temper your own high-handedness! I'm scarcely accustomed to being treated in such a vile manner, and by a creature such as you!"

"Arse-lickin' pig!" she shrilled, planting her hands on her hips in outrage. "Bloody worm! Begone from my sight. I wouldn't hire you if you was starvin'. You with your soft hands and your high-flown ways. You ain't no man! I reckon you runs from a woman, your prickle hangin' useless atween your legs."

That was too much. Not a man? With a growl, he grabbed her shoulders, pulled her close and ground his mouth down on hers. Her lips were full, delicious... and yielding. She sagged in his arms, all soft surrender. She smelled of lavender from the moors.

But after a long, heart-pounding moment, she stiffened, broke free, pushed roughly at his chest. She bent and scooped up her hammer, holding it menacingly above her head. "Begone, villain, lest I dent your pretty face!"

"As you wish," he drawled, lazily picking up his coat and then his hat, which he planted firmly on his head. He turned and made his way back along the path, grinning as he went. She'd wanted his kiss, welcomed it. And though he regretted his prideful anger, he knew with certainty that she could be won. He'd find another way.

He glanced back once more. She stood where he had left her, looking stunned, one hand to her heaving breast.

"Gloriana," he whispered softly, still enchanted by the sweetness of her kiss. "I'll have you yet."

Chapter Four

The cold rain beat down on Gloriana's hooded cloak, chilling her to the bone. A fierce wind whistled up from the sea far below her, tangy with salt. She reached forward and gave Black Jack's mane an encouraging pat. The poor beast was as drenched as she was, and surely weary from fighting the ceaseless wind that had long-since bent the scrawny trees that dotted the edge of the cliff.

"You be daft, my girl," she muttered, tempted to turn around and return to her cozy cottage. But she was more than halfway to Whitby at this point, following the road that overlooked Robin Hood's Bay. Better to stop for a tankard of warm mulled cider at The Eagle when she reached Whitby, and wait out the storm. Black Jack would welcome a dry stable for an hour or so.

Foolish jade! She should have known when she left her cottage that the storm would grow worse. No passing shower, but a savage assault of wind and rain from the northeast. But she had been desperate to get out, breathe deeply of the sea air, clear her head. She hadn't really needed a new sack of flour, but it had served as a convenient excuse. She knew she wasn't merely escaping from her cottage. She was running from a disturbing memory.

The man. Tall and strong, with a beautiful face, and a body that made her mouth water. And his kiss—she shivered, and not from the cold. Never in her life had a man's touch so shaken her. She could still recall his scent, that intoxicating mix of manly sweat and tobacco, of fine soap and pampered living. His lips had been soft, yet firm and burning, demanding her passionate response. She'd yearned to drag him to her bed upon the instant.

And now? Regret gnawed at her. Perhaps she *should* have hired him.

No! She needed a man who wasn't afraid of hard work, a man of strength and courage. Time enough for kisses and such if she became a successful tradeswoman—let the countrymen woo her when she'd made her mark in the parish. She was mad to keep thinking about him. He was so far above her, so clearly refined. She cringed, recalling her gutter language, her crude insults. Surely he had kissed her only out of anger. She scarcely needed scorn from *his* sort.

She glanced down at the sea, then reined in Black Jack. Bloody hell! Far below her, a ship seemed to have foundered, dashing against the rocks of a narrow cove. She saw men running across the sand, bodies bobbing in the surf, small boats fighting the undertow and relentless wind to reach the ship.

Perhaps she could be of help, she thought. There was no way down to the sea from this vantage point, but the village of Robin Hood's Bay had been built on the sides of a jagged cleft in the mountainside. She turned Black Jack around and headed back toward the road that led to the beach. The rain had almost stopped, but the cobbles would be slippery, and the headwinds would be difficult to buck. She dismounted and led her horse down the steep path, passing ancient stone cottages on either side. Several men raced ahead of her, carrying coils of thick rope.

She reached the end of the village and moved onto the beach, leading Black Jack and swinging around a spit of land to get to the cove where the ship lay. All was chaos here. Men running, shouting. Fishing boats pushing toward the sinking vessel, fighting winds, currents, the merciless sea. Several small fishing boats had overturned, and frantic groups of men dragged fresh boats into the water to rescue their comrades.

One of the boats had managed to reach the large ship; someone had thrown down a line, and the sailors were scrambling down the rope toward the small vessel. As the last man descended, the large ship seemed to groan—one last cry of defeat before it split in two and sank beneath the raging waves.

Gloriana, standing near a group of womenfolk, watched in helpless dismay as the boatmen struggled against their oars to reach the shore. Above the wind, she could hear the sound of one man shouting orders, calling out the stroke to maintain the oarsmen's rhythm. As the boats reached land, the women rushed forward to help the stricken men, lead them to the village, embrace the friends who had been miraculously saved—and briefly mourn the ones who hadn't survived. Gloriana helped as much as she could, wading into the shallows to pull men to the beach.

One by one, the boats made it to shore, until there were only two still bobbing on the tide. As Gloriana watched in horror, the farther boat capsized, sending the men into the roiling water. Several of them managed to climb on top of the capsized boat, but the others were washed away or dashed against the rocks.

The last boat had nearly reached the shore, with no room aboard to go back for more survivors. One of the men—the one who seemed to have been shouting orders—leaped out into the shallow water. He motioned for the others to follow. They formed a human chain—joined by others on land—and waded through the pounding surf until they were close enough to the capsized boat to urge the survivors to come to them. Slowly, hand to hand, they passed the sailors along, until the beach was littered with exhausted, gasping men, grateful to be alive.

The man who had led the rescue was the last to come ashore. He staggered toward the beach and collapsed in a heap on the edge of the sea. While the townsfolk comforted their friends and family members, he seemed to be ignored, his head buried in his arms, his dark hair soggy around his face, the rough current lapping at his legs.

Gloriana clutched at the sleeve of a woman hurrying past. "What of that cove, there? Don't he be worthy of attention?"

The woman managed a tight smile, reflecting a small town's hostility to newcomers. "You be Mistress Cook, what lives in the dingle, ain't you?"

"Aye. But what of that man?"

"An outsider. Just come to town. But welcome, the Lord knows. First man out when the ship foundered. Hours ago."

Gloriana shook her head. "He must be plumb wore out! Will no one care for him?"

The woman shrugged. "We has our own to care for first, and take 'em home. Mebbe you could get 'im to the church. A stranger, after all."

As though that should matter, thought Gloriana, remembering the open friendliness of the London streets. "Aye. I be doin' that." She hurried toward the stricken man, managing to enlist the help of a passing fisherman. Together, they dragged the man out of the water and onto the beach. He shook back his hair and looked up at them, his eyes unfocused and glazed with fatigue.

Gloriana gasped in recognition. "Bloody hell!"

The fisherman scowled at her. "Be this a friend o' yourn, mistress?"

It took her a fraction of a second to decide. "This be my manservant, John Thorne," she said with pride. She thought quickly. She could never get him back to the cottage on her own. But with Black Jack...?

She turned to the fisherman. "I be askin' a favor o' you, mate. That be my horse yonder. I'm Mistress Cook, livin' in the old Wickham cottage in the dell. You know the place?"

"Aye."

"I can run on ahead, and get a fire goin' in the grate. If you can get him on my horse and bring him to the cottage, it would be a blessin', upon my oath."

He hesitated. "I be needed here."

She fought to keep her temper from exploding. "There'll be a half-crown waitin' for you when you gets there."

His mouth quirked in a sly smile. "And a tot of rum?"

"Burn and blister me! Will you do it, or no?" She glared

at him, daring him to refuse.

He dropped his own gaze. "No need to get raspish with me, mistress. I'll get 'im there." He bent to help Thorne to his feet.

"Wait!" The word emerged as a croak from Thorne's throat. "My *shoes*. My hat and coat."

Gloriana was surprised at his urgent tone. "What matter? I'll get them tomorrow."

"No! I must have them." He sagged in the fisherman's arms and rubbed his hand across his face. "Christ Jesus, I'm tired." He pointed to a small shack hugging the edge of the cliff. "I left them there."

Gloriana turned toward the shack. "I'll get them." She turned back to the fisherman. "Mind he don't fall from the horse, my gallows-bird, or I'll have your ears as a keepsake!"

She fetched his belongings, then raced up the steep path of the village, grateful to have the wind at her back. She had left a small fire in the grate and was pleased to see it was still burning when she reached her cottage. She tossed an armload of fresh wood on the fire, watched it catch and burn, and warmed her cold hands for a moment in front of the flames. She stripped off her cloak, then her soggy skirt—her petticoat was fairly dry, except for the hem. But her shoes and stockings were a ruin; better to go barefoot than squish with every step she took!

Wait a moment. She might need to go outside to help with Thorne. She slipped into a pair of old mules—far from comfortable, but they would serve.

"Now what?" she said to the empty room, placing her wet clothes on a chair near the fire. There was a small trundle bed tucked under her own bed upstairs, but it would take time to drag it down and place it near the fire. "Towels, my girl, and a coverlet or two. That be the ticket." She fetched the bedding and spread one of the quilts on the floor as close to the fire as she could. Then, noting that it would soon be nightfall, she lit a few candles around the room and nodded in satisfaction at her handiwork.

At the last moment, she remembered what she had promised the fisherman. She wasn't about to let him see where she kept her coins! She lifted her strongbox from its wicker hamper in a corner of the room and pulled out a half-crown, then placed it on the table along with a bottle of brandy from her pantry closet, having decided that rum wasn't strong enough after what Thorne had endured.

She shook her head, still finding it hard to believe his bravery. First man out, the woman had said. Who would have thought it? Clearly, he was more a man than she had given him credit for.

"But there'll be no more kisses, my fine jack-a-dandy," she said with determination. She wasn't about to tolerate another insolent servant, as she had at Baniard Hall. Best he understood that from the beginning!

She heard Black Jack's whinny outside the door and rushed to throw it open. Thorne sagged on the horse, holding the saddle with lax fingers. She jerked her head toward the coverlet and scowled at the fisherman. "Put 'im on the floor, next to the fire. I'll stable the horse. There be your reward on the table. And some brandy. Mind you take a swig, not the bottle. I be needin' it for him."

By the time she had seen to Black Jack's comfort and feed, the fisherman had gone. She closed the door and crossed to the fireplace, kicking off her muddy mules as she went, and noting with distaste as she passed the table that the scoundrel had taken a very healthy gulp of the liquor. "Welladay," she muttered. She had scarce known a man— except Da and Grey Ridley—to be anything but selfish at his heart.

Thorne sat hunched on the coverlet—his arms around his body, his knees drawn up to his chest—shivering violently. Gloriana fetched the brandy and held out the bottle, urging him to drink. She had to steady his hands as he brought it to his mouth, so fierce were his tremors.

"Thank you," he said, through chattering teeth. "Did you find my shoes and things?"

"They'll be dry by mornin'. Never you fear." She tugged at his shirt, pulling it from his breeches. "Out of these wet clothes, now."

He groaned, attempting to lie down on the coverlet. "Just let me sleep."

"Be you quarrelin' with me, caitiff? I'm not of a mind to nurse you with a fever!"

He glared at her, but allowed her to strip off his shirt. She reached for a towel and began to vigorously rub his wet hair, then moved on to his muscular back, noting—in spite of herself—the smooth perfection of his flesh. She next toweled his hairy chest, grateful to see that his trembling had stopped. But when she began on his arms, he pushed weakly against her hands.

"Leave me be," he growled. "Just let me sleep, woman."

"I be doin' what needs to be done!" she snapped. "And you mind your manners, or I'll throw you out into the night."

His gray eyes were like cold steel. "My *manners*? By God…" They stared at one another for a long, angry moment, then he dropped his gaze and ran his hand across his face. "I forgot. Forgive me, mistress." He sighed. "Do your worst."

She pushed him onto his back and pulled off his soaked knee-breeches and stockings, drying his feet and working her way upwards. By the time she reached his knees, she saw that he was half asleep. She leaned back on her heels and took a moment to scan his form.

He was beautiful. From his shoulder-length black hair to his broad chest and narrow hips, he was everything a man should be. She stole a glance at his groin, the dark patch of curls cradling his considerable male parts. *Everything.*

Afraid to disturb his sleep, she toweled him more gently, stroking his hips and thighs with tender hands. She returned to his chest and arms, her movements like a caress. She felt her own body growing warm from his seductive presence, the familiar ache in her lower regions.

He moaned softly in his sleep, a wisp of a smile curling the full lips that she could still taste.

"Bloody hell," she whispered. His manhood was now quivering, stretching to its full height. She watched in fascination, her desire growing to a fever pitch.

Did she dare? Her own hunger conquered common sense; lifting her skirts, she straddled him and slowly lowered herself onto his body. She gasped at the hard fullness of him inside of her, then glanced hurriedly at his face.

Though his eyes were still closed, his smile had grown into a quirk of pleasure. He gave a contented grunt, his hips rising eagerly to meet hers. His hands circled her waist, holding her in a firm grip as she moved up and down on his shaft with an ever-increasing need. She had never felt such satisfaction in her life. He was large and hard—so unlike Charlie, whose prickle had been as shriveled as his soul. She felt an urgent tension rising at her very core, like a line stretched tight; then the line snapped, bringing blessed release. At the same moment, he gave a strangled cry; she could feel his seed flooding within her. He sighed and grinned in his sleep.

She rolled off him, and then stood, moving quickly to reach for the towel and clean herself. She wiped the telltale signs from his own body, praying he wouldn't notice in the morning. Time enough to figure out what she would tell him when he awoke—she wasn't about to let him know what she had done.

"Not if I can help it, my fine cove," she whispered, knowing she should feel remorse for taking advantage of him, but unable to erase the warm glow of satisfaction that filled her body.

He opened his eyes, momentarily alert. "What?" he muttered with a frown.

She covered him with a blanket and stroked back the hair at his forehead. "Hush," she murmured. "You be dreamin'. Go back to sleep."

She laid out his clothes to dry, picked up a candlestick and mounted the stairs to her bedroom. No need for a fire. The storm was already passing—it would be warm by morning. She unlaced her stays, pulled off her petticoat and lay down in her shift, wrapping herself snugly with a coverlet.

"For what you just did, my girl," she said to the empty room, "you should suffer the pangs of Hell." But she couldn't keep the contented smile off her face as she drifted off to sleep.

• • •

Thorne awoke slowly to the sunny morning, every muscle aching. Then he remembered the shipwreck. Christ Jesus! What had he been thinking yesterday? What mad impulse had driven him to risk his life, his own safety, for a bunch of sailors he wouldn't have noticed if he passed them on the High Street? But Gloriana's words had touched something deep within him. *Soft? Not a man?* He had wanted to prove to himself that she was wrong. And surely he felt an unfamiliar glow of satisfaction, knowing that he had helped to save so many lives.

He was suddenly aware of his surroundings. Naked—except for a thin coverlet—in front of a cold cottage fireplace. Gloriana! He felt at his groin, stunned to discover the signs of something he only remembered in fragments. It was true, then! The brazen hussy had had her way with him. He grinned. It would be damned easy to win his wager, and then some.

He stood up and stretched, easing his tired muscles. He heard Gloriana's voice outside the cottage. Talking to someone? He reached for his shirt and breeches, pleased to see they were almost dry. He carried them to the half-open door and surreptitiously watched her.

She was alone. She stood with a rake, scraping at the downed branches and leaves in the yard. "Burn and blister me," she muttered. "Stupid storm."

He smiled. Sweet Gloriana. She talked to herself. He found it charming. He dropped his clothing to the floor. After last night, there was no need for modesty. He waited for her to turn away, then strode quickly toward her, grabbing her around her waist and kissing the back of her neck. "Where the devil are my shoes, woman?" he murmured in her ear.

"Bloody hell!" She spun around and swung at him with her rake, holding it in two hands like a weapon. He dodged the blow and reached for her arms, managing with some difficulty to twist the rake from her grasp. They wrestled for a moment—he was stunned to discover how strong she was. But at last he managed to kick at her ankles and bring her to the ground, falling on top of her and pinning her arms at her sides. He felt his manhood hardening at the feel of her lush body beneath his.

She shook her head from side to side. "Let me go, villain!"

"Not yet, my sweet Glory," he said, remembering at the last moment that that was the name she used here. His mouth slashed down on hers, stilling her frantic movements. This time, she didn't respond to his kiss as he had hoped. She bit down on his lip and he jerked his head up in pain, grunting and feeling for the spot with his tongue.

She took the opportunity of his surprise to roll out from under him and leap to her feet. "Be you daft, man?" she cried. "I'll set the Watch on you!"

He sat up and scratched his head in bewilderment. "But after last night..."

Her eyes opened wide. "What about last night?"

He grinned despite his injured lip. "I distinctly remember an intimate encounter—initiated by you."

"Pah! You be losin' your mind, caitiff."

"I *did* find evidence on my person this morning," he said with a sly smile.

"Oh, that," she sneered. "Whilst I was dryin' you, you

must have had a wicked dream. Your knocker stood up and you rogered the air. Disgusting. I had to clean you up best I could."

"A dream?" It had been so real, the parts he could remember—the feel of his hands around her waist, the tight imprisonment of his manhood—that he found it hard to believe. "A dream?" he said again, shaking his head at the humiliating thought of having ejected his seed in her presence.

"Aye." She put her hands on her hips, all brisk business. "Now, seein' as how you turned out to be stronger than I guessed, the job is yours, if you want it. Twenty pounds per annum, and room and board. And I don't haggle over the price."

He had to keep from snorting at that. He seldom carried coins that small in his purse, leaving minor costs to his servants. "I'm agreeable, mistress."

"Good. Now go and get dressed. You might think bein' naked is fine, but I looks at you and sees a bull in heat. You ain't *never* to be around me unless you be properly clothed. Do you understand, rogue?"

He was still burning with embarrassment over his behavior of last night; her autocratic tone further irritated him. "You needn't bark orders like a drill captain," he muttered.

"Bloody hell! Listen to me, my fine fellow. I be mistress here. I be givin' you any orders I choose. And I expect you to follow 'em. Humbly! I'm makin' that clear now. If you can't swallow your stiff-necked pride, then begone!"

Damn! He ground his teeth together. If he was ever to make it into her bed, he would have to forget that his usual habit was to swat insignificant people who stood in the way of what he wanted. "I understand, Mistress Glory," he said reluctantly.

"Good. Now get dressed and go in for breakfast. There be cold porridge on the table and a pint of ale."

"*Cold?*"

"If you wants it warm, you can kick up the fire. I'll not be servin' you. And move your lazy arse. There's work to be done."

He stormed back to the house, painfully aware of his nakedness, and wondered if the blows to his pride were worth a tumble with this perverse creature—no matter how seductive she was.

Chapter Five

He came striding out of the cottage with easy confidence and smiled as he neared Gloriana. *As if he owned the world and all in it,* she thought with disgust. Or perhaps he hadn't accepted her lie about last night? She prayed it wasn't so, and twisted her face into a haughty sneer.

"And what be you grinnin' about, my fine jackanapes?" she asked.

He chuckled. "Much as I hate to admit it, your cold porridge tasted delicious. I didn't expect you to be such a good cook."

Was there an edge to his laughter? She wouldn't stand for it! She stamped her foot. "Be you mockin' me?"

The smile faded from his face, to be replaced by a bewildered frown. "Why, no. Are you so unfamiliar with approbation that you misread my words?"

"I... I... that is..." She fought against her blush, feeling stupid in his educated presence. "What do you mean by that?"

"Praise," he said gently. "That's the meaning of the word."

"Burn and blister me!" she said, jutting out her chin in defiance. "I knew that."

"Of course you did, mistress. Forgive me." He seemed genuinely apologetic.

His unexpected kindness made her uncomfortable. She wasn't about to let him forget he was her servant. Nor use his charm to take advantage of her. She turned about and stormed back into the stable. "Follow me, rogue," she ordered. "I needs your two strong arms."

He ducked through the doorway and scanned the small space. "I'll be damned. You've turned it into a smithy shop." He gestured toward the large brick fireplace and chimney, then surveyed the various wooden tables piled neatly with tools, the hooks on the walls that held more. "And a right fine place it is."

She snorted. "Took me weeks and a pretty penny to get the scoundrels from Whitby to put in the forge. We quarreled over the price of every bloody brick!" She crossed to the back of the space, where a small enclosure had been set aside for Black Jack. She nuzzled her face against the animal's forelock and stroked his mane. "Sorry to crowd you in, pet."

"A fine horse. I don't think I could have made it back here without him. And I thank you for that."

Was he trying to charm her again? "You were a bloody fool to risk your neck in the sea," she snapped. "A stranger to these parts. And scarcely a seaman. Be you daft? What made you do it?"

He shrugged. "Damned if I know. I've always been

impulsive, I suppose." He hesitated. "That is… I do things without thinking sometimes."

She didn't know whether to be angry or grateful for his gentle tutoring. "Well, I don't," she said sourly. "Now roll up your sleeves and pick up a spade. We needs to get the anvil set up." She indicated the large tree stump in the center of the room. "We'll sink it about halfway into the ground to keep it steady."

He whistled through his teeth. "That's a heavy load. How the devil did you get it here?"

She snorted. "Two thievin' caitiffs from the village. Took me half a day of arguin' to get 'em to do it. If I had me a wagon, Black Jack could have done it—and with no insolence."

He quirked an eyebrow at her. "Do you quarrel with everyone?"

That stopped her for a moment. Was she a shrew, as he seemed to suggest? "Only them what don't show me no respect," she said in her own defense. "And them what don't do as they're told! Pick up the bloody spade and get to work. I'll not pay good money for sluggards."

She saw the flash of anger in his eyes and stared him down. Then his clenched jaw relaxed and he sighed. "As you wish, mistress."

Working together, they dug a deep hole in the earthen floor, until Gloriana was satisfied with its depth. They lifted and dragged the tree stump into the hole, pounded it in firmly with sledgehammers, and packed the extra dirt around its base. By the time they had set the heavy iron anvil on top of the stump, they were both bathed in sweat.

Gloriana mopped her brow with her sleeve. "I'm that

dry, I couldn't spit a sixpence. I be needin' a drink."

He nodded. "A fine idea."

She jammed her hands on her hips. "Well? There be the ladle and bucket."

His mouth twisted into a frown. "Am I expected to…?"

"You be my manservant, be you not?"

He rolled his eyes and pulled the ladle from its hook on the wall. "God save me," he muttered. He dipped the ladle into the bucket of water, held it for her to drink, and then slaked his own thirst. He replaced the ladle and stared at her, his eyes unreadable. "Is it too much for me to hope for a word of thanks?"

His words stung. She remembered that even Allegra was quick to thank the servants. She lashed out with her only weapon—blind rage. "Bloody hell! You mind your insolent tongue, caitiff!"

"I have a name," he said in a tight voice. "I don't think you've used it once."

"Pah! John? Too common for a snot-nosed pig like you. I shall call you Thorne."

He seemed to be teetering on the edge of anger again. Then his expression softened and he chuckled. "I pray I'll not be a thorn in your side, mistress."

His easy humor took the edge off her own dark mood and she joined in his laughter. "Wicked devil." She hesitated, then nodded graciously in his direction. "But I thank you for the drink."

His beautiful eyes glowed with warmth. "You do me honor, mistress."

Flustered by her own reaction to his seductive gaze, she turned quickly, picked up a pair of tongs and placed half a dozen long bolts onto the coals of the forge, directing Thorne to work the bellows that would increase the heat of the fire. When the bolts had turned a glowing red, she put on a leather apron and handed another to Thorne.

"Do I need it?"

She snickered. "Only if you needs your man parts to work as they should. If you stands too close, the sparks could toast your prickle."

With her tongs, she pulled one of the bolts from the fire, then picked up a small hammer. The bottom of the anvil had been pierced with small holes; she inserted the red-hot bolt into one of the holes and pounded it in, curving the last few inches of the bolt over the foot of the anvil to anchor it securely to the tree trunk.

Thorne watched her closely as she worked, asking an occasional question and ducking the sparks that flew from every blow of her hammer. "May I try the last one?" he said, as she reached for the final bolt.

"Pah! You're scarce ready."

"I'll wager I can do it."

She eyed him with suspicion. "Wager? Be you a reckless gamblin' man?"

He grinned. "As a matter of fact, I am. Within reason, of course. And I never lose."

"Arrogant dog! I'll take your wager. What are your stakes?"

"As much as I enjoy a good tankard of ale, I like a bottle of wine from time to time." He smirked. "My 'high-handed' past, you understand. If I win, you allow me to go to Whitby tomorrow and purchase a bottle."

She snorted. "With whose coins?"

"Mine, if I lose. Yours, if I win. Agreed?"

I must be mad, she thought, then nodded. "It be on your head, braggart. Agreed." She offered him the tongs, clicking her tongue in annoyance as he held out his hand. "Bloody hell! You be left-handed."

"All my life. Does it matter?"

"Don't be a thick-skull. Of course it matters. How am I to teach you to hold any tools proper-like?"

Unexpectedly, he stepped behind her and encircled her with his arms. "Like this."

She wriggled in his embrace, her back rubbing up against his hard chest. "Cursed whoremonger! After this morning, you dare to...?"

"Be still!" he hissed. "This way we can both see our hands, and I can copy what you're doing with your right hand with my own left." He laughed softly as she relaxed within his arms. "I don't fancy another wrestling match today. Do you?"

She felt her face burning. His gesture had been innocent; it was she who had read a darker meaning into it. But his nearness unnerved her. She took a steadying breath and managed to sound indifferent. "Pah! You only won because you cheated and kicked at my ankles."

He chuckled softly behind her. "True enough. Now show me how to hold these blasted tools."

He was a surprisingly deft pupil, studying her movements with her right hand and transferring them to his left. And when he had pounded in the bolt and bent it to his satisfaction, he threw down his tools and laughed in delight. He grabbed her around the waist and swung her in a circle. "I'll be damned! What do you think of that, woman?"

"Put me down, caitiff!" She pounded at his chest until he released her. She didn't know what angered her more—that he had won his bet or that he had dared to touch her so brazenly again. "I bean't your 'woman'," she snarled. "I be mistress here!" She tore off her leather apron and added it to the tools on the floor. "Now pick all that up, and put 'em where they belongs. 'Tis time to eat. I'll be cookin' up some meat pies. I expects you to muck out Black Jack's stall. There be a wheelbarrow and a shovel by him. Dung pile is out back."

He looked truly stunned. "What? You expect me to do such a filthy job?"

"Only if you expects to *eat*. I'll pay for your blasted wine, but I'll feed you naught save pig-slop if you forgets your place again!" She saw the clench of his fists, the hard set of his jaw, and prepared herself to dismiss him on the spot. Then he closed his eyes for a moment, muttered something under his breath, and bent to the tools.

She swirled to the door, grinning in triumph. "It ain't like powderin' your master's wig, caitiff, or shinin' his boots, but it be good enough work for the likes of you. And don't forget to wash up near the cottage when you're done. After we eat, we'll pull out the trundle for you, and then you'll fetch water from the stream yonder."

She sailed toward the cottage, hearing the angry clank of iron tools bouncing off the stable walls. "So much for you, thorn-in-my-side," she said aloud. The hot-headed fool would only have to pick up the tools he was tossing around in his fury. He might have a temper to match her own, but she'd won this morning's battle, wager or no wager. And she intended to win all the rest, blast his soul!

• • •

"Will you have another mutton chop, Your Grace?"

Thorne put down his fork, wiped his mouth with his napkin and finished the last of his wine. "No. That was delicious, Dobson. Gads! I don't know how I'll endure only porridge and meat pies and bread and cheese. Plentiful, to be sure, and she cooks well enough, but I fear I'll be thoroughly sick of the menu before the week is out." He tapped the rim of his empty glass with an impatient finger. "And don't call me Your Grace. Someone might overhear. I'm Thorne to you as long as we're in Whitby."

Quick to obey his master's silent signal, Cleve Dobson picked up the wine decanter and refilled Thorne's glass, his nose twitching almost imperceptibly as he bent low to the table.

Thorne frowned, at once alert to the sudden change in his valet. "What is it?" he demanded.

Dobson cleared his throat delicately. "Begging your pardon, Your... Thorne, but you smell like a stable. I can ask the serving girl here to wash your shirt, if you wish."

That stung his pride. He had always been impeccable with his toilette, as befitted his lofty title. Then he sighed. "No. I'll stay as I am, more's the pity. We had both better get used to it, if I'm to keep up this pretense. Though I may purchase another second-hand coat one of these days. The one you bought me itches like the devil." He surveyed the comfortably furnished bedchamber of the inn and grunted. "And I'd trade my lumpy trundle for your bed in a moment, if I could."

Dobson shook his head. "Bad food, bad clothes, bad

lodgings. And a virago for a mistress. I think, if you'll pardon me, that this was one of your more reckless wagers."

He was beginning to think the same, but he wasn't about to let his servant know it. "I didn't give you leave to offer your opinion," he said coldly. "But I have until the end of September. Nearly three months. And I don't think it will take me that long to bed the wench."

"And a lock of her hair as proof?"

He gave a smug smile. "Once I have her in my bed, I can persuade her to do anything I want." He glanced up at his valet's face. "You don't approve of this, do you, Dobson." It was a statement more than a question.

Dobson shrugged. "'Tis not my place to approve or disapprove. Except for your wager, she's no different than any other woman you've seduced and jilted."

"And she's a strumpet, lest you forget. The very symbol of faithlessness." He took an angry swallow of his wine. "And speaking of faithlessness, is there any news from Sussex? How is my beloved mother, the Dowager Duchess, faring in the country?"

"Comfortably settled in for the summer. Your secretary, Rogers, will keep me abreast of any news concerning both domestic and business affairs, should you need to be informed."

Thorne stood up and stretched. "Gads, I ache all over. I can't wait to conclude this business. That woman is a terror. Always with some new back-breaking chore for me to do. This morning she had me hoeing the damn garden, and scarcely allowing me the time to stop and piss! The perverse creature is high-handed, arrogant, hot-tempered. It's all I can do to contain my own rage, sometimes. And she's proud and haughty, though it's unseemly for one of her low class, to my way of thinking."

Dobson turned away, but not quickly enough to hide the smirk on his genial young face.

Thorne scowled. "That amuses you, sirrah?"

Dobson hesitated, smoothing back the crown of his blond hair and fussing with the dishes on the sideboard. "If I may be frank, *Thorne*," he said at last, "that description could fit any number of gentlemen I have met in the four years I've been in your service. *Any* number. And try not to call me 'sirrah', if you please, whilst we are in Whitby. 'Tis an insulting word, even for an underling. I am a visiting scholar, lest you forget. You, on the other hand, are a lowly manservant who happens to smell of horse dung."

Thorne allowed himself a moment to quell his annoyance at Dobson's frank words. Then he smiled ruefully. "A fitting rebuke, my friend. I tolerate such imperious behavior from my own kind. And excuse it in myself. Why should she be any different? Though she might temper it with a little graciousness from time to time."

"Perhaps she's afraid."

"That shrew? Of what? She's fearless, it seems to me."

"But think of her position at Baniard Hall. A street whore, suddenly cast into nobility. I'm sure Lord and Lady Ridley were unfailingly kind to her, but what about the servants? They can be cruel, and far more conscious of a person's station than the gentry."

Thorne scratched his chin. "I never thought of that. She did say that she quarrels with those who don't show her any respect."

"And she might see insolence behind every innocent

remark. And feel the need to defend her pride."

"Hmm. I can see I shall have to tread more carefully if I intend to have her." He grinned up at Dobson. "But she is worth it. Gads! Wait till you see her. My hands itch to touch that body. And as for my other parts… I fear I shall have to wear my breeches loose to hide my desire!"

Dobson chuckled. "And, in the meantime, you'll become a blacksmith. The great Duke of Thorneleigh."

"By the horn of Satan, if you ever breathe a word of any of this, I'll sack you upon the instant! I'd be the talk of London for months." He reached for his battered hat. "'Tis time for me to go, before the wench takes my lateness for insolence."

"Have you forgotten your wager? The wine."

"Ah, yes." He laughed. "I think it was rather clever of me to find a way to come to Whitby and see you. I knew you'd be wondering what had become of me."

"Indeed. I was concerned when I heard talk in the village about the shipwreck and the 'stranger.' I feared it was you. A reckless but brave act. I should like to gossip about *that* when we return to London."

"Not a word! Lord DeWitt would mock me for my stupidity."

"Pshaw! His lordship's ration of courage would scarcely fit a thimble, if I may be so bold. I am exceedingly proud to call you my master, Your Grace."

Thorne nodded his acknowledgment of Dobson's praise and reached for his coat. "The wine?"

"I'll have the innkeeper bring up a bottle."

"No, wait." Thorne fished in his pocket and pulled out a handful of small coins. "This is all the tight-fisted witch gave me to spend. Scarcely enough for a cheap bottle of gin, let alone wine. If I'm to endure common food, the least I'm owed is a decent portion of good French wine. Get me the best that the innkeeper has to offer, as well as a common vintage, then switch the contents."

Dobson grinned. "Very clever. As was the wager for it. Did you doubt you'd win?"

"In truth, I was a trifle uneasy about that blasted bolt and my newly acquired skills. But I could think of no other way to come here alone and assure you that I was well and safe."

"And your coins?"

"Still safely in my shoe heels."

"And, of course, by winning the bet, you've maintained your unbroken streak of good fortune. I know you set great store by that."

That gave him pause. Had he heard an edge of scorn in Dobson's tone? That a man should measure his worth by something so trifling as the winning of a wager? Yet when he thought about it, he realized what his real triumph had been. "To tell you the truth, Dobson," he said, surprised at his own frankness, "what gave me joy at that moment was knowing I could *do* something, even such a simple chore as hammering in a bolt."

Dobson chuckled. "I suspect you may gain more from this mad adventure than merely the lady's favor."

Chapter Six

"Damme!" Thorne glared at the broken horseshoe draped over the anvil, lifted it with his tongs and thrust it into the bucket of water. It made a loud sizzling sound. "By the horn of Satan, why does the blasted thing keep breaking?"

Gloriana finished trimming Black Jack's hoof, gave him a soothing pat and turned to Thorne. "You're too quick to take the rod from the fire. Wait till it's white hot afore you starts to hammer it. Fetch another bar and start again."

Thorne tossed a cold iron bar into the red-hot forge and gnashed his teeth against his frustration. "How many days have we been at this? And still I can't get it right."

"You ain't the one who should be complainin'. Poor Black Jack here has had more new shoes this week than Queen Charlotte in her palace."

"And you've done them all." He slammed down his hammer and tongs on the work table. "You make it look so easy. I feel like a helpless fool." He cursed himself silently for admitting such a weakness to this high-handed creature.

Another reason for her to mock me, he thought sourly, and steeled himself for her usual sarcastic reply.

Instead, she laughed softly. "You're no fool, Thorne," she said. "'Tis only that you're... *impulsive.*"

He had to smile at that, remembering the word he had explained to her nearly a week ago. She might be uneducated, but she clearly wanted to learn. "Indeed I am. Forgive me, mistress." He pulled the ladle from the wall, dipped it in the bucket and brought it to her lips. "While we're waiting for the rod to heat..."

She took a small swallow of water, then murmured a soft, "Thank you." *Another lesson learned,* he thought.

She stared him full in the face, stunning him, as always, with her breathtaking beauty. Her lips were full and rosy, seeming to beg for his kiss, and her green eyes had softened to a mossy hue. He felt his insides quivering, and wondered if he should reach for her. But she turned away quickly, a blush rising in her cheeks, and crossed to the back of the smithy. "You must have more patience," she said in a voice that seemed to tremble, "if you wants to master the craft. I remember a tailor in London who used to say, 'Measure twice, cut once.' That be the ticket for any skill you learns."

He cursed himself for not taking her in his arms when he'd had the chance. Surely the look in her eyes had been an invitation. But the moment had passed. Best to cool his own desires. "You lived in London?" he asked in what he hoped was an offhand tone.

"Aye. Born and raised there."

"And that's where you learned to be a blacksmith?"

"Aye. Old Diggory Dyer. He were a master, were Old Diggory. My Da always said we would open a shop someday, when he had us enough coins."

"And is your father still alive?"

A shadow darkened her face. "No. He be gone near on to two years now."

"And still you miss him." He could read the grief in her eyes.

She sighed. "He were the only man I ever loved."

In some odd way, that pleased Thorne—that she hadn't loved her husband. *Fool!* he thought after a moment. Why the devil should he care? A whore, after all, lest he forget—how could love ever matter to her?

She turned away, but not quickly enough to hide the tears that had sprung to her eyes. Tears for her father, no doubt. He took her by the shoulders, turned her about and wiped at her cheek with tender fingers. She shook off his hands and scowled. "Bloody sot! You tryin' to be saucy with me again? I thought we settled that long-since!"

He forced himself not to smile, finding her fragile pride unexpectedly appealing. "Not at all, mistress," he said gently. "You had a smudge of soot on your face."

That seemed to satisfy her. "Well, then. Work them bellows to get the fire hot. We're wastin' the whole afternoon yammerin'."

Determined to get it right this time, Thorne concentrated on his work. He pulled the white-hot rod from the fire, carefully bent it into the proper shape on the curved horn of the anvil, then flattened its rounded sides. With Gloriana keeping Black Jack steady, he held the horse's foreleg between his knees and carefully placed the hot shoe against its hoof, pleased to see that it fit well.

Gloriana grinned. "You ain't so useless after all. Now

back to the work table and punch in the holes for the nails."

He did as she asked, carefully spacing the holes evenly around the horseshoe. Then he plunged the shoe into the bucket of water and grinned in his turn. "Now if Black Jack doesn't attack me…"

"Mind you aim the nails toward the outside of his hoof, so you don't hit the quick. I don't reckon I wants to patch your skull if he kicks you."

It took Thorne a few minutes to soothe the horse and win his trust, but at last he was able to nail the shoe onto the horse's hoof to his satisfaction, and finished the job by filing the rough edges of the horseshoe. He threw down his file and laughed. "By God, I did it!"

"So you did. Your first horseshoe." She glanced out the door at the sky, which had begun to turn pink. "And about time! Be you as hungry as I am?"

The thought of bread and cheese didn't excite him, but he was hungry. And they'd been at the forge all afternoon without a break. "Famished," he said.

"I think, in honor of your first success, we should have a bit of a celebration. I have me a nice smoked ham in the larder."

His spirits rose at that. "And will you join me and share my wine?" She had refused up until now, finding her common ale more to her liking.

She gave a little curtsy. "I should be pleased, sir."

He stared at her glowing face, cheeks pink from the heat of the fire, and shook his head. "What a lovely smile you have."

She stiffened. "Are you forgettin' your place again?"

He was about to answer angrily at this fresh insult to his

noble pride, then he remembered what Dobson had said.
A woman unused to flattery would be suspicious of every
kind word. "No, Mistress Glory," he said in as humble a
tone as he could manage, "I was merely trying to give you a
compliment. The ladies I have known are usually pleased to
be admired."

She tossed her head, but he could see the blush rising
up from her chin. "Humph! What makes you think I wants
to be a lady?"

Of course she does, he thought, realizing in a flash of insight
that her lack of polish must have been what had caused her
to flee the Ridley household. "Whatever you want to be," he
said, "you're a damn fine woman—and I won't apologize for
saying it."

She almost ran for the door. "Stuff and nonsense!
Put away them tools and feed Black Jack. And be sure you
wash up afore supper. You looks like a blackamoor with all
that soot!"

• • •

Gloriana held out her goblet to Thorne. "I'll have a bit more
wine, if you please."

Thorne smiled ruefully at her from across the table and
turned the wine bottle upside-down. "Alas. Not a drop left."

She felt a pang of disappointment. Supper had gone
wonderfully, the warm wine filling her belly and her soul,
giving her an unfamiliar glow. It was a pity for it to end so
soon, and all for the lack of more to drink. "I do have a
jug of rum…" she began, then shook her head. "No.
Too wasteful."

His lower lip puffed in a little-boy pout. "But this is my celebration dinner. Don't I deserve it?" The pout dissolved into a contented smile. "And the ham was delicious, by the way. A bit of rum would be a fitting end to such a splendid supper."

"No."

"What if I make a wager on it?"

"Be you daft? What stakes?"

He swiveled on his bench and looked toward the fireplace. "See the two logs at either end of the fire? The ones that are nearly burned through? I'll wager that the one on the right will break and collapse first."

She studied the logs carefully. They both seemed equally burned, and it was a silly wager. But she was feeling giddy. "Agreed," she said. "But the left one will go first."

They stared at the logs for a few minutes, absorbed in the bet. Suddenly, with a small crackle, the side of the right-hand log tipped and broke off, dropping into the fire with a burst of sparks.

Thorne cackled. "Ha! I told you I never lose a wager."

Conceding graciously—and oddly pleased that the bet had turned out the way it had—Gloriana crossed to the larder and reached for the rum, spying a small dish of stale sweet cakes sitting on a shelf. "They be a trifle hard," she said, placing the bowl on the table in front of Thorne, "but we can dip 'em in the rum. In honor of your first horseshoe."

He poured them both a generous portion of rum, then grinned in satisfaction. "And my first blister."

She frowned. "Show me." When he held out his left hand to her, she clicked her tongue. "Fool! You should have told me. I could bind it for you, with a bit of ash from the fireplace to help it heal."

He looked at her, his silvery eyes shining with pride. "No. 'Tis my badge of honor. You have my gratitude, mistress. I confess that I've never made anything before with my own two hands."

"In your whole life?" She eyed him with sympathy. "Never built a toy house of twigs? Or made paper boats as a child?"

He shook his head. "I always had carved wooden boats that the servants made for me."

"Servants?" The word aroused her suspicions. "What was your life afore this?" she asked, squinting at him.

He looked embarrassed for a moment, like a little boy caught in a lie. He took a deep swallow of his rum, then stumbled out his reply. "I... that is... I was raised in a prosperous household, but then my father lost everything and I had to hire out as a valet."

"And a soldier?" She was still suspicious.

"That was a lie, I do confess." He had the grace to blush.

His unexpected honesty eased her doubts. And his humility made him all the more attractive. She had seen his pride, his temper, his arrogance, but the softer side that he was revealing tonight was charming. "Poor child," she murmured. "Did you have no childhood dreams?"

He shrugged. "I was too pampered to think of anything but my immediate desires, which were always fulfilled."

"And now? No dreams for the future?"

He was silent at that, his face a mask of surprising despair. He took another swallow of rum and smiled stiffly at her. "And what of your dreams?" he said at last.

She finished her rum and poured a bit more into her

goblet. "To be a successful tradeswoman, of course."

He puffed out his chest. "With a skilled blacksmith at her side!"

"Well, you ain't as bone-lazy as I thought you'd be."

"And you *aren't* as fierce as you pretend," he said gently.

She knew he was correcting her speech, but his tone had been kindly, not mocking. She nodded in acknowledgement, her old lessons from Baniard Hall coming back to her. There would be no danger in improving herself in his presence. "You be... you *are* a rum gent," she said, "and that's the truth."

"And you're a wonder," he murmured.

The conversation was growing too intimate for her comfort. "We should talk about the morrow," she said crisply. "I think we'll go to Whitby. I have purchases to make. And perhaps we can talk up the smithy and see if we can get us a few customers."

They spent the next quarter of an hour discussing their plans for the next day. Safe talk, though the rapidly emptying jug of rum was beginning to give Gloriana a mellow buzz. "Let me see to that blister," she said at last, rising from her bench to cross to the fireplace. He followed. She pricked the blister with a pin, then found a scrap of fabric. Scooping a bit of cold ash from the side of the fire, she placed it carefully on his blister, then tied the bandage around Thorne's palm. She patted it with a motherly hand. "There you be."

He put his unbound hand over hers. His flesh was warm, sending a thrill down her spine. "You're a tender nurse," he said, his eyes soft with desire. "Thank you." He smiled. "I should very much like to kiss you at this moment."

Why did he have to spoil their lovely evening, reminding

her of her own longings? She would be foolish to give in, to make him think he was her equal. "You go too far!" she burst out, pulling her hand away.

"How can I earn a kiss, then?"

"What makes you think you deserve one, caitiff?" she sputtered. It seemed a good time to remind him of his inferior station.

But instead of becoming annoyed at the word, he laughed. "I didn't say I deserved it—I simply thought it would be a pleasant ending to our celebration. Come. You took my foolish wager before. What say we bet on a kiss?"

She thought about that, weighing the possibilities. If she won, it would put him in his place once and for all. She had a sudden idea. "But I name the stakes," she said with a crafty smile.

"I'm agreeable to that. What is your wager?"

"Indian wrestlin'. The way the savages do in the New World. Arm to arm, until one arm is pushed to the table."

"But that's absurd! I know you're strong, but you *are* just a woman."

She was growing more and more confident she could best him. She had seen him at his work, knew what he was capable of. "Ah, but you be left-handed. If you use your right hand against my right hand, that should even the odds."

"Even so, I fear I'd break your arm."

She smirked, egging him on. "Be you a coward? Afraid to lose a wager? Ain't you the great gamblin' man who never loses?" She knew, from the sudden flash of anger on his face, that she had hit him where he lived—in his pride.

He sighed in resignation. "So be it. But I think you're mad." He crossed to the table, rolling up his sleeve as he went. They sat facing one another, elbows firmly on the table, right hands clasped together. At a signal from Gloriana, they began to push against each other's hand.

She closed her eyes and imagined herself back in the gladiators' ring, all her focus on her right arm. She could feel the power of Thorne's muscles, hear his grunts from the effort—it only made her more determined to win. She took a deep breath, then, marshaling all her strength, she gave a sharp cry and pushed violently against him, slamming his forearm onto the table.

She opened her eyes. His face, bathed in sweat, was dark with fury. He released her hand and jumped from his bench, storming toward the fireplace and smacking his palm against the mantel. She couldn't tell if he was angry at losing his bet or losing his kiss. His turned back was stiff with injured pride.

"Come," she said gently. "Can you not be gracious in your losin', though you be arrogant when you win?"

His shoulders relaxed a bit and he turned, a thin smile on his face. "'Tis only that I'm disappointed." He crossed back to the table and emptied the last of the rum into their goblets. He picked up a sweet cake, dipped it into the liquid and chewed it slowly, as though he hadn't a care in the world.

But she knew he was fighting with his pride. In a strange way, she felt guilty for hurting him. She indicated two rush armchairs in the corner. "Draw up the chairs to the fire," she said. "'Twould be pleasant to warm our toes while we finish our rum."

She could see gratitude in his eyes—that she didn't intend to humiliate him by crowing over her win. While he pulled the chairs toward the fire, she carried the cakes and goblets. "Do you smoke?" she asked, after they had settled themselves comfortably before the hearth.

He looked surprised. "In point of fact, I do. But where...?"

"The last tenants here left pipes and tobacco." She had bought them for Charlie, but he had always been too impatient, pacing the room with angry strides, for the relaxation of a pipe. She fetched the fixings and watched Thorne go through the motions of filling the clay pipe and lighting the tobacco with a taper from the fire. He moved with an easy grace, the golden glow of the candles softening the lines of his angular jaw, his patrician nose.

He settled back in his chair and blew out a mouthful of smoke. "Is that the way you treat all the men you meet? Force them to arm-wrestle for your favors?" There was no lingering resentment in his voice, only good humor.

"Don't be daft." She thought suddenly of Charlie, who had simply taken what he wanted. His kisses had been offhand and passionless—his only thought had been to satisfy his prickle in bed. But Thorne's kiss... she felt her insides melting, remembering the day they had met. *Foolish jade!* she thought after a moment. This was not the time to think about kisses from a servant, when she had just shown him she was mistress here. "Shall we talk more of the trip to Whitby?" she said quickly. "We needs flour and salt and butter. A few carrots for the pies. And a new jug of rum for cold nights."

"And wine, mistress?"

"Pah! Don't give me none o' your hang-dog look. You shall have your wine, my pampered princeling."

"Thank you, Mistress Glory. And didn't you say we

needed more iron rods for the forge?"

"Aye. And more seeds for the garden. The way the lettuce is growing, we shall have salad with our supper soon enough."

He shook his head in wonder. "Damned if I can get over how fast it grows! Every day when I hoe, I can't wait to see it."

She laughed at that. "Bloody hell. We shall turn you into a gardener as well as a blacksmith!"

They lapsed into silence, lulled by the warmth of the fire, the sweet aroma of tobacco smoke, the soothing rum. Gloriana felt her head dropping forward, her eyes closing. *I should really go to bed*, she thought. *I should...*

She gasped in surprise, feeling herself lifted and cradled in Thorne's strong arms. "What are you doin'?" she cried, wriggling in his embrace. "Put me down!"

"Shhh," he crooned. "You were falling asleep where you sat. I doubt you have the will to stumble up the stairs yourself. Take up that candle to light the way." He bent low to allow her to reach the candelabra.

She knew she should insist that he put her down, but she felt warm and secure, and oddly comforted to be cossetted like a child. She reached for the candle and allowed him to carry her up the stairs. He kicked open the door to her room and laid her gently at the foot of her bed, taking the candle from her; then he stripped back the coverlet. Kneeling at her feet, he removed her shoes, discreetly untied her garters below her knees and pulled off her stockings. She lay still, enjoying his kind attentions. But when he reached for her bodice and began to untie her stays, she sat up in alarm.

"What are you doin'?"

"You can't have a decent night's sleep when your ribs are crushed. Keep still." He undid the laces, then held up a folded handkerchief that had fallen from her bodice. "What is this?"

She gasped. Her keepsake—Billy's lock of hair. She snatched it from him and shoved it under her pillow. "That be mine! None o' your business."

He shrugged. "Whatever you say." He lifted her once more and placed her head on the pillow, pulling up the coverlet to her chin. Then, with a wicked grin, he leaned down and planted a soft kiss on her mouth.

She was suddenly wide awake, ready to do battle. How dare the rogue take such liberties?

But he was already backing away toward the door. He gave a humble bow. "Good night, Mistress Glory," he said, his face a mask of boyish innocence. Then he was gone. She could hear him whistling softly as he descended the stairs. Heard the scrape of the trundle bed as he dragged it before the fire.

The poxy villain! she thought. Smug and proud because he'd had his kiss after all. Well, by thunder, she would see to it that he walked several paces behind her in Whitby tomorrow. The way a proper servant should.

But it was hours before she could sleep, still tasting the sweetness of his mouth on hers.

Chapter Seven

"Lift your bloody feet, you sluggard, and follow along o' me! We ain't got all mornin'." Gloriana glanced back at Thorne and gave him a withering scowl.

Struggling with his armload of packages, Thorne swore under his breath. The great Duke of Thorneleigh indeed! To be treated like a beast of burden. He'd even had to walk behind her on the trip to Whitby, while she rode Black Jack. It was all he could do to keep from throwing down his load and giving up his mad wager. The witch seemed determined to bedevil him today, to play the lordly "mistress." Bundles piled upon bundles, heavy purchases that seemed chosen merely to increase the weight he was forced to carry. He stumbled on a loose cobblestone on the Whitby street and swore again.

Clearly he had gone too far when he'd kissed her last night. And now he was suffering because of her injured pride. *I must be going mad,* he thought. More and more she was getting under his skin, like a burr on his saddle when he rode in the woods. He felt torn between the urge to smack her rounded bottom with the flat of his hand, or toss her down and take her on the smithy floor and satisfy his hungers once and for all. And all the while knowing he could do neither, but had to maintain his humble pose, no matter how often she irked him or provoked his growing desire.

"If you please, Mistress Glory," he said as calmly as he was able, "I saw a basket-seller down the lane." When she turned, a sour expression on her face, he managed a thin smile. He juggled the awkward packages. "If I could purchase a basket, I could carry all these on my back."

"Burn and blister me! You be free with my money, bean't you."

He ground his teeth together. "Damn it, I'll pay for it myself."

She snorted. "And where be you findin' coins? Under a rock?"

"I have a few coppers of my own."

"Well..." She glanced down Church Street, crowded with Friday morning market stalls. Flower sellers jostled with onion farmers for a bit of space on the busy street, and an angry sausage maker, his stall festooned with garlands of his wares, shook his fist at an equally angry goose girl, whose creatures had ventured beyond their pen and were trying to snatch at the strings of meat. Among the crowd, Thorne could see an occasional customer or tradesman with a bit of black crepe pinned to a garment—in memory of a lost one from the recent storm, he guessed.

Gloriana shrugged. "If you must, softling," she sneered, "go and buy your basket. We be needin' more charcoal for the forge. And there be my man yonder. You get your basket while I talks to him about bringin' round a new delivery."

Thorne threaded his way through the throng of people on the narrow lane, dodging a milkmaid with a yoke of pails on her shoulders. He tried to ignore the cold faces that turned toward him, the people who barely made way for him as he passed—he was still a stranger, an outsider in the community. *Small towns*, he thought with a mental shrug. Perhaps, before he left Whitby, he'd find acceptance. Though why it should matter to him, he couldn't fathom. Common people, after all.

When he finally reached the basket-seller, he was pleased to be unexpectedly greeted by a friendly smile on the young woman's face. He took a moment to appraise her charming features and full, rounded breasts, then dumped his packages on the crowded table in front of her. "I need a basket."

She laughed, allowing her gaze to travel the length of him with a brazenness that surprised him. "That you do, my fine cove," she said. "Though, if you be the blacksmith for Mistress Cook, as I hear tell, you be strong enough to carry that load."

He snorted. "Only if I'd studied to be a juggler at a county fair."

She lifted a basket from a pile on the ground—a strong wicker with heavy leather straps. "I think you have the shoulders for this size. A fine strapping man like you. And only tuppence. At least for a man who knows what he wants." She favored him with a suggestive smile, clearly meant as an invitation.

He was glad he'd thought to pull a few coins from his shoe before the trip to Whitby. He fished the silver coin from his pocket and handed it to the girl. "Worth the price." With her eager help, he loaded his packages into the basket and hoisted it to his shoulders, pleased at the comfort and convenience it gave him.

She came around from her table and adjusted the straps across his shoulders, her hands lingering on his broad chest. She gazed up at him, pursing her lips in a seductive pout. "There you be. And if you be coming to town soon again, you can find me down the lane in the shop."

An easy conquest, he thought. But when had it ever been difficult for him? He wondered if he should kiss her right here and now. God knew his body was painfully eager for a woman. He could make the arrangements with Dobson, have her waiting at the inn the next time he visited Whitby.

But the image of Gloriana suddenly danced in his head—her lush body, her beautiful face—and suddenly he knew that he didn't want just any woman. He wanted *her*, with a passion that was eating away at him. Which was absurd, of course. Why should his only desire be for a faithless whore? "I don't come to town often," he said gently, and watched the girl's smile fade with disappointment.

He hurried away from the stall and made his way back to Church Street. He heard Gloriana's shrill voice long before he reached her, arguing with the charcoal man. He quickened his steps.

• • •

Gloriana rolled her eyes in exasperation. Was she never in her life to be treated in a proper manner? "What do you mean, caitiff," she shrieked, "you can't deliver the charcoal tomorrow? When I pays you good money, I expects service!" The man bared his teeth at her. "I told you, Mistress Cook, you'll have to wait till Monday. I have two other deliveries tomorrow. And a bad back besides."

"I don't give no tinker's damn what ails you! When I asks—" Gloriana stopped in mid-sentence, feeling a strong hand on her arm, tugging her away from the stall. She whirled about and scowled. Thorne! "What do *you* want, thorn-in-my-side?"

He pulled her away from the crowd and gave her arm an angry shake. "Must you always quarrel to get your way?"

"That man didn't give me no respect."

"*Any* respect," he hissed. "You screamed at him like a fishwife. Why should he show you respect?"

The man was impossible—correcting her speech, lecturing her as though he was her equal. "What do you know of respect, knave? Kissin' me last night as though you had a right!"

She expected a sharp reply. Instead, he hung his head, refusing to look her in the eye. "You're right," he said softly. "I should never have done that, mistress. I apologize for my lack of respect." He lifted his head and looked directly at her, his soft gray eyes opening wide, as though a sudden idea had caught him by surprise. "I never thought of it before. No woman should have to give up her favors just because a man wants them. And to take advantage, as I did last night... Forgive me."

How could she remain angry with him when he seemed genuinely sorry? She managed a small laugh. "Perhaps we both had a bit too much rum last night."

He smiled his relief. "Indeed. Are we friends again?"

She cocked an eyebrow at him. "Friends? As much as we can be. Mistress and servant, after all. But as friendly as we can be."

"I'm agreeable to that."

She scanned his form, strong and upright with his burden. "That be a fine basket. I should have thought of it myself." She rummaged in the pocket of her skirt and pulled out a few coins. "How much did it cost?"

"No, no, mistress. You needn't reimburse… pay me back."

Reimburse. A nice word. She must remember it. "But I'll pay for your wine. And the rum, lest we forget." She pressed a silver bob into his hand.

"Thank you. Now, as to the charcoal… if we're careful, we can make it last until Monday. Now that I've got the knack of it, I can make a few horseshoes without wasting the fire on my mistakes." He gave her a doubtful smile. "That is, if the man is still willing to deliver."

"Humph!"

He put a gentle hand on her arm. She could feel the comforting warmth of his flesh through her sleeve. "Go back to him. Make your peace."

"Go back? Be you… *are* you mad? When he never showed me no… *any* respect?"

"Why should he? You can't demand respect. You expect it, by showing respect in turn. And then you receive it. A true lady doesn't have to be haughty. She knows her own worth. 'Tis not an accident of birth that gives a woman true nobility. 'Tis the purity of her respect for others."

His voice was soft and kind—a helpful tutor not a scolding tyrant, as that little worm at Baniard Hall had been.

And perhaps he was right. She had always felt so small, so unimportant among her betters—even Charlie, fallen to a lawless life, had been able to bully her most of the time because of his noble birth. She looked helplessly at Thorne. "But what am I to do? To say?"

"To start, don't always be so defensive."

"What does that mean?" she asked. His manner was so understanding, she didn't mind showing her ignorance a bit.

"Ready to quarrel all the time. It isn't necessary." He grinned. "Remember, you can catch more flies with honey than with vinegar." He stroked the side of her cheek with soft fingers. "And with that beautiful face, it should be easy for you. Expect to be respected. Believe in it. People will see it in your eyes. Hear it in your voice."

His touch made her shiver. And his words warmed her heart, gave her courage. "Do you truly think so?"

"I do. Go back to him and try again. You can do it." He stopped her with a hand on her arm as she turned toward the charcoal seller. "And one more thing. Try to lower your tone. Your voice can be quite shrill. Highborn ladies practice speaking in a soft, deep voice. Think of a cat purring."

She laughed at that. "But cats have claws."

"Ah, but they only show them when it's necessary, not for every minor annoyance."

Encouraged by his confidence in her, she approached the charcoal seller once again. She took a moment to concentrate on lowering her voice and remembering her grammar. Then she smiled and spoke slowly, carefully choosing her every word. "I do ask you to forgive me, sir." She hoped he'd be pleased with her use of the gentlemanly address. "I was hasty before. Too...*defensive*. I have spoken to my blacksmith. We would be satisfied with a Monday delivery. You with your bad back, and all."

He grunted. "A touch of the lumbago is all, even on warm days."

She remembered her aching muscles after she'd been in the gladiator ring. She clicked her tongue in sympathy. "You b...*are* a man in pain, more's the pity. But perhaps a hot pack? And, foolish though it may sound, you might have someone stand on your back whilst you are lyin' down." She chuckled. "Not too heavy a cove, you understand!"

"That be very kind of you, mistress. To take notice of my misery." He scratched his chin. "If I can get my boy to do one of my local deliveries, I think I can manage to get the charcoal to you tomorrow."

"No, no..."

"No trouble, Mistress Cook. It would be my pleasure."

"Thank you." She favored him with a dazzling smile, then turned back to Thorne, scarcely keeping her jaw from dropping in wonderment. "But that was so easy," she whispered, staring up into his grinning face.

"I knew you could do it. And if we weren't in a crowded market, I'd kiss you as a reward. But only with your permission," he added quickly, as she glared at him.

"Only if you wins it by arm-wrestlin', knave." Her words were more harsh than she'd meant them to be. She softened her tone by smiling up at him.

"You're a hard woman, Mistress Cook," he said, his own smile showing her he hadn't taken offense.

"Come along, then, and don't bedevil me, rogue," she said with a small laugh. "There's more to buy afore we picks up Black Jack at the stable and heads for home." She made her way down the street, almost sorry that he had fallen into step a few paces behind her.

"Wait a moment, mistress." When she turned, he pointed to a large sign over a shop. "Look. That might be the way to get business for the smithy."

She stared at the sign in bewilderment. "Oglethorpe—Fine Calligraphy and Advertisements" it said. She bit her lip. The only words she could understand were "Fine" and "and." "If you think so," she said uncertainly.

He studied her face with searching eyes. "You can't read, can you?" he said at last.

She felt a hot blush flood her face. "Burn and blister me! 'Course I can." But when he continued to stare, his gray eyes warm with understanding, she lowered her head in shame. "I... I been learnin', but some words..."

He lifted her chin with gentle fingers and smiled. "'Tis no crime. I've known many a fine man who never learned. And many a well-read London fop who's as ignorant as a country bumpkin." He pointed to the sign again. "Master Oglethorpe there can print us handbills advertising... *telling about* our trade. And, for a few extra pence, I'm sure he could find a young lad to hand them out all over the town. We can talk about what you want to say on them, and I can arrange it with the printer when next I come to Whitby."

She nodded. "Yes. Thank you. A fine idea." She lifted her chin boldly, no longer afraid of his scorn. "What does that other word mean? Colli... colli...?"

He laughed. "Calligraphy. It's simply a high-handed word for fancy writing. Master Oglethorpe can write letters for people, with many loops and curls and such." His mouth twisted in a wicked smirk. "Say if you were to wish to write a letter to an eager lover…"

She poked him playfully in the chest. "Oh, get on with you, John Thorne. Always teasin' me. I ain't about to let you into my bed."

He bowed humbly, but she could see the glint of mischief in his eyes. "Of course not, mistress. I'm not about to forget my place."

She wasn't sure he would *ever* know his place. "Humph!" she said to cover her confusion. She turned briskly and continued down Church Street, toward the quay. "We'll go this way. Fish for supper, I think."

The streets near the river were even noisier than Church Street had been. Several shipbuilding factories had been set up alongside the quay, and half-finished vessels swarmed with busy workers. But above the clank of iron fittings and the thud of countless hammers, Gloriana suddenly heard the sweet, shrill sound of a flute. She and Thorne moved closer, where a small crowd had gathered. A young man, dressed in dark and simple clothing, sat on a bench, playing a lively song that Gloriana had often heard sung by the sailors at the port. In front of the man, several children danced to the merry tune.

Thorne let out a gasp. "I'll be damned!"

His outburst had been so unexpected that Gloriana turned in alarm. "What is it?"

She had never seen him so rattled. "That… man…" He took a deep breath. "That is… I met him when I came to Whitby before. Dobson, I think his name is. A scholar visiting from London. We chatted for a bit. I was surprised to see him playing the flute, is all. He never mentioned it when we spoke."

"You gave me a fright. I thought the sky was fallin'!"

He laughed and took her by the arm. "Come. I should like you to meet him." He steered a path through the crowd and approached the man. "Master Dobson, sir," he said. "I'm John Thorne. You remember we met when last I was in Whitby?"

Dobson put down his flute and rose to his feet. Gloriana noted his fine features, his clear blue eyes, the golden hair tied back with a black velvet ribbon. He smiled warmly at Thorne. *A fine man*, she thought, without the haughtiness she had seen in more than one scholarly man in London. "Thorne," he said. "Ah, yes. How nice to see you again."

Thorne indicated Gloriana. "I should like you to meet my mistress."

Dobson reached for her hand. "Mistress Cook, is it not?" Instead of shaking her hand, he lifted her fingers to his lips and kissed them softly. "'Tis my pleasure, ma'am."

Thorne coughed loudly beside her. "You aren't at a fancy ball, Master Dobson." Gloriana was surprised to hear a note of irritation in his voice.

Dobson scowled. "Please do not speak to me in that insolent tone, John. Your mistress is a beautiful woman who deserves every honor I can show her."

Thorne's smile was tight with controlled fury. "Your pardon, sir."

Gloriana rolled her eyes. What was it about men that they had to compete with one another at every turn? Though she couldn't imagine why they seemed to be on the edge of a quarrel. Best to change the subject. "You play a fine flute, Master Dobson," she said quickly.

"Thank you, ma'am. I have been studying the songs the

seamen sing at work. A most interesting field of study."

Thorne seemed to make an effort to control his feelings. "But the flute, sir. You never spoke of your talent. That is, when last we met."

Dobson smirked. "I have many talents. It only takes inquiry to find them out."

Thorne nodded. "Indeed. I have been thoughtless. Not to have asked," he added humbly.

Dobson smiled, showing dimples in his cheeks. "No matter." Several townsfolk crowded toward him, begging him to play again. "Perhaps tomorrow," he said, shaking hands with a number of people and waving to an elderly couple who were passing by.

Thorne raised an eyebrow. "You seem to have made a number of friends in town. And in a short time."

Dobson scanned them both, a puzzled frown on his face. "And you have not?"

Gloriana blushed, feeling shamed by his question. How could she have made friends, when she quarreled so often with the townspeople? "We... come to town so seldom... and the cottage is so... so..." She couldn't think of a proper word.

"Secluded," Thorne said quickly. She shot him a smile of gratitude.

Dobson chuckled. "Why then, we must remedy that at once." He motioned to the couple, who hurried to join them. "Master Wilson," he said, indicating Gloriana, "I should like you and your charming wife to meet Mistress Glory Cook, who has opened a blacksmith shop just outside of town."

Gloriana smiled, welcoming their warm handshakes. "'Tis my pleasure, sir. Madam."

Wilson returned her smile. "Ah, yes. Are you not in the old Wickham place just above Robin Hood's Bay?"

"Aye. That we… *are.* A cozy cottage." She turned toward Thorne. "And this… *is* my manservant and blacksmith, John Thorne." She nodded regally at him. "Make your proper salute to these fine people, John."

She saw the familiar flash of anger in his eyes for what he took to be an insult to his pride, but he managed a small bow. "Sir. Madam," he said in a tight voice.

Dobson nodded, a sly smile on his face. "Very humbly done, John," he said in a lordly voice. "Good for you." Gloriana saw Thorne's fist curl in fury, and wondered why Dobson seemed to be deliberately provoking him. Then the man went on smoothly, as though he were unaware of the effect of his words on Thorne. "Master Wilson, I understand that John, here, is a most skilled blacksmith. You might ask your friends to visit Mistress Cook's shop."

The old man nodded. "A fine idea, sir." He turned to Gloriana. "And can your man fashion other things besides horseshoes?"

"Yes indeed, sir. Soup-ladles, wrought-iron fences, all manner of tools." She ignored Thorne's look of panic. She'd been turning out goods like that for Old Diggory for ages.

"I'll certainly spread the word, ma'am."

Dobson's expression was suddenly serious. "One other thing, Master Wilson. You recall the shipwreck last week, of course."

"Dobson! No!" Thorne leaped toward the man as though he intended to strangle him.

Dobson's blue eyes narrowed. "Do not interrupt me, sirrah. I *will* tell it." He smiled at Wilson and gestured at

Thorne with a wide sweep of his hand. "This fine man here was the stranger who so bravely directed much of the rescue effort."

"You don't say! Good job." Wilson patted Thorne on the shoulder, while his wife, her eyes wide, turned to a nearby group of women and began to whisper excitedly to them. In a moment, Thorne was surrounded by half a dozen townsfolk, all praising him and eager to shake his hand. He seemed embarrassed by all the attention, his cheeks turning red.

Gloriana giggled softly. Who would have thought that such a proud man could suddenly turn so shy? She knew it was wicked of her, but she turned to him and smiled innocently. "Say a few words to these fine people, Thorne."

"Mistress…" His eyes were full of pleading.

"No. You must. I insist on it."

He glared at her, then cleared his throat. "I only did what had to be done. If you wish to show your gratitude, bring your business to Mistress Cook here."

After a few more minutes of congratulations, the crowd slowly drifted away, taking Dobson with them. Gloriana turned to Thorne and giggled again. "I do believe you be shy, Thorne."

"I'm not used to praise for something I've actually done," he growled. "Now, weren't you going to buy fish for supper? And I still need to get some wine and rum."

He seemed so uncomfortable that she wanted to make her peace with him. *More flies with honey*, she thought. She gave him her warmest smile. "I'm sorry, John. I reckon I wanted to tease you a bit, as you like to tease me."

He relaxed at that. "Fair enough. I suppose I deserved a

bit of your revenge." He pointed to the crowd, still buzzing with Wilson's news. "And I think we won't lack for customers in Whitby now. Nor friends."

"Thanks to your Master Dobson." She indicated the clock in the town square. "I'll meet you at the stable at half after the hour."

"I'll be there, mistress."

She watched him go, striding purposefully back to Church Street. *Friends.* They would have friends in town. When she thought of it, she realized that, though she had known many people in London, she had never felt that they were true friends. And now she was to have what she had missed in her life.

And of all of them, the dearest friend, she knew with a sudden flash, had become—in such a short time that it made her head spin—John Thorne. As though she had known him for ages.

"I shall cook you a fine supper tonight, John, my friend," she whispered softly.

Chapter Eight

Thorne tore off a chunk of bread from the fresh loaf and mopped up the last of the fish stew in his bowl. He savored his final taste of strong mackerel, potatoes, and rich cream, then washed it down with a large gulp of his wine. "Damme, but that was good," he exclaimed, smacking his lips.

Gloriana shrugged in seeming indifference, though he noticed that she could scarcely hide the satisfaction on her face. "That were... *was* nothing."

"No, really. You are a superb cook."

"What does that mean? Superb?"

He noted with pleasure that she no longer seemed embarrassed to ask about words. "The best of the best," he explained.

"Humph. You were just hungry."

That was true enough. After their morning shopping in Whitby, they had spent all afternoon in the forge. Thorne had successfully hammered out half a dozen horseshoes in various sizes, now pegged neatly on the wall of the shop, then watched in amazement as Gloriana had fashioned ladles and pothooks and assorted iron tools with a skill he could only hope to master. "But hungry or not," he said, "your cooking was delicious." He smiled slyly at her. "How can I thank you for supper? My usual thanks to a beautiful woman?"

"You *are* a devil, John Thorne." She pushed aside her plate, rolled up her sleeve, and anchored her elbow firmly on the table. "Win it then. If you can."

He couldn't avoid her challenge, though he was determined not to sulk if he should lose this time. *If* he should lose. She wouldn't take him by surprise, as she had last night. He positioned himself across the table and clasped her hand. At her signal, he strained mightily against her, his teeth clenched in concentration. But it was no use. He felt his arm slowly giving way to her superior strength, and allowed himself a small muttered curse as she slammed his arm onto the table. He forced a smile. "One of these days, mistress…"

She grinned. "But not tonight, John. Alas." She rose from the bench and cleared the table. While she rinsed their bowls, he pulled the armchairs near the hearth. She indicated a small basket set on a shelf. "Fetch my sewin', Thorne. I'll do a bit of mendin', I think. Will you smoke?"

"Not yet. And I have something better than your sewing tonight." When she raised a questioning eyebrow, he crossed to his coat, fished in its pocket and pulled out a small volume. "A gift for you."

"Will you read to me, then?"

"No. You'll read to me."

She shook her head. "You know I can't… that is…" She

stamped her foot. "Will you shame me, caitiff? And in my own house?"

"'Tis not meant to shame you. How can you learn to read if you don't practice?" He held out his hands, palms upward, and pointed to the growing calluses, the blister that was beginning to heal. "If you can make a blacksmith out of a 'softling,' as you've called me, why can't I make a reader out of you? I've been angry at myself from time to time, but only at my lack of skill. Not because I was ashamed."

She looked down, seeming to struggle with her pride. "What is the book?" she said at last, lifting her chin and staring boldly into his eyes.

"'Tis called *Colonel Jack*, by Daniel Defoe. I've heard it's quite a lively story." When she still hesitated, he smiled. "You can do it. Did you not charm the charcoal seller this morning?"

"That be... was different. I can't charm the words out of a book by smilin'."

"True enough." He crossed to the table and indicated the bench. "Sit beside me. I'll read to you for a bit. Follow along with the words as I read, and stop me if you need a word to be explained. You can take over when you feel ready."

She nodded in relief and took her place beside him. He found it difficult to concentrate on the book, with her seductive body pressed close against his, but he began at last to read. She followed along, occasionally interrupting him to ask about a word.

It was indeed a lively story, concerning a young bastard son of a gentlemen brought up by a foster mother with two other boys similarly disadvantaged. And the description of their lives in the back streets of London, as they spiraled into petty crimes, made him chuckle. He was surprised that

Gloriana sighed unhappily at every humorous misadventure. "Don't you find it amusing?" he asked at last.

She looked up at him, her green eyes glistening with the beginning of tears. "I have known too many boys like that," she said. "Poor children, fightin' for every crumb of bread. They winds up in prison, or starvin' to death. I were a bastard, too. But at least I had my Da, and we got along. We didn't live in the streets."

"What did he do, your father?"

"I makes no excuses. He were a thief." She spat out the words like a challenge, but he could read the uncertainty in her eyes.

"'Tis not for me to judge," he said gently. And surely it was so, he thought with sudden realization. He'd never thought about it much, the grinding poverty of the London streets. He'd enjoyed his privileged life, seldom noticing or caring about those whom he considered beneath him. He'd given generously to his church, to charity, of course, but he'd never been particularly interested in where his money went. "And what did you do, as a child, when he was engaged in his work?"

"I helped him, of course. I'd sit in a dark alley and cry, as if I was lost. And when some soft-headed 'mark' came to help, Da would politely ask him for his purse. When I got older and riper, I'd make calf-eyes at the 'mark' and lure him into a dark corner where Da was waitin'. And then, I worked at Old Diggory's forge to bring in a few extra coins. That's all. And we never wanted for a loaf of bread." She looked embarrassed for a moment, as though she were reluctant to say more, then pointed to the book. "I be... am ready to read now."

He noted that she had carefully neglected to mention that she'd been a whore, which must have been degrading to her. And here she was, struggling to better herself, to rise above her coarse beginnings. What had *he* ever accomplished in his whole worthless, wastrel life?

She began to read, one slim finger moving across the page, her voice hesitant at first, then growing stronger as her confidence grew. Occasionally, he would help her sound out the letters, or explain a difficult word, pleased that she took his help with a grateful nod of her head. She read a dozen pages or so, then yawned. "Enough. I be needin' my sleep. Can we read again tomorrow?"

"Of course." He bid her goodnight as she rose from the bench and picked up a candle. "I'll have my pipe before I sleep."

About to mount the stairs, she turned, her exquisite face illuminated by the candle flame. "I think we'll have salad tomorrow. Your lettuce looks fit to pluck."

He smoked in front of the fire, one leg thrown over the arm of the chair. *Your* lettuce, she had said, giving him credit for all his hoeing and weeding and watering. He grinned to himself. He was bone-tired, his muscles ached, and his feet hurt from all the walking and standing he had done that day.

But he had never felt more content in all his life.

• • •

Gloriana smiled at the farmer. "Never you fear, Master Wallace. My man will finish the job in jig time." She watched in satisfaction as Thorne hammered out the last shoe for the farmer's horse, measured it against the animal's hoof, then plunged it into the water bucket.

The farmer nodded. "That looks to be a fine job, Mistress Cook. I needs my horse for a special occasion, and he can't be throwin' a shoe at the wrong time!"

"Indeed?"

"My wife and I be takin' our new baby to his christenin' tomorrow. A fine boy," he added with a satisfied grin. "You'll be wantin' a baby someday for yourself, ma'am. You couldn't do better than our bouncin' Jacob."

The smile faded from her face as an image of her sweet Billy rose in her mind. *No! Best not to think of him.* She concentrated on Thorne, watching as he hammered in the shoe, filed it smooth, and gave the animal a pat on the head. He had learned quickly in the month he'd been in her service, taking to his work with a cheerful willingness that still surprised her.

She turned to the other visitor in the shop, a handsome young gentleman who smelled of fine perfume and an easy life. "Now, milord," she said, indicating the wrought-iron gate leaning against a wall, "there b… is your gate. As promised. I hope you are satisfied."

He crossed to the gate and fingered its elaborate curves. "Excellent. Exactly to my specifications. I'll have it installed this very afternoon." He smiled warmly at her, his eyes flickering from the top of her head to the tips of her shoes. "You are a woman to be admired, Mistress Cook."

She wasn't sure his words were meant for the work on the gate. It gave her a thrill of pleasure to know that she could catch the eye of someone as important as he was. She smiled coyly at him. "For the gate, milord?"

He laughed. "That, too. Indeed, it was finished more

quickly than I would have imagined."

She nodded. "When we promise on time, we deliver on time." She suppressed a yawn. She was more tired than she cared to admit. Since their trip to Whitby three weeks ago, and the good will that Master Dobson had spread their way, the shop had bustled with customers for most of every day. She had been forced to work in secret in the evenings, turning out the more complicated ironworks that some of the customers demanded, lest they discover her unladylike skill. And, with cooking and the nightly reading she and Thorne had shared, she was exhausted.

But she couldn't have done it without him. He had even begun to try his hand at pothooks and ladles, simple jobs that he could master, to save her the extra work. And his gentle tutoring while they read—urging her to lower her tone, correcting her faulty grammar—had made her feel that he was a friend who cared about her.

She smiled in his direction as he bid the farmer good afternoon and crossed to her side, then turned to the gentleman. "John, here, will take the gate out to your wagon, milord."

He gave Thorne a patronizing nod of the head. "You do good work, sirrah. And you are fortunate to have such a beautiful mistress." His eyes narrowed. "I trust you don't take advantage of that."

Gloriana could almost hear the crunch of Thorne's jaw. *God save us if he loses his temper*, she thought. "Oh, milord," she said quickly with a girlish giggle. "I set my sights higher than that."

The gentleman relaxed, his face twisting into a leering smile. "I shall remember that." He pulled out his purse and fished out several gold coins. "'Tis more than we agreed upon," he said, pressing the coins into her hand, "but consider it an advance on future... work." He held tightly to her hand for a moment, then leaned forward and kissed her on the cheek.

Thorne let out a growl and stepped toward the man. Gloriana pushed against his chest and glared at him. "John! Take the gate to the gentleman's wagon and see that his man loads it properly. Now!"

He hesitated, his eyes flashing, then sighed deeply and did as she asked. The gentleman followed him out, his hand on his sheathed sword, as though he were prepared to do battle should Thorne anger him further.

Gloriana drew in her breath, one hand to her breast. Her heart was beating like a captured bird in a cage. She turned away from the forge door, afraid to see the look on Thorne's face when he returned.

His voice behind her was harsh with accusation. "You behaved like a strumpet."

She whirled to him. "How dare you! I'm your mistress!"

"You flirted with him like the lowest whore on the London streets!"

"What did you expect me to do, fool? He's Lord Arthur Pritchett, cousin to the Cholmleys, the family that lords over Whitby."

"Pah! A baronet? Low-ranking provincials."

She snorted. "Low? And who are *you*? The Duke of Buckingham?"

He clenched his teeth, as though he were fighting with his pride. "Merely your servant, mistress," he muttered at last.

"Just so. And I saw the defiant look in your eye. You were ready to fight with him, lay hands on him. And then what would become of our business?"

"And so you let him kiss you?" He could scarcely hide the resentment on his face.

"Burn and blister me! You're just jealous because you haven't won your own kiss yet." They had wagered for his kiss almost every night in the past few weeks, and Thorne had never succeeded in besting her at arm-wrestling.

He grabbed her in his arms, his hands tight on her shoulders. "You beguiling witch," he growled. "You know I want more than just a kiss."

She felt herself crumbling with fatigue, with longing. She wanted him as much as he wanted her. But if she gave in, she would lose her authority over him, lose her self-respect. "Oh, John," she said, her voice quivering, "leave me alone. I'm too tired to quarrel with you today."

At once he released her, his eyes warm with sudden sympathy. "Forgive me, mistress. You're exhausted. You've been working too hard. And you're right, of course. We need the good will of the gentry to succeed." He took her by the arm and steered her gently toward the door. "Go and take a nap. I'll work here for a little while, then heat the meat pies. You've been working late for too many nights."

She sniffled. "What else can I do? It wouldn't be proper for the folks to know I does... I do much of the work."

"Sleep now." He stroked the side of her face, a tender gesture that made her ache with desire.

She squared her shoulders. "No. There's too much work to do. All those tools for the carpenter. We won't read tonight. I'll go to bed early. Tomorrow is Sunday. I can nap for half the day."

"As you wish. I think I can turn out a goodly number of horseshoes before we finish." He turned to the forge and picked up his tongs. "But I'm glad not to work tomorrow. 'Tis devilish hot today, and likely to be so on the morrow."

"Perhaps, if I'm rested, we can swim. Do you swim?" She beamed with pride. "I do."

"I know."

What an odd answer, she thought. "How do you know?" she demanded.

He reddened. "That is… I… I guessed you did," he stammered. "You're so skilled at everything you do—forging, cooking, gardening. And you've come so far in your reading, I can scarcely believe it. I couldn't imagine that swimming wouldn't be one of your many accomplishments."

She felt flustered by his praise. She picked up her hammer. "Enough of your blather. There's work to be done."

They worked for several hours, hammering away at the iron. Tired as she was, Gloriana felt oddly refreshed, basking in the glow of his compliments.

She went to bed early, thinking she would sleep soundly. But her dreams were filled with Billy—his gurgling laughter, his precious smile, his sweet scent. She awoke at last, her heart breaking, and gave way to her sobs.

• • •

Thorne sat up abruptly in his trundle bed, blinking against the thin moonlight that streamed in at the window. What had disturbed his sleep? Then he heard it—the sound of a woman crying. Gloriana! He jumped to his feet, then reached for the tinderbox, struck the flint, and lit the candle on the mantel. He padded quickly up the stairs in his bare feet, conscious of the cool night air on his legs beneath his long shirt.

Her door was open. She sat hunched up on her bed, arms around her knees, weeping uncontrollably and rocking back and forth with every sob. It broke his heart to see such a strong woman brought so low.

"Mistress," he said, hurriedly setting the candle on a small table. "What is it? A bad dream?"

She shook her head, unable to speak, and waved him away, her hands flapping helplessly toward him. "Leave me in peace, John," she said at last.

"Nonsense. I'll do no such thing." He sat beside her on the bed and pulled her into his arms. "I've always heard that a strong shoulder is the best to cry on. Mine may not be your favorite shoulder, but 'tis the only one here."

She managed a small laugh at that, then leaned her head against his chest and began to cry again. Her body was soft against his, and her silky hair beneath his chin smelled smoky from the forge, yet scented with the sweetness that only a woman seemed to possess. He found himself stroking her back with gentle hands and kissing the top of her head, praying that his comfort would ease her unknown pain.

At last she quieted, raised her ravaged face to his. "Thank you," she murmured. She sniffled and touched her tear-stained face. "I must look a fright."

He smiled. "A little the worse for wear. Have you a handkerchief?"

She indicated a small chest in the corner. He fetched a handkerchief from its contents, returned to the bed, and handed it to her. She wiped at her face, blew her nose and managed a rueful smile. "I'm sorry to wake you. Go back to bed."

"No. Not until I'm sure you've quite recovered from… a bad dream?" He regretted his words the minute he said them; at once her eyes began to fill with fresh tears. "Please don't cry again. Your face is too lovely to spoil." He stroked at her wet cheeks with tender fingers. Her skin was as soft as the down on a peach, and golden from the kiss of the sun. And her lower lip, ripe as cherries, still trembled. Impulsively, he put his two hands around her face, leaned forward and kissed her softly on the mouth. His head spun from the sweetness of her lips, molded so perfectly to his.

But after a moment, he broke free, knowing he had crossed the line again, and that she would soon berate him for taking advantage of her. It took all his willpower, desire burning within him, but he started to rise from the bed. "Forgive me, mistress," he said. "I'll go now. I trust you will be able to sleep peacefully for the rest of the night."

To his surprise, she wrapped strong arms around his neck and pulled his mouth close to hers. "No," she said in a seductive growl. "Don't leave me tonight."

Chapter Nine

Her body was on fire, aching for another kiss and burning with a hunger that she had denied for weeks. She smiled up at him, her lips pursed in invitation.

Instead, he unwrapped her arms from his neck and put a gentle hand on her shoulder. "If I stay tonight," he said softly, "I will want to stay every night."

She glared at him, his words reminding her of his inborn arrogance, despite his humble tone. He dared to be so forward and demanding? "Snot-nosed, insolent dog!" she said, her voice rising. "I offer myself and you forget your station? Your pride will ruin you someday, caitiff. But for now, quit my side!"

He jumped to his feet, his anger matching her own. "Damn you! You speak of pride? I swallow my pride every time you give me high-handed orders or call me 'caitiff' with such contempt. And now I'm expected to beg for your favors? To share your bed only when it suits you? I think not!" He snatched up the candle and headed for the door.

"Those b… are my terms," she said defiantly.

He whirled back to her, his face stiff and cold. "And these are my terms. Out there…" he gestured vaguely toward the stairs, "…we would continue as we always have. As mistress and servant. But here in this room, we would be equals—merely a man and a woman with the same passions and needs. If *your* pride is too stubborn to accept that, I bid you good night."

She felt torn. Yearning for him, yet fighting with her pride. Equals, he had said. Not the way it had been with Charlie, lording it over her every minute of their lives together, even when they were in bed. She hesitated for a moment, fighting her desire, then held out supplicating arms to him. "Wait," she whispered.

His handsome face showed relief, not triumph. He slammed down the candle, moved quickly to her side and snatched her into his arms. His kiss was hard and demanding, wringing a groan of pleasure from her. She clung to him, her fingers tangled in his hair, and opened her mouth to his searching tongue. His strong hands moved impatiently down her back, then slid to the front to squeeze her full breasts.

She felt a shiver of wild anticipation and broke free from his kiss, panting. She tugged at his shirt, lay back against the pillow and clasped his hard shaft, poised and waiting for her. "Come into me now," she gasped, desperately trying to guide his manhood to her burning loins.

He gave a throaty laugh. "You impatient witch," he said. "At least give me the pleasure of seeing you."

While he pulled his shirt over his head, she fumbled with the drawstring of her shift, nearly tearing it in her eagerness. She settled herself once more on her pillow and spread her legs. "Now, you devil. For the love of pity."

He placed himself between her legs. She closed her eyes, waiting. Instead, he laughed again, a sound filled with wonder and delight. Her eyes sprang open. "Beautiful Glory," he said, his searching gaze enveloping her body. "You're the most tantalizing creature I've ever known."

"I don't give no damn what that means," she sputtered. "I'll kill you if you make me wait any longer!"

"I'll explain it later," he said, and drove into her with such force that she gasped in delight. He was hard and full, filling her, arousing her with an intensity she had never known. Her hips rose to meet his every impatient thrust— they were two bodies in perfect, wild rhythm, responding to one another with all their pent-up longings. He rode her like a madman; she received his ever-quickening movements with an equal degree of passion, clutching at his hips to increase his pressure.

She was floating, flying, all her thoughts concentrated on the tension that built and built in her core, waiting for the moment when she would explode in perfect fulfillment, yet wishing the tension would never end. He increased the force of his frenzied thrusts, his head thrown back, teeth clenched in passionate concentration.

Then, suddenly, it was over. Her body trembled violently with her climax and she cried out at her release. At the same moment, he gave a final thrust and groaned in satisfaction, collapsing against her breast. She curled her hands around his body, glorying in the firm flesh beneath her fingers, the magical waves of warmth that still filled her.

They lay entwined for several minutes, bathed in sweat, too exhausted to move. Then he rolled off her and flopped onto his back. "Gads, you're a wonder," he panted. "You're everything I dreamed you'd be."

She felt as giddy as a child with a new toy. "And … tantalizing?"

"It means I watched you for weeks, wanted you, and suffered for my wanting. And feared you'd be forever beyond my reach." He swept her into his arms, pulling her body close to his. "And here you are at last. I think I must be dreaming."

"As to your dreams…" She hesitated. She couldn't believe she was confessing to him. "That first night, after the shipwreck…"

He sat up and let out a shout of laughter. "I knew it! It always seemed too real to be a dream."

She felt herself blushing, though she felt no shame for what she'd done. "Well, I have my needs as well. And you were very… tantalizing."

He clicked his tongue, but he could barely hide his smile. "Wicked woman. To take advantage when I was helpless."

She sat up, her hands on her hips. "I didn't take advantage of you. I was only drying you. You invited me."

He snickered. "I don't remember being able to talk, let alone issue a formal invitation."

"Oaf! Your damned prickle stood at attention. A regular soldier it was, daring me."

He crowed with laughter. "And so you took advantage."

She shook her head. "And you? That first day when you kissed me. Didn't you try to take advantage of me?"

"If you hadn't threatened to crown me with your hammer, I might have taken more than a kiss."

She giggled. "Then we're well matched, John."

"As to that, since we're equals here, may I call you Glory in this room?" He frowned. "'Tis not a name that is pleasing to my ears. Is that your Christian name?"

"I was baptized Gloriana."

"A lovely name. A royal name. The poet Spenser used it as a name for Queen Elizabeth."

She preened at that. "Indeed."

He chuckled. "Now don't get puffed up about it. 'Tis only a name."

She eyed his strong body, sitting so temptingly beside her. His shoulders were wide and muscular, and the black curls on his chest led down to a dark patch that cradled his limp manhood. The sight of him made her senses quicken, raising a returning tingle at her very core. "The only thing I want 'puffed up' at this moment is you."

He groaned, a sound that seemed to blend both proud satisfaction and suffering. "Greedy creature. Give me a few moments, at least!"

She snorted. "Seein' as how you're just a man, maybe you need some help."

He reached out and pinched her playfully on the rump. "Seeing, not seein', remember? And what kind of help did you have in mind?"

She pushed him onto his back and straddled him with her body. She leaned down and kissed him softly, then let her lips stray to his cheekbones and drift to his ear. She blew softly, enjoying his shiver of pleasure, then gently stroked his ear with her tongue until he moaned in delight. She leaned back and fondled his chest, glorying in the strength of his muscles, the hard planes beneath her wandering fingers, the silky thatch of dark curls. At last her hands reached his manhood, and she caressed its length, her fingers ever more demanding, until she felt it stir and harden. With a contented sigh, she lowered herself onto him, the power of their mutual desire trembling between them.

To her surprise, he pushed her off him and rolled her onto her back, kneeling above her. "No," he said with a wicked smile, "you're not going to have it so easy this time. You like teasing, you devil? Well, what's sauce for the goose..." He curled his hands around her breasts, squeezing gently, then leaned down and suckled at one tender nipple. She drew in a sharp breath, enchanted by the waves of feeling that swept through her. He kissed her on the mouth, drawing her tongue between his lips; all the while his hands roamed her body, finding sensitive spots she had never known existed, telling her with his caresses that she was honored and admired. And when he slipped his fingers within her, she was in heaven. She had never known such tender lovemaking.

When at last he entered her, every fiber, every nerve of her being responded to him. He was gentle this time, content to bring them both to climax in a leisurely manner, adding fire to her forge one charcoal at a time. And when it was done, and the flames had consumed her and subsided to a flickering ember, she curled up on her side and began to weep.

"Gloriana," he cried in alarm. "What did I do to make you sad again? Did I hurt you?"

She shook her head. "No. 'Tis only tears of happiness. I never knew it could be so sweet." Charlie had been selfish and crude, using her for his own satisfaction, without a thought to her emotions. Her body had been satisfied, but somehow she had always felt that something was missing. And now

Thorne had shown her the full glory of making love.

"You enchantress," he said, lying down behind her and drawing her into his embrace. "Will you never cease to surprise me? Come. Sleep now. I think we've had enough waterworks for one night."

She felt warmed by his chest against her back, comforted by the strong arm that circled her waist. She smiled into her pillow. "As to waterworks, I shall best you at swimming tomorrow."

He chuckled "Is that a wager, mistress?"

"If you wish it, John. But for now, I need my rest." She sighed, settled herself more comfortably in his arms, and drifted off into a contented sleep.

• • •

Gloriana awoke to a beam of sunlight streaming in through the narrow window. She allowed herself a few moments to luxuriate in the feel of the sheets on her bare flesh, to relive the passion of the night before, to glory in the satisfaction that filled her body.

But as she slipped into her shift and mules, washed her face and cleaned her teeth with a sponge, she began to have doubts about Thorne. Would he be high-handed now that he'd won his prize? No! She wouldn't tolerate it. She put a determined frown on her face and marched purposefully downstairs.

To her surprise, she found a small fire in the grate, with a pot of oatmeal set on a hook over the coals, filling the room with its warm scent. Thorne was nowhere about. She stepped out into the sunshine. Stripped to the waist, his dark hair tied back with a string, he stood before a small mirror, his face covered in lather, a razor in his hand.

At sight of her, he turned and gave a deep bow. "Good morrow, mistress," he said in a humble voice. "I trust you slept well?"

Was that a smirk trembling around his lips? "You might have wakened me," she snapped.

"You needed your rest," he said. "And I needed time to reset the carrot seedlings before the day grew too hot."

"Humph! Did you remember to feed Black Jack?"

"Of course."

"And you put up the porridge, I see." His very competence was beginning to annoy her. And the sight of his tempting bare flesh only made it harder for her to remember that he was beneath her station. "Oh, do continue shaving," she said with a queenly wave of her hand. "I give you leave."

He raised a questioning eyebrow but nodded politely in her direction. "Thank you, mistress."

She watched as he scraped the razor across his chin, started on his cheeks, ran the blade carefully across the top of his lips, the lips that had burned against hers so passionately last night. "Oh, bother," she said at last, giving in to her desires. "Come and kiss me, fool!"

He grinned, threw down his razor and swept her into his arms. His kiss tasted of soap, and a dab of lather landed on her nose. By the time the kiss was ended, they were both laughing. He wiped the bubbles off her nose and grinned again. "What happened to our arrangement? I was prepared to be servile—"

"And I was prepared to be high and mighty," she said with a rueful smile. "For the sake of my pride."

He held her face in his hands and looked deep into her eyes. "Needless pride. I promise I shall never do anything to humiliate you. You have my oath on that."

She gulped and blinked back the tears that sprang to her eyes. "Oh, pooh," she said, turning away to cover her moment of weakness. "I'm hungry. I want to see if your cooking is as skillful as your flattery."

He laughed at that, wiped the remains of the lather from his face and shrugged into his shirt. "We shall see. And I have a wager to propose."

"Indeed?"

He took her arm and steered her into the cottage. "If you find my cooking agreeable, you must answer a question for me."

"And that is…?"

He shook his head. "No. I'll not tell. Not unless I win."

That made her uneasy and hopeful at the same time. Was it mad of her to wonder if he'd ask to stay forever? His behavior last night had shown that he cared for her. And she knew that she would say yes in a moment. To live and work here together for the rest of their lives, to raise children and ease the ache of Billy's loss…

She dished out the porridge and they sat down to breakfast, facing each other across the table. To her surprise, the porridge was quite good, though she teased him by making a face and declaring that it was a bit lumpy.

"Humph. Well, Mistress Slug-a-bed, if you hadn't slept late you could have made it yourself. Now, do I win my wager or not?"

"It was good enough for your first try," she conceded. "Ask your question." She held her breath, wondering, hoping.

His gray eyes were dark with sincerity. "Did you enjoy last night?"

"Oh! That's *all?* Of course I did."

"But you wept."

"'Twas only that… I… had a husband once. He be… is dead now. He was good to me sometimes, but never as kindly as you were last night."

"Did you care for him?"

She snorted. "What does that matter? Where I came from, there were few choices. It seemed the wisest thing to do. And I was…" she struggled for a word, "…connected."

He frowned. "That's an odd word to use."

"How can I tell it? All my life, I've always felt alone, except when Da was around. I remember once, as a child, we were in a wood, and I got lost. And I looked up at the stars and I felt so small. Then Da was there, and held my hand. And I was safe again. That is part of what it feels like when… when a man is… inside me."

"Connected," he said in a hoarse voice, clearly moved.

"Yes. Even a man as thoughtless as my Charlie was."

"My adorable Gloriana," he said, rising from his bench to sweep her into his arms.

She tucked her head into his shoulder, feeling a hot blush burn her cheeks. What had possessed her to be so open with him, telling him things she had never spoken of to anyone else? She pulled away from him and busily gathered up the porridge bowls. "Are we going swimming before the day gets too hot?"

"Of course."

"And we should find a secluded spot, so we don't alert the gossips."

He grinned. "I shall remember to walk two paces behind you, as befits a proper servant. But as for my wager on a swimming race…"

She was grateful their conversation had turned to a lighter topic. "I'm agreeable, though I know I'll win." She ignored the confident shake of his head. "What are your stakes?"

"If I win… *when* I win… we come back here and spend the rest of the day in bed."

"Arrogant dog! And if you lose?"

"No. You name your terms."

She eyed his strong body, the hands that had held and caressed her, the lips that set her heart to pounding. She laughed. "If I win, we come back here and spend the rest of the day in bed."

• • •

Dobson placed a sheath of papers before Thorne. "This is the last of the deeds, Your Grace. If you would be so good as to sign, Rogers will finalize the sale."

Thorne picked up the quill pen, dipped it into the ink and carelessly scrawled his name. "A fair exchange. I'd rather have that rolling piece of land overlooking the river than a couple of marshy plots." He dusted the paper with a sprinkling of sand to blot the ink and shook it clean. "Here you are. When I get back to London, I might have Rogers look into building me a private retreat on the new site." His mouth curled in scorn. "When I've had my fill of my mother for a season."

Dobson reached for the papers and frowned. "If I may be so bold, Your Grace, your hands are…" he cleared his throat delicately, "...somewhat the worse for wear. Scarcely what I'm used to seeing."

Thorne laughed and surveyed his thick calluses, the ragged and broken fingernails, the dirt that rimmed his cuticles and nails. "Gardening and forging are messy businesses."

"Perhaps when this is over, you should make a visit to a spa. The waters of Bath are quite fine this time of year, are they not?"

"I should prefer Epsom or Tunbridge Wells, I think. The gambling is better."

"And, speaking of gambling, how goes your pursuit of the woman?"

"By the cross of St. George, she is a difficult creature to win over. No success as yet." Thorne turned away, fearful that Dobson would see the look on his face and guess the truth. It was almost two weeks since he and Gloriana had first shared her bed, and every day was more wondrous than the last. She brought a breathtaking passion to each encounter, her needs as strong as his, yet with a fragile vulnerability that touched his heart.

He knew he should end the matter, go back to London, announce his triumph and collect his winnings. But he didn't want to leave. And a new thought had begun to trouble his conscience—the shame he would bring to her if she should ever find out about his mad wager.

Thorne rose from his chair to cross to the window of Dobson's room and stare out onto the street. "In point of fact," he said at last, "I have begun to think she's not worth my effort. Perhaps this is one wager I should concede with grace."

Dobson whistled. "I never thought I'd see you give up

so easily. And you still have well over a month to conclude the matter successfully."

He gave a careless yawn. "I've begun to miss good food, fine clothes, a comfortable bed. If God had meant me to be a peasant, I would have been born to that low degree."

"If your mind is set on leaving, I can notify your gaming opponents and arrange to pay them off."

Thorne whirled to face Dobson. "No!" The sharpness of his reply surprised him until he thought about it for a moment. He wasn't ready to leave Gloriana. He glanced uneasily at his valet, whose head had snapped up at his forceful answer. "That is…" he stammered, "…perhaps I… should give myself a couple of weeks more, to see if she can be persuaded. And there's to be a fair in town next week. It should be amusing, to learn how the country folk disport themselves."

"As you wish it, Your Grace. But, sooner or later, you must remember your duties to your tenants and return to Surrey. Whether or not you manage to bed the wench." Dobson's piercing blue eyes bored into Thorne, seeming to search for clues to his master's state of mind.

Thorne turned and picked up his battered hat. It was becoming too difficult to maintain the lie. He slung his basket filled with purchases across his shoulders and headed for the door. "'Tis time I was getting back. There's work to be done before the sun sets." He hurried down the steps of the inn and emerged onto Church Street, feeling welcomed and accepted by the smiles and nods of the townsfolk. He had become oddly comfortable in his humble disguise, enjoying the simple wisdom of the country farmers, the practical advice of rugged tradesmen and sailors.

But he was still the Duke of Thorneleigh, lest he forget, with obligations and responsibilities he couldn't avoid forever.

What in the name of Satan shall I do? he thought. He wasn't ready to leave this pleasant village, his satisfying work—or Gloriana. Especially Gloriana. Which was absurd, of course. He'd never found it difficult to jilt a woman, to take what he wanted and then cast her aside. And his usual conquests had been high-born ladies, not trollops. Why should he fear to hurt Gloriana? Her own loose ways had surely taught her that men were impermanent and faithless. Hadn't his own mother's betrayal of his father taught *him* that women were fickle?

But as he moved down the street, he quickened his steps, eager to mount the Whitby stairs, pass the ruins of the old abbey and see her radiant face again. There was something about her that was so real, so genuine—so unlike the artificial people he had known for most of his life.

And she needed him. He had wanted only her body in the beginning, but the loneliness she had haltingly revealed to him had been a surprise. In all his privileged life, he had always felt a sense of uselessness, an unimportance in spite of all his riches and inherited honors and lordly burdens. But here he was *needed.*

He grinned as he neared the steps. Perhaps, if they finished their work early, and spent a shorter time on her reading, they could go to bed. He wanted to enjoy her body in a leisurely manner tonight, to see the glow of contentment on her beautiful face. And then they would fall asleep together, nestled warmly in each other's arms. It was a new experience for him; always before, when he was finished with a woman, he would rise from the bed and seek the solitary comfort of a pipe or a glass of wine.

He was so preoccupied with his thoughts that he nearly ran into an elderly woman coming down the stairs with her companion. He stepped back. "Forgive me, madam," he murmured, then reeled back from a vicious slap to the side of his head, knocking his hat to the ground. Fists clenched, he glared at his assailant, almost automatically prepared to strike back at a man who had so little respect for his station.

Damme! he thought. The man was Lord Arthur Pritchett, the rogue who had dared to kiss Gloriana in his presence. As tempting as was the thought, he realized that if he attacked Pritchett, there would be the possibility of an arrest and the inevitable exposure of his disguise.

He took a steadying breath and scooped his hat from the ground. "Milord. Milady," he said, managing to give a humble bow. "I beg your forgiveness. 'Twas careless of me." He found it difficult not to choke on the words.

Lord Arthur snorted. "Have you any idea whom you nearly capsized, sirrah?" He indicated his companion, a white-haired, finely dressed woman with a kindly face. "This is Lady Cholmley, whose son, Sir Hugh Cholmley, allows you to inhabit his town at his sufferance." He gave a smug toss of his head. "And my most esteemed aunt," he added.

The elderly woman smiled innocently, her rosy cheeks like round apples on her face, but there was a mischievous twinkle in her eyes. "Oh, don't be such a prig, Arthur," she said. "The man scarcely intended to offend."

"The man is a common peasant, Auntie, lest we forget."

Thorne forced his hands to stay at his sides and even managed a tight smile. "Are you enjoying your new gate, milord?"

Pritchett's eyes flashed, his hand going to the sword at his hip. "Do I know you, sirrah? Who are you, to speak to me in such a familiar manner?"

I'll skin you alive when I get back to London, thought Thorne savagely. It would take only a few conversations with the right people to ensure that this pompous ass was never invited to Court again. He contrived to hold his smile and speak in a civil voice. "My mistress, Glory Cook, owns the blacksmith shop in the dell."

At her name, Pritchett relaxed. "Ah, yes. Of course. And you were the jealous lout who couldn't hide his envy at my station and my courting of your mistress. A very beautiful mistress," he added, turning to his aunt.

Lady Cholmley nodded. "So I've heard. And growing quite successful in Whitby, they say. I should like to see this beauty."

Pritchett scratched his chin. "With the fair next week, and Hugh's assembly ball in celebration..."

"A fine idea, Arthur. It can be arranged." She smiled at Thorne. "Give my regards to your mistress, my good man, and tell her she may expect an invitation to the assembly."

The smile he returned to her was genuine. Gloriana would be delighted. One step further on her path to becoming the lady she longed to be. "Thank you, milady."

He bowed again to them both, then hurried up the steps. Despite the growing heat of the afternoon, he took a rapid pace, becoming more and more eager to see the look on Gloriana's face when he told her the news. He felt almost as excited as though it were his own first assembly ball.

He heard the clank of Gloriana's hammer as he neared the smithy. Working hard as usual, despite the warm day.

He pulled off his basket, tossed down his hat and rushed through the door. "Gloriana!" he shouted happily, bursting with the news.

"Oh!" She whirled at his cry, one long red curl coming loose from her pinned-up locks and dropping down to graze the red-hot piece of iron on the anvil. The smithy was suddenly filled with the acrid smell of burning hair.

"Dear God!" Thorne was before her in an instant, frantically clapping his hands around the thick strands to extinguish the sparks. Then, with a relieved groan, he pulled her into his arms. "Forgive my stupidity," he murmured, kissing the top of her head. "I didn't mean to startle you."

She pulled away and smiled up at him. "'Tis only hair. I should have pinned it more carefully."

"But I might have lost you."

"Dearest John. Be at peace," she said, examining the singed curl. "The only thing lost is a few inches of my hair. And it wants cutting anyway. 'Tis too thick and heavy in this hot weather."

For the first time, he noticed the dampness on her face, the rivulets of sweat that ran down her neck. "And you work too hard on a hot day like this." He pulled out his handkerchief, crossed to the water bucket and moistened the cloth. With tender hands he dabbed at her face, ran the handkerchief across the back of her neck, stroked her soot-stained arms. "Enough work for now. Into the cottage. A pint of cool ale from the larder is what we both need."

"But—"

"Not another word. I insist." He gently took the hammer from her, then scooped her into his arms and carried her into the cottage.

134

She giggled and lifted a finger to tickle his ear. "And what will follow the ale?"

He gave her a leering smile. "I leave that up to you." He could feel his body growing warm with his need of her.

She smirked. "I think you should cut my hair."

"What?" He set her roughly on her feet.

"Oh, don't pout like a little boy. Bed will come later."

"You wicked tease," he said, and kissed her, glorying in the feel of her body pressed against his, the sweetness of her mouth. She clung to him, returning his passion with a fervor that made his head spin.

At last they separated. While Gloriana fetched scissors and comb, Thorne set a chair in the center of the room and found a towel to drape around her shoulders. She unpinned her hair and sat in the chair. He combed the long tresses, marveling at their silky texture, the vivid color that, as always, took his breath away. But as he worked, his thoughts drifted back to his conversation with Dobson.

Willy-nilly, he had obligations, another life besides this bucolic domesticity, people who depended on his presence, his judgment. And the happy times here with Gloriana would just be a fading dream, to be recalled in nostalgic moments. He felt like a child about to be deprived of a treasure. He worked mechanically, cutting Gloriana's hair a few inches shorter at her direction, but his heart was heavy. And when the job was finished, and she fetched a broom to sweep up the curls on the floor, he snatched up a lock of her hair and cradled it in his palm. At least he could have something to remember her by.

She laughed. "You're a softhearted fool, John Thorne."

He turned away to cover his embarrassment, but held

tightly to the curl. "Humph. Weren't we going to have some ale?"

"Indeed. And then, perhaps you can tell me why you rushed into the smithy like a madman."

"Damme, I'd nearly forgotten." While they drank their ale, he told her of the meeting with Lord Arthur Pritchett and Lady Cholmley, and their invitation to the assembly ball. Gloriana was as excited as he had hoped she'd be, laughing and clapping her hands in joy.

"But you must come with me, John," she said, her face suddenly darkening. "I'd be fearful to go alone."

"Nothing to fear. 'Tis only a country assembly."

She stuck out her chin at a stubborn angle. "The gentry bring their servants, don't they?"

"Of course."

"Then so shall I."

He thought about it for a moment. There was really no need for him to fear that anyone would recognize him from London. He usually wore his periwig in the city, and the only aristocrat who might regularly venture from this backwater to Court was Sir Hugh, whom he had never met. Whitby gossips had mentioned that Sir Hugh and his wife had made an infrequent visit to Court last season, when Thorne had been abroad. "Very well," he agreed.

"And you must have a new coat." She crossed the room to a wicker hamper in the corner and pulled out a strongbox, setting it on the table and lifting the lid.

Thorne knew he was prying, but he stood up and peered into the box. He was astonished to see a large pile of gold coins within. He whistled. "Miser!" he said with a laugh. "The way you hoarded money, I thought you were nearly destitute. Poor," he explained.

She blushed. "My late husband... left me some jewels. Enough to buy this cottage and set up the forge. And some left over. But that doesn't mean I can't be thrifty," she added defiantly. She counted out a few coins and dropped them into his hand. "For your coat."

He stared at the money and tried not to look disappointed. Thrifty was scarcely the word to describe her tight-fisted offering. He would have to settle for another scratchy second-hand garment. "And what of you?" he asked. "You'll need a new gown."

"Oh, I shall find something in town."

"No. You should have something better than what Whitby has to offer. Let me take Black Jack and go to Scarborough. They have finer shops there."

She snorted. "And finer prices, I'll wager."

"No matter. I want you to look beautiful that night." He smiled warmly, hoping to persuade her. He had already decided to spend whatever he had of his own money, to see her magnificently dressed. "Will you not allow me the pleasure of choosing a gown for you?" When she looked uncertain, he tried one more argument. "With my past experience in the duke's household, I'm more accustomed to seeing what the fashionable ladies are wearing now." And he intended to take Dobson with him, trusting in the man's taste.

"Very well." She reluctantly counted out a few more coins and handed them to him. "But nothing too... extravagant? Is that the word?"

"Indeed." He hesitated, remembering her easily wounded pride. "Forgive me, but I must ask. Do you dance?

Or shall we have lessons this week?"

She lowered her head, unwilling to look him full in the face. "I… had been learning, but we can practice, if you don't mind."

He lifted her chin with gentle fingers and smiled warmly in reassurance. "For the joy of holding you in my arms, I won't mind at all."

She returned his smile, but her emerald eyes had suddenly turned dark with desire. "No dancing now. I'm hungry," she whispered.

Her unexpected words surprised him. "But 'tis not time for supper."

"I'm not hungry for supper," she said with a suggestive grin. She slipped one hand around his body and patted his buttocks through his breeches.

He shook his head. "Gads, woman, you're insatiable."

She frowned in suspicion. "What does that mean?"

He tried to hide his grin of pleasure. "It means you're never satisfied, and always want more."

Her frown had turned to a wispy smile of uncertainty. "Don't you?" she asked in a timid voice.

He cursed himself for having shaken her fragile self-esteem again, if only for a moment. "Always, my sweet." He held out his hand in invitation. "Lusty wench," he growled. "Come along."

Fingers entwined, they raced up the steps together, laughing as they went.

Chapter Ten

Stooping before her small looking-glass, Gloriana finished tying the last pink bow across her bodice. She ran her hand over her pale green taffeta skirt, luxuriating in the feel of the silky fabric under her fingers. She had worn fine dresses at Baniard Hall, but never one as handsome as this, with its snug waist and belled skirt. She glanced at a grinning Thorne, lounging against the doorway. "Oh, I wish I had a larger mirror, to see how I look."

"Let me be your looking-glass." He appraised her from the top of her head to the pointed tips of her new shoes and nodded in satisfaction. "You look exquisite. That is—"

"Bloody hell! I know the meaning of that word."

He chuckled. "The pupil advances beyond the tutor. And try not to say 'bloody hell' tonight. It doesn't go with your gown."

Gloriana made a face at him. She picked up her comb and smoothed several long curls around her finger, carefully placing the locks over her shoulder to rest against the bodice of her shift. At the last, she pinned a tiny muslin cap to her topknot—the smallest one he could find, Thorne had said, so as not to cover too much of her vivid hair. "I don't know how you managed all this with the coins I gave you. The gown, the petticoat, the cap and shoes." She patted the stiffness that sprang from her waist beneath her gown. "And even a whalebone hoop. How did you do it?"

He stirred uncomfortably at her question. "I… I know how to bargain. And then… I had a few extra coins of my own to contribute."

"Not from what I pay you! 'Twould never be enough for all of this."

He shrugged apologetically. "Truth be told, I'm as miserly as you are. I'd saved a bit of money, thinking to buy a horse."

"And you spent it on me?" Her heart swelled with the wonder of this man, his warm generosity, his loving thoughtfulness.

He crossed the room and pulled her into his arms, kissing her with a passion that took her breath away. "Dressing you like this brings me more satisfaction than would a stable full of horses."

She smiled tenderly at him and blinked back the tears of gratitude that had welled in her eyes. *I love this man*, she thought in sudden wonder, feeling a surge of emotion she hadn't experienced since Da had died.

He dabbed at her eyes with gentle fingers. "Are you going to get weepy again, when your triumph awaits tonight?"

She snorted. "I have no doubt many a fine lady will outshine me."

"Would you care to make a wager on that?"

She turned away, all her old self-doubts returning to haunt her. How could she compete with women who had been born to fine living, gracious manners, cultured speech? "I shall lose, of course."

He shook his head. "Not bloody likely. But if you lose, you must sell all these splendid garments and—"

"*Reimburse* you?" she interrupted, pleased she had remembered the word.

He laughed. "Indeed. And if you win, which I know you shall, what are your stakes?"

"If I win, you must tell me that I'm beautiful every day for a whole week."

He stroked the side of her face and kissed her softly on the mouth. "That's not a fair wager. I could tell you that every single hour."

"Even with soot on my face?"

"Even then." He turned and picked up her plain woolen cloak, draping it carefully around her shoulders. "'Tis time to go. I've saddled up Black Jack. We can ride double until we near Abbey House. Then I'll dismount and lead you to the door, as a proper servant should."

She smiled wickedly. "'Tis astonishing how you've changed since you came here. Burn and blister me, I thought you'd choke those first few weeks, every time you had to be humble!"

He smoothed back his dark hair, neatly tied with a ribbon. "Truth to tell, humility wasn't one of my virtues. And perhaps I've benefitted by having my pride knocked down occasionally." He cupped her full breast with a gentle hand. "Of course, I've been compensated handsomely."

"What does that mean?"

"Rewarded, my sweet." He gazed at her with hungry eyes that yet held a twinkle. "What say we forgo the ball and go to bed instead?"

"Oh, get on with you, John. Always teasing. I didn't spend all this time dressing just for *you* to see me."

He grinned. "Come along, then."

She perched in front of him on Black Jack, feeling the warmth of his strong arms around her, like a comforting cocoon. And when they reached the cliff road, his body was her shelter from the salty winds that blew up from the sea below. The sun had set, but its rosy glow remained, a pink halo in the west. She scanned the darkening sky, noting the pale orb that hovered over the water. "The moon is almost full," she said. "'Twill be a lovely night."

"Indeed. I have fond memories of a moonlit night." He chuckled softly, an odd, faraway laugh, as though he was sharing a private joke only with himself.

"Oh, tell me."

"Perhaps, some day, I shall."

They rode slowly past the Gothic ruins of Whitby Abbey, stark and foreboding. Beyond the church lay Abbey House, home to the Cholmleys, its gray stone walls dark against the fading sky. Lighted torches had already been placed along its drive, and Gloriana could see liveried servants running about, helping guests from their horses or carriages. Despite the comfort of Thorne's arms, she felt a twinge of anxiety. She glanced at the old ruins, crumbling columns still in orderly rows. *Like prison bars*, she thought. Was her past a prison she could never escape? Surely tonight she would be exposed as a fraud, pretending to be someone she wasn't, nor ever could be. The guests—and even the servants—would see through her fine clothes to the common London street urchin she had been. She shivered.

Thorne reined in Black Jack. "Are you cold?"

"No. Just… a little frightened."

He dismounted and lifted her from the horse, pulling her into his embrace. "Foolish child. Frightened of what?"

She was almost choking on her fears. "Oh, John," she said, "I don't belong here!"

He stared at her for a long minute, then shook his head. "No, you don't. You belong in a palace. You should be a queen, a princess." He dropped his arms and let out a shout, as though he'd been struck by a thunderbolt. "Gads! What a fool I've been! You should be a *duchess*."

His words of praise restored her common sense and she giggled. "And where is the duke who would be mad enough to marry me?" she said with a snort.

He hesitated, then swept the cloak from her shoulders. "Time enough to talk later. Your adoring admirers await you." He kissed her tenderly, then set her back on Black Jack. "One more addition to your toilette." With a grin, he fished in his pocket and pulled out a fan. "Every proper lady needs one," he said, handing it up to her.

She opened it, noting the fine lace, the painted scene of lords and ladies, the dangling wrist-ribbon that just matched the pale pink of her bows. "Oh, it's lovely. And to buy it for me…" She felt as though her heart would burst with all his kindnesses.

"If I could, I'd buy you that moon, my moon-kissed duchess," he said fervently. "Now come along." He tucked her cloak behind Black Jack's saddle and led the horse down

Abbey House drive. He helped her from Black Jack, handed the animal's reins to a waiting groom and dropped several paces behind her.

Gloriana stared at the imposing entrance to the banqueting hall—a recent addition to Abbey House—squared her shoulders in resolve and sailed through the door. A uniformed majordomo, resplendent in blue velvet and gold braid, waited in the antechamber. Thorne stepped forward and whispered to him. At once, he threw open the inner doors to the hall, ushered Gloriana inside and announced in a loud voice, "Mistress Glory Cook!"

The great hall was elegantly furnished, with small tables and chairs scattered at its corners, and lit with several blazing chandeliers; it swarmed with people, dressed in their finest, milling about and chattering away. Gloriana could hear music coming from another room. At the majordomo's announcement, all conversation had stopped. Gloriana gulped. It seemed as though all eyes were turned toward her. She managed a gracious smile, then sighed in relief as Lord Arthur Pritchett hurried toward her, decked out in a bright scarlet brocaded coat and breeches, an elaborate periwig over his close-cropped hair.

"Mistress Cook. What a pleasure to see you." He slipped her arm through his and led her toward the center of the room. "Give me the honor of presenting you to Sir Hugh. And then you must meet his mother, my aunt. She is most eager to make your acquaintance."

Gloriana allowed Pritchett to lead her through the crowd of guests, aware that Thorne followed close behind. Her confidence grew as she noted the admiring stares of the gentlemen, the whispers among the women, carefully examining her costume over their fans. She briefly glanced back at Thorne. He was grinning in pleasure, as if to say, "I told you so."

Sir Hugh was polite, though somewhat distant in his greeting, but his mother, Lady Cholmley, seemed delighted to meet her. "My dear," she said with a warm smile, "you are every bit as lovely as Arthur said you were. And your gown is exquisite. Where on earth did you find it? Not in Whitby, surely."

Gloriana nodded in Thorne's direction. "My manservant, Thorne, made a trip to Scarborough on my behalf."

"A blacksmith with taste. You're very fortunate, my dear." She swept her plump arm around the large hall, indicating several doors leading to other rooms. "Dancing is through that door. The retiring rooms are over there. That's the door to the tea room, where you will find refreshments to your liking, I trust. And there's the door to the garden. You can also reach it through the dancing room, should you feel the need of a cooling breeze."

"And that room, milady?" Gloriana pointed with her fan to a door in the far corner of the hall.

Lady Cholmley shrugged. "Oh, that's for the fools who think that cards and dice are the whole purpose of an assembly ball. But you, my dear, will be far too busy dancing, I suspect, from the look of the gentlemen who seem to be assessing their chances." She nodded to Thorne, who still hovered behind Gloriana. "You may rest assured, my good man, that I shall take excellent care of your mistress this evening. You may join the other servants below."

He gave a polite bow. "If you please, your ladyship, I should prefer to take my place against the wall, to be at hand should my mistress need me."

"As you wish. Good manners as well as an eye for fashion. Now, my dear," she said, turning back to Gloriana, "let me introduce you to Master Collins, a fine shipbuilder, who hasn't taken his eyes off you since you arrived."

Collins seemed a pleasant older man, slightly portly in his velvet coat, but his eyes twinkled with youthful merriment. He ushered Gloriana into the dancing room, where the orchestra—seated in a gallery overlooking the space—had just begun a lively reel, and led her to the polished floor. Gloriana noted that Thorne had discreetly followed and had taken his place near the door to the garden, arms folded in satisfaction.

She danced the reel with Collins, several minuets and a saraband with assorted gentlemen who crowded toward her the minute Collins released her hand, and a gavotte with a sighing young man who had barely begun to sprout whiskers.

The evening flew by in a dizzying whirl. Sir Arthur took her in to supper, lavishing compliments on her as they ate, and complaining about all her other admirers. They danced again, but he was soon kept at a distance by the many gentlemen who wished to dance with the most beautiful woman in the room.

And through it all, Thorne watched her. Her heart ached that he couldn't be a part of her triumph. After a particularly fast-paced reel with a clumsy dancer, which left her gasping, she excused herself and stepped aside, snapping open her fan to cool her hot face. At once, Thorne was before her, his handkerchief at the ready, to mop her moist brow, as he had done so often in the forge.

She looked up at the longing in his eyes, her emotions

matching his. "I want to dance with you," she whispered. "Only you."

"They've begun another minuet," he said softly. "Go through to the garden. I'll meet you there."

"But what will people say?"

"The devil with what they say. We won't be seen if we stay in the shadows. And I want to tell you something. Something I should have confessed about myself weeks ago."

"That sounds... *ominous*," she ventured. "Are you secretly a pirate?"

He snorted. "Not bloody likely. Now go, before I kiss you right here and scandalize the whole village!"

She hurried out to the garden, waving off the men who clamored to accompany her. "I wish to be alone for a few minutes," she murmured.

The moon had risen to its apex, bathing the garden in its brilliant glow. She stepped off the terrace onto the carpet of grass, inhaling the perfume of a thousand roses in the air. She moved around the corner of the building, out of the view of the windows. The stately cadences of the minuet vibrated on the night air, filling her heart with joy. Had music ever sounded so glorious to her? She was aware that every pore, every sense, every fiber of her being was awakened to the wonders around her—the sights, the scents, the sounds. Even the soft caress of the night air on her face.

Then Thorne was there. He bowed deeply to her curtsy and held out his hand. They danced effortlessly together in the moonlight, turning, pointing graceful toes, gliding across the lawn in perfect rhythm. There was no need for words—their bodies were in sublime harmony, responding to the music, to each other, as though they had danced together forever.

When the dance was over and they had made their final bows, Thorne pulled Gloriana into his arms. "I don't know how many hearts you've broken in there," he said softly, "but you've surely conquered me tonight."

Gloriana gazed up at his handsome face, illuminated by the bright moon. She wished she could see his eyes, read into his heart. Surely he must love her as much as she loved him. "Oh, John, you great oaf," she blurted out. "Why don't you marry me?"

His laugh was gentle, enveloping her in its warmth. "You brazen hussy. Perhaps I shall. But first we must talk." He held her tightly, as though he feared to lose her. "Oh, God," he said with a groan. "Come home now and hear my confession. And then we'll speak of marriage, if you still want it."

"Not want it? Do you think I'm a fool?"

"No," he said, shaking his head. "I'm the fool, as you shall soon learn." He propelled her around the corner, past the dancing room, to the terrace that led to the great hall. "Now go and say your farewells. I'll follow and get Black Jack. Meet me outside the antechamber. Wait!" He pulled her into his arms. "One more kiss. It could be the last," he said sadly.

His kiss was deep and searching, almost desperate, demanding her most passionate response. She felt a thrill of uneasiness. Surely his "confession" was something he dreaded to give. She stepped up on the terrace, decorated with large potted bushes that shadowed her as she moved toward the door. A slightly disheveled man had just emerged from the gaming room and was staggering unsteadily toward the door in front of her, clutching his groin. She had not seen him before. She stepped aside as he brushed past her, grumbling under his breath.

"Need to piss," he muttered. "Damned cards!"

The drunken fool, she thought. To waste this lovely evening on too much wine and the mindless pleasures of gambling. She was about to step inside when she heard his shout of surprise.

"Begad! Thorne, is it you?"

Someone who had known John before? She felt guilty for eavesdropping, but she concealed herself behind one of the tall bushes, curious to hear the conversation out.

Thorne's voice was low, tight and controlled. "I fear you've mistaken me for someone else, milord."

"Not at all," the man sputtered. "I may be drunk, but I'm not blind. You're John Havilland, Duke of Thorneleigh. Haven't seen you since the races at Epsom. What the devil are you doing here in Whitby? And dressed like a peasant."

"I assure you, milord, you are mistaken."

"Balderdash! Must I acknowledge you to the company?"

At the sound of Thorne's muttered curse and heavy sigh of resignation, Gloriana felt her heart contract. A *duke?* That would explain his natural arrogance, his fine manners, far above those of a mere valet. But why his elaborate ruse, the masquerade he had maintained for nearly two months?

"Keep your voice down, Nescott," he muttered. "I don't wish to be recognized."

Nescott laughed. "Aha! Pursuing one of your many conquests? And how soon will you jilt her as you've jilted the rest? To keep up your reputation, of course."

Gloriana gasped at his words. Was that all she had been to Thorne? Another conquest?

Thorne's voice was suddenly aristocratic and hard—a tone she had never heard before. "Are you forgetting your place, you insignificant worm?"

"I... I... not at all, Your Grace. I speak from admiration, not disapproval. Your exploits are the talk of London. And your mad wager in May, the most reckless gamble you've ever proposed... Tell me, did you ever find the Baniard woman? And bed her? Your adversaries are still buzzing, waiting for your admission of defeat, or the lock of her hair as proof of success."

Gloriana suppressed a cry, her hands going to her mouth. A wager! He had known all along who she was. Had pursued her only to win a bet. She wanted to die of shame.

"Listen to me, Nescott," Thorne growled in a menacing voice. "You will say nothing! Either to this company or anyone else. You will not recognize me if we should meet in Whitby. Do you understand? I can be very dangerous when I'm crossed."

"Y... Yes... yes, of course, Your Grace," Nescott stammered. "You shall not see me again this evening if that pleases you. I intend to find a bench and take a nap in this garden. Rest assured, I would never do anything to harm anyone as... as influential as you are. I take my leave, Your Grace. Forgive me for my impertinence."

Gloriana could no longer control herself. She burst into heartbroken sobs, her body shaking with grief.

Thorne was suddenly before her on the terrace, his arms reaching out to her. "Oh, my God! You heard it all."

She slapped at his arms. "Don't touch me, you monster!"

"Gloriana, listen to me! I forgot that absurd wager weeks ago."

"You poxy villain!" she cried through her tears. "Before or after you bedded me? Or perhaps after you sent the lock of my hair to your vile companions in London. And collected your winnings, no doubt."

He groaned. "I had forgotten about the hair. I wanted it only as a memento."

"Do you now add lies to all your other sins?" She had never hated anyone as much as she hated him at this moment.

"No! I intended to tell you the truth tonight, and ask you to be my duchess."

"A marriage proposal? Another wager? Another amusement for you and your friends—before you jilted me and preserved your reputation? *Your Grace?*" she added with scorn.

"No, never! Oh, Gloriana, my sweet. Please forgive me. Come home to our cottage, so we can talk."

"'Tis not *your* home, caitiff. 'Tis mine. And you are not welcome there. Not ever again!"

"Let me make it up to you. Let me…" He tried to reach for her again, but she eluded his grasp and dashed back into the great hall, choking on her tears. She saw Sir Arthur across the room, speaking with several other gentlemen, and dodged the clusters of guests on the floor, seeking him out like a starving beggar desperate for a crumb of kindness. Thorne pounded after her, finally managing to clutch at her arm as she reached Pritchett.

"Let me go, you dog!" she cried. "Sir Arthur, I beg you… help me!"

Pritchett's eyes flashed. "Take your hands off the gentlewoman, sirrah!" He gestured to his friends, who immediately leaped to pull Thorne away from Gloriana and hold him fast. He struggled vainly against the men who held him, cursing savagely. The room had gone quiet. The guests crowded around, wide-eyed, whispering among themselves.

Sir Arthur planted himself before Thorne, his lip curling in contempt. "You dared to attack this kind lady, to bring her to tears? I intend to have you horsewhipped. But first... something I've wanted to do since the moment I met you—a cur who clearly doesn't know his place..." He swung back his arm and drove his fist into Thorne's jaw—once, and then again. Gloriana could hear the crunch of bone on bone. Thorne sagged between the men who held him, his eyes glazed in near-insensibility. Rubbing his bruised knuckles, Pritchett turned back to Gloriana. "Now, my dear, may I see you home?"

She felt suffocated, drowning in her sorrow, scarcely able to breathe with the staring faces so close. "No. I want to be alone. My horse..." She brushed past the crowd, hurried to the door and fled outside, shrilly demanding that Black Jack be brought to her at once.

As she galloped home in the moonlight, her thoughts were in turmoil. She couldn't stay in Whitby. The town, the cottage, her happy life here—all had turned to poison in her heart, corrupted by the venom that Thorne had brought to every day they had spent together. She could taste the bitterness in her mouth, remembering his final kiss, now irreversibly altered by his deception.

But where could she go? Back to the streets of London? It was where she belonged, she could see that now. She had been a fool to think she could ever be a lady. Thorne had probably been laughing at her the whole of their time together, as the servants had at Baniard Hall, using her for his own satisfaction. His seeming warmth, his kindnesses, had merely been a sham—only instruments for his vile seduction.

She sobbed aloud in the darkness. Perhaps his betrayal had only been her proper due in life. The bastard child of a Gypsy and a thief. Common clay. What had ever made her think that she could rise above her beginnings?

• • •

Thorne shook his head to clear it of the last cobwebs. His jaw throbbed like the devil. Damn Pritchett! He struggled to stand tall and proud, despite the men who still clutched his arms. He stared at Pritchett with contempt, managing with difficulty to control the fury that raged in his heart.

"You will have your men release me, Pritchett," he said in a stern tone. "At once."

"Pah! And who are you to give me orders, sirrah?"

"I am John Havilland, Duke of Thorneleigh. And your superior in every way."

Pritchett was clearly rattled by his announcement, delivered with supreme confidence, but he managed to sound skeptical. "Indeed, sir?"

"Nescott is in the garden. He recognized me. Send for him." Thorne glanced briefly at the two men who still held him. "And call off your dogs. I'm not in the habit of being pawed."

Pritchett hesitated, then stepped aside as Sir Hugh Cholmley, summoned from the dancing floor, made his way through the gathering.

"What the devil is going on here, Arthur?" he demanded.

Pritchett pointed a scornful finger at Thorne. "This

rogue claims to be the Duke of Thorneleigh. And he had the temerity to assault Mistress Cook."

Sir Hugh raised a questioning eyebrow. "Thorneleigh? Mistress Cook's blacksmith? An improbable tale. I would have met that esteemed gentleman at Court last season and recognized him at once."

Thorne forced himself to remain calm. He outranked every man in this country backwater, and he found it maddening to have to explain himself. "I was abroad last season, Sir Hugh. I came to Whitby in disguise. On a whim, if you will. But if you send for Nescott in the garden, he will identify me. In the meantime, have these men release me."

Cholmley nodded. "Let the man go. And find Nescott. We'll resolve this dilemma soon enough."

Thorne chafed with impatience as several footmen ran into the garden. He couldn't see Gloriana among the crowd. She must have gone back to the cottage while he was regaining his wits after Arthur's attack. What a mess he'd made of the whole business. Would she ever forgive him? He should have told her the truth weeks ago.

At last, Nescott came stumbling into the hall, his periwig askew, his waistcoat unbuttoned. He planted himself unsteadily before Cholmley and gave a polite nod of his head. "You sent for me, Sir Hugh?"

"I did. Who is this man?"

Nescott looked at Thorne, an edge of fear in his eyes. "I know not, milord. A stranger to me."

Thorne gnashed his teeth. "You may tell the truth, Nescott. I release you."

"I never saw this man before, I tell you."

Thorne took a menacing step toward Nescott. "Damn

it, man! I'll have your head on a pike."

Nescott began to blubber, waving his arms helplessly in front of him. "I… I want nothing to do with this business. I've said my piece. I'll say no more." He bowed to Sir Hugh. "By your leave, milord, I'll withdraw." He turned about and fled the room.

Pritchett sneered at Thorne. "Well, sirrah, what do you have to say now?"

Thorne rolled his eyes in frustration. There was no help from a spineless coward like Nescott. But perhaps… "In the village. Master Dobson. You all know him well. He's my valet. Send for him."

It seemed forever until Dobson appeared. Thorne had never been so happy to see the man in his life. "Tell them who I am, Dobson."

Dobson bowed politely to the gentlemen. "Milords. This is John Havilland, Duke of Thorneleigh, of London and Sussex." He turned concerned eyes toward his master. "Are you safe and well, Your Grace?"

Thorne ignored the gasps of surprise from the assembled company, the bows and curtsies. He accepted Sir Hugh's apologies with polite but hasty grace. All he could think about was Gloriana. He had to reach her. "I need a horse. At once, if you please." He was about to leave, when he had one final thought. He turned to Pritchett with a scowl and rubbed his sore jaw. "You had best stay clear of me, *sirrah*!" He was pleased to see the man cringe in fear.

He galloped through the night, his heart pounding as fiercely as the horse's hooves on the narrow path. He smelled the smoke before he reached the clearing. The forge was ablaze, shooting flames high into the sky. He dismounted and raced to the cottage, calling her name. He took the steps two at a time and burst into her bedchamber. On the floor was her silken gown, torn to shreds. He threw open her small chest and found it empty. Returning to the room below, he saw that her strongbox was gone.

Too late, he thought with a heavy heart.

He dropped to his knees and groaned, cursing himself for his stupidity, for his thoughtless arrogance. "God help me, I'll find you again, my sweet," he whispered.

Chapter Eleven

Thorne stumbled along the cobbled street in Tunbridge Wells, his head spinning. That last glass of claret had been his undoing. Perhaps he'd take to the mineral baths on the morrow. They could restore his body, if not his soul. He kicked at the fallen leaves on the pavement, golden in the early twilight. October had come too soon, blotting out the warm days of summer. He glanced back in annoyance at Cleve Dobson, who followed behind. "Oh, go back to my rooms, Dobson," he muttered. "I don't need a chaperone at Lady Pelham's reception."

His valet frowned. "By your leave, Your Grace, would it not be wiser for you to retire for the evening? I fear there was far too much wine around the gaming table this afternoon."

"By the cross of St. George, you sound like a maiden aunt! I won, didn't I? Sober enough to best the fools who thought I'd lost my edge after the Baniard debacle. Including Felix." He sighed, reluctant still to accept his self-imposed defeat. He was almost sorry he'd impulsively decided to forfeit the wager. "They're all paid off, are they not?"

"Of course, Your Grace. Rogers was naturally vexed by the expense, but you can afford it." Dobson hesitated. "Truth to tell," he said at last, "I'm surprised you didn't succeed with the Baniard woman. I've seen you seduce more difficult creatures with ease."

Thorne studied his valet's face, a mask of neutral propriety. He wondered if Dobson had guessed the truth. After all, the man had witnessed his weeks of moping after they had returned from Whitby, a sadness he had not been able to shake until he'd begun to throw himself back into his old life of easy pleasures. The comfort of the familiar. "Pah!" he said with a snort. "I lost interest. The creature was a strumpet, and I was never able to see beyond her stained past." He pointed down the street. "Now go back to my lodgings. The evening air will clear my head before I reach Lady Pelham's rooms."

He watched Dobson turn the corner, then sighed again. He must have been mad this summer, still intoxicated with the memory of Gloriana dancing in the Shropshire moonlight. She was nothing but a whore. The very symbol of a woman's faithlessness. More wanton even than his mother had been. What a fool he'd been to entertain the possibility of marrying her. To lower his pride, his family honor, to such a level. How soon before she would have tired of him, sought out other men, disgraced the title he had almost been prepared to bestow upon her?

No. A woman like that lived only for the moment, filled with unending desire for a man. *Any* man. He recalled her behavior each time he had bedded her—her immodest responses, her brazen eagerness for their next encounter.

She had used him only to satisfy her prodigious lust. How soon would she have abandoned him, once her hungers had abated?

And of course she was desperate to pass as a lady. And he'd been her dupe, her willing tutor. He cringed, recalling the many times he'd had to swallow his pride, to pretend that he was not better than she, or anyone else in Whitby. The sooner he forgot that shameful episode, the better off he would be. He was glad now that he hadn't set his men to finding her again. It humiliated him to remember how he had behaved—like a besotted mooncalf—those last few days with her.

He climbed the steps to Lady Pelham's rooms, grateful that he felt a bit more sober than when he'd left the gaming hall. He handed his hat to a waiting footman, smoothed his hair—unencumbered by a bothersome periwig—and entered the lady's parlor, almost automatically surveying the room to see what beauties were present.

"Damme," he muttered in consternation. At his entrance, a bewitching blond, elegantly clad in fragile pink, had risen from her chair and was now gliding toward him. He bowed, a frozen smile on his face. "Lady Penelope."

Lady Penelope Crawford gave him a simpering smile. "Thorne, my dear."

"What brings you to Tunbridge?"

Her blue-eyed gaze was innocent, yet enticing. "*You.* I missed your presence over the summer. So when I heard you were coming to take the waters here, I made it my business to follow you."

He cleared his throat. "If you mean to remind me of your absurd wager..."

She laughed, an aristocratic titter, so unlike Gloriana's boisterous guffaws. "Oh, do forgive me, my dear. That was offered in a moment of madness. I don't intend to force you into vows you don't wish to take. I merely wish to enjoy your company, which I have sorely missed."

He smiled his pleasure and relief, took her hand, and kissed it. "You are too gracious, milady." He wondered why he had been preparing to cast her aside. She was so polished, so cultured. Everything he had always admired in a woman. He had kissed her more than once, and enjoyed it, though it would never have occurred to him to invite her into his bed and insult her refined sensibilities. "How long do you intend to stay here?"

She tapped the side of his cheek with her fan, smiling suggestively. "As long as you want me to," she said in a voice that sounded like the purr of a contented kitten.

He was feeling better and better. "I must be back in London in a fortnight, but we shall spend as much time together here as we can, if it pleases you."

"Nothing would please me more." She indicated a room from which came the sounds of music. "But now you must dance with me. I want to feel your strong arm around my waist." She took hold of his sleeve and squeezed. "And your arm seems to be so much stronger than I remember it," she said with a girlish giggle.

"All the better to hold you tightly," he said, realizing, as he never had before, that her lips were full and rosy, and dimples appeared in her porcelain cheeks when she smiled.

They danced for what seemed like hours, while he noted that her movements were effortless, unlike Gloriana, who had often seemed to be counting out the beat silently as they danced. And when he took her to her lodgings, she curled her hand around his neck and pulled his mouth down to hers. Her kiss was soft and maidenly, sending delightful shivers down his spine.

He whistled as he made his way back to his own rooms. It would be very easy to forget Gloriana with Lady Penelope Crawford at his side.

• • •

Sarah, the Dowager Duchess of Thorneleigh, smiled thinly at her scowling son sitting next to her in their box at the Drury Lane Theatre on Brydges Street in London. "There's no point to this ridiculous charade, John, if you refuse to smile at me the whole time," she said softly.

Thorne dragged his eyes away from the players on the stage and lifted his chin in his usual signal. At once, his valet, sitting discreetly behind them, leaned forward in his chair. "Dobson, please tell my mother that she may take my arm when we go below during the interval. And I vow to smile." Dobson nodded, but said nothing.

As though her son had replied to her directly, Lady Thorneleigh answered him. "Merciful heaven, John," she said with a sigh. "How many years must we play this game? I find it absurd. Why not simply banish me to the countryside for the rest of my life and be done with it? Lock me away in a tower somewhere, if you will. Is your pride so stubborn that you cannot openly admit your dislike of your mother? Instead we must come to the theatre often, stroll on the Mall, pretend to the world that we are devoted to one another. And poor Dobson here. I speak to you, you speak to me only through him. He must find it tiring. I certainly do."

Thorne nodded to the couple in the next stall, then pasted a false smile on his face and turned to his mother. "Dobson, please tell my mother that 'tis not pride that impels me to keep up this pretense. 'Tis shame. That the world should know how... this woman... betrayed my father."

Lady Thorneleigh closed her eyes and bit her lip. "But nearly ten years, my boy. Am I never to be forgiven?"

Thorne shrugged. It was all the response she deserved. Nearly ten years. And still the images haunted him, like ghosts in the night—his father sinking into depression, turning to drink, listless, devoid of hope and joy. And the final horror: The sight of the poor man, discovered by his heart-stricken son, hanging from a beam in his bedchamber, dead by his own hand. And all because he could not endure life with his faithless wife for another day, another hour.

Lady Thorneleigh opened her eyes and sighed. "Unless you are enjoying the play, John, I should very much like to return home. I feel a sudden weariness coming upon me."

Thorne glanced back at his valet. "The weight of my mother's conscience, no doubt," he said with a sneer. "Dobson, take the lady home. I shall stay for a while. If the play begins to bore me, there are other amusements here. I'm told there's a very ribald dancer in one of the smaller rooms below. Willing to perform privately for a gentleman. Or perhaps a cockfight. I feel lucky tonight."

"Shall I send the carriage back for you, Your Grace?"

"No. The devil knows when I shall tire of the sport. We're close to the Thames. I can find a waterman to row me home when I've had my fill of pleasures."

Dobson frowned. "But the streets near the river are far

from safe, milord. All manner of scurvy creatures haunt that neighborhood. And late at night…"

Thorne clapped his hand to his hip, patting the sword that rested against his leg. "I'm armed. Scarcely helpless. But if it will mollify you, I'll hail a sedan chair directly as I leave the theatre."

Lady Thorneleigh rose from her chair, smoothing her skirts. Her son stood in his turn, and even managed to kiss her hand as she swept from the box, Dobson close behind.

Thorne turned his attention back to the stage, then swore under his breath. His conversation with his mother had distracted him long enough to lose the thread of the play, and he had scant interest in trying to follow the actors' dialogue and pick up the plot. He felt restless tonight, as though he were ready to jump out of his skin. If he admitted it to himself, he missed the physical activity that working at the forge had given him. Perhaps he'd see if, on the morrow, Felix would be willing to engage in a bout of swords.

And of course, more reluctantly, he had to admit that he was becoming horn-mad. More than two months since he'd had a woman, and he'd awakened on more than one morning to discover his member rigid and primed. Perhaps it was time to press Lady Penelope to grant him the last favors. He thought she might be agreeable, given her coquetry and warmth these last few weeks since they'd returned from Tunbridge.

But in the meantime… The thought of the naked dancer was intriguing. That sort of woman was usually willing to go beyond mere dancing, especially if he was generous with his praise and his coins. He made his way to the bowels of the theatre, hearing tell-tale noises from the various closed doors—the bark of fighting dogs, the shouts of bettors on this or that game of chance, the clank of chains from the bear-baiting space.

The door to the dancer's room was open. He entered quickly and closed the door behind him, nodding to the raven-haired beauty who stood on a table, a tambourine in her hand. She wore a loose shift that barely reached her knees, and her face was rouged and powdered to accentuate the fullness of her lips, the sharp lines of her cheekbones. He slapped a gold crown on the table and settled into one of the nearby armchairs.

She put one hand to the drawstring of her shift and raised a questioning eyebrow. "Yes, milord?"

"Yes," he growled. He scanned her lush body as the shift dropped at her feet, noting the fullness of her breasts, the seductive patch of dark curls at her groin. She was a beauty. He smiled in satisfaction as she gyrated slowly before him, keeping time by tapping the tambourine against one sensuously curved hip. He felt his cock growing hard with desire.

The dance was finished. She gave a little curtsy, then glanced to the corner of the room, where a small cot sat in shadows. "Is there more that you be wantin', milord?" she purred.

He threw another coin on the table, stood up and began to fumble with the buttons on his breeches. Then he hesitated and shook his head. He would get as much enjoyment from pleasuring himself as he would with this creature. She would moan and cry out with as little sincerity as the actors on the stage upstairs. All to earn her pay.

But Gloriana's joy had been real, her passion genuine,

making him feel at those moments of physical joining that they were connected in so many other ways besides their writhing bodies. "Never mind," he muttered, and fled the room, ignoring the dancer's thanks for her unearned coins.

He wandered through the dim passageways, seeking a way out to the street. It would be better to go home and drink himself into a stupor, hoping he could blot out the memory of Gloriana's seductiveness.

He stopped abruptly, hearing shouts from behind one of the closed doors. It sounded like the voices of a score of men, whooping with enthusiasm. "Glory! Glory!" they cried.

Curious, he pushed open the door and stood, dumbstruck, at the scene before him. A gladiator's pit, similar to the one he'd visited with Felix all those months ago. But the stage was almost on a level with the floor that held the standing crowd, who continued to shout and throw purses onto the shallow platform. To one side of the stage was a fallen woman, her arm bleeding profusely, her limbs almost as red from numerous blows. Several men tended to her wound.

But it was the half-naked victor, brandishing her bloody sword, parading about and acknowledging the plaudits of the spectators, who caused him to swear aloud.

"Sweet Jesus! Gloriana!"

His shock soon turned to anger. How could she lower herself to such a degree? To fight like a savage, to exhibit her body in such a shameless manner. Impulsively, he pushed through the crowd, leaped up to the platform and swung her into his arms, throwing her over his shoulder like a sack of grain. Her sword dropped to the stage with a loud clank. "Are you mad, woman?" he cried.

She wriggled furiously against him, pounding on his back with fierce blows. "Let me go, you pig!"

He could only think of getting her out of there. He saw a small open door at the back of the stage and headed in that direction, kicking it shut behind him. He spied another passageway and a small staircase leading upward; he took the steps two at a time to reach the ground floor. His sword clanked against his hip as he ran. Gloriana continued to wriggle and curse him, using crude oaths that blistered his ears. "Hold your tongue, woman," he growled, and smacked her bottom with the flat of his hand. "To shame your family name in such a vile manner. What would the Baniards think if they could see you now?"

"I am what I am," she said, her voice catching in her throat. "And the devil with the Baniards."

They reached the top of the stairs. Thorne looked around for another door, the safety of other patrons.

He felt Gloriana stiffen over his shoulder. "Jeremy!" she cried. "Jem Royster!" He suddenly found himself surrounded by three men, as evil-looking as any trio could be.

The tallest one, clearly the leader, smiled, exposing broken teeth behind his smirk. "Never you fear, Glory, my girl," he said, his voice confident and menacing at the same time. "This cove ain't going nowhere with you." He pulled a pistol from his pocket and aimed it at Thorne's head. "Put the lady down, sir. My best gladiator ain't your property."

Thorne hesitated, then set Gloriana on her feet. He had no choice, with the pistol so close. At once, Royster's companions clutched at his arms and held him fast. He muttered a curse, feeling helpless.

Gloriana spat at him, then slapped him hard across the

face, rattling his brains for a moment. His periwig flew from his head; Gloriana scooped it up and scowled at it as though it were a foul living creature. She turned to Royster. "Thanks, Jem. What are we to do with this cove?"

Royster pulled Thorne's sword from its sheath, taking a second to admire its fine workmanship. "This will bring in a pretty penny." He nodded to Gloriana. "Get his purse. And then we'll haul him outside and throw him in the river."

"No! Wait." Gloriana turned to Thorne, hatred burning in her emerald eyes. "I have a better idea. I know who this fine gentleman is. The great Duke of Thorneleigh. His people would pay a deal of money to see him safe. We'll take him to my room." She jerked her chin in the direction of the two other men. "Rafe and Sam, there, can go to his house and demand a ransom."

"A fine idea, my girl." Royster gave a mocking bow to Thorne. "Your Grace. Will you come with us?" Despite Thorne's struggles, Royster pulled his neckerchief from his neck and tied Thorne's hands firmly behind his back, then borrowed Rafe's neck-cloth to gag Thorne. They carried him, squirming and grunting, out to the street. Thorne could smell the strong odor of the river nearby, feel the dank cold of the night air on his face. The dim street was deserted, trash-filled and foul, with only the light from a few disreputable grogshops to show the way.

After a few minutes, they entered a small building, carried Thorne up the stairs, and threw him into a chair in a corner of a tiny room, tying him firmly against the chair back. Royster pulled the gag from Thorne's mouth and was immediately greeted with a storm of curses, delivered in a loud voice. "Shout all you want, Your Grace. Ain't no one pays attention in this part of London." He took Thorne's periwig from Gloriana and examined it with care. He snorted. "Look, Glory. Such vanity. His coat of arms even inside his wig."

She laughed sharply. "Bloody hell. A lion in his crest." She glared at Thorne, bound and helpless. "And there be the King of the Jungle," she said with mockery.

Royster handed the wig to Rafe. "This will prove the truth of our threat. You can show it to his people and ask for a thousand pounds for his lordship's release."

"I have no doubt his life is precious to *some* people," Gloriana sneered.

As Rafe turned toward the door, Royster stopped him. "Wait. Find out where the rogue lives, then come back here. We'll write a proper ransom letter. Show them we ain't savages."

After the two men had left with Thorne's wig, Royster put his arm around Gloriana's waist. "Shall we amuse ourselves while we wait, Glory?"

She looked at Thorne with disgust, then deliberately turned and kissed Royster on the mouth. Thorne gnashed his teeth in fury. "Have you sunk so low, woman?"

"Your high-toned manners don't matter here, caitiff," she said. "I do as I wish."

Royster grinned, pulling Gloriana toward a small bed on one side of the room. "And as I wish?" he said with a leer.

"No. Not now." She twisted away from his arm, crossed to Thorne and pulled his purse from his pocket. "They'll be looking for us, after the ransom is paid. Take this and go and find a carriage to carry us out of London for a spell. 'Twill be safer. Rafe and Sam can stay. No one will look for them.

But you and I had best leave the city."

Royster nodded reluctantly. "Aye. 'Tis best." He brightened. "But with your skills, we can find another town to set up a ring."

When he had gone, jingling Thorne's purse in one fist, Gloriana turned to Thorne with a contemptuous smirk. "Not feeling so high-and-mighty now, are you, Your Grace?"

"Curse you, woman!" he spat, struggling against his bonds. "Flaunting your body for all the world to see. Not content with whoring in private—"

"I was *never* a whore!" she cried. "Except with you," she added bitterly. "You made a whore of me, with your vile wager."

"And that... Royster, there? How many times has he enjoyed your favors?" Thorne's sharp pang of jealousy was something he hadn't expected. He glared at Gloriana. "Wanton woman. I'm only surprised you didn't swive him in front of me, to exact your revenge."

"And you would have enjoyed it, you filthy gambler. You could have made a wager on which one of us would come first."

He closed his eyes for a moment, trying to collect his thoughts. It was pointless to quarrel with her. They would only end up saying hateful things to one another, spiteful insults that could never be retracted. And he needed all his wits about him to get out of this place before the men returned. He lifted his head and managed a gentle smile. "Gloriana. I beg you to accept my forgiveness for that shameful wager. I regretted it from the bottom of my heart. To bring dishonor upon you. I had put it out of my mind long before that night at Abbey House." He shook his head. "In faith, you are the kindest, most worthy woman I've ever known."

If he had hoped to win her over, he was disappointed. She laughed, an ugly bark. "Bloody hell! What a pack of lies. If you had been so concerned with my honor, you would have left long before Abbey House. Or told me the truth. But instead you stayed. To satisfy your prickle every chance you could." She eyed him with scorn. "And you still want me, you villain. I can read it in your eyes."

He turned his head aside, unwilling to let her see the hunger that was rising in him. "Don't be absurd," he muttered.

She stepped closer, bending down so her full breasts nearly touched his face. He breathed in her scent and felt his senses reeling. She laughed and stood straight, pulling the cluster of ribbon bows from her hair and unfastening the ribboned belt that held her short gladiator shift close to her waist. She stripped off her shift and stood naked before him. He felt his cock growing hard despite his strong will. "Absurd?" she purred.

"For the love of God," he said in a strangled voice. He fought against the ties that held him fast. "Untie me, you witch."

"Not bloody likely," she said. "This is my... *recompense* for your villainy. Wasn't that one of your high-toned words?" She reached down and undid the buttons on his breeches, burrowing among the folds to clasp his hard member. He groaned in agony. "Poxy rogue," she said with a laugh. "I'm minded of how you teased me with your words. 'Tis far more satisfying to tease you thus." She caressed his cock, squeezed it rhythmically, until he thought he'd go mad with desire. "And thus," she added, and bent her mouth to his.

Her kiss was as sweet as he remembered it. He strained forward, thrusting his tongue against her closed lips until she opened for him. She responded with unexpected passion, meeting his eager tongue with her own. He inhaled her lips, drowning in the ecstatic feel of her mouth on his.

When she finally lifted her head, he saw that her eyes were hazy with a desire that matched his own. "Untie me, love," he whispered. She nodded, her frantic hands tearing at his bonds. He jumped from the chair and pulled her into his arms, propelling her swiftly toward the bed and onto her back. He opened his breeches, poised himself above her spread legs and plunged. She gasped in pleasure, her hips rising to meet his every wild thrust. He prayed to last as long as he could, to prolong the sweet tension for them both. A frenzied dance of pleasure, given and received.

"Harder!" she cried. "Harder." She wrapped her hands around his buttocks and pulled him closer, increasing the force of his penetration. He slammed into her again and again, reveling in the tightness of her core that enclosed him. They climaxed together, with a great cry of release. He collapsed beside her, holding her naked body close to his beating heart.

"Gloriana," he said with fervor. "Don't ever leave me again."

Chapter Twelve

Gloriana stirred in Thorne's arms and leaned up on one elbow to look down at him. His eyes were closed, his beautiful mouth slack with spent desire. She felt her heart tearing into little pieces, scattering like the sparks from the forge. She hated him. She loved him. "A pox on you," she muttered, "for making me want you."

He opened his clear, gray eyes. "Was there not more between us than simple desire, my sweet?"

She couldn't let go of her bitterness and hatred so easily. "Yes. There was dishonesty, deception. I can never forgive it. You treated me like common dirt, lower than your lowliest scullery maid. A whore, you called me, and think it so. Just someone you can boast about to your friends."

He sat up in his turn. "Let me make it up to you. Let me—"

"No! 'Tis over between us. No matter what you say. I will always see the contempt in your eyes." She sighed and pulled her thoughts together. This was madness, to quarrel about feelings at a time like this. At any moment, Royster might come back. She rose from the bed and grabbed for her clothes. "Quickly, now. We must leave. I may still hate you, but I don't wish you dead. And Royster will kill you even after the ransom is paid. I know the man." She jerked her head toward the table, where Royster had placed Thorne's sword. "Fetch your weapon."

As Thorne replaced his sword in its sheath, she hurriedly dressed—shift, petticoat, skirt, and stays. "Will we head for the river?" he asked.

"Aye. If we're lucky, we'll find a waterman willing to take you home." She finished tying her garters, then slipped into her shoes. She glanced around the small room. She knew with a certainty that she could never come back here. Had she forgotten anything? A warm jacket—the nights were growing cold. And money! She pulled a small sack of coins from a box under the bed. "These can pay for the waterman. And see me safely out of London and Royster's grasp."

Thorne put his arm around her. "You'll come with me, of course."

She shook her head. "No. As long as I can't forgive you, I can't stay with you." She turned to the bed. "Oh! My keepsake." She fished under the pillow and pulled out the handkerchief that held Billy's curl.

Thorne leaned in close. "You guarded that every moment when we were in Whitby. May I see it at last?"

She hesitated, then unwrapped the handkerchief and showed him the tiny red curl, like spun copper, tied up with a blue ribbon. "'Tis my son's," she said, her voice catching.

"Yes, of course. Sir Charles' child. Will you return to the family?"

"No," she said softly. "He's better off without me." It broke her heart to speak the words.

"But to give up your child, never to see him again…" He put a tender hand on her arm.

She sighed and shook off his fingers. "Then we have both lost something in this game." She reached for his hand. "Now come. No time to waste."

She guided him hurriedly through the few narrow streets that led to the banks of the Thames. The only light on the narrow cobblestoned way came from a nearby dilapidated inn, its lamp-lit windows casting glowing oblongs onto the pavement.

Gloriana scanned the dark waters of the river, seeking a torch that might indicate a nearby waterman. "Bloody hell," she muttered.

"Perhaps if we go back to the Strand," Thorne said. "A busy street, even at this time of night. We might find a sedan chair or—"

He was interrupted by the soft click of a pistol being cocked, just behind them. He and Gloriana whirled about to stare into the barrel of Royster's gun. The villain smiled. "I knew I couldn't trust you, wench. The carriage will wait until I've dispatched His Grace and dealt with your betrayal."

Gloriana swallowed her dismay and thought quickly. "Don't be a fool, Jem. The noise of your pistol will raise a hue and cry." She gave a helpless, apologetic laugh. "'Twas only a moment's weakness, pet. I thought to enjoy the gentleman's favors before you returned. And then I didn't want to see him dead. Let's go back to our old plan. The ransom will be enough. We needn't have blood on our hands besides. Certainly not the blood of this weak, scurvy dog, who couldn't lift a finger to help himself." She looked at Thorne, praying he would understand her words.

Thorne nodded, seeming to read her thoughts. "Indeed, sir," he said in a pleading voice, so unlike him. "Collect your ransom, allow me to go safely home. And I won't press charges. I swear it." He held up his hands in surrender, slowly stepping closer to Royster. "I am your prisoner."

The pistol wavered in Royster's hand. "Well..."

At that moment, Thorne leaped forward and knocked the weapon from Royster's fingers, sending it spinning toward the river bank. Royster swung at Thorne and they grappled for a long minute; then Thorne reared back and landed a heavy blow on Royster's chin, driving the man to the pavement. He took a second to grin at Gloriana. "My strong left arm, thanks to you." He unsheathed his sword and handed it to her. "Watch him while I retrieve his pistol."

She nodded and took the weapon, admiring Thorne's bravery and quick mind, and remembering absurdly at that moment how he had rescued the seamen at Whitby. A fine man, in spite of the ugly wager. Perhaps she could forgive him after all. She smiled at his bent back as he stooped to the pistol at the water's edge.

She turned toward Royster, but not soon enough to catch him as he reached behind his collar and pulled out a dagger. "John!" she screamed. But it was too late. The dagger flew through the air and caught Thorne between his shoulder blades. He gasped and turned, eyes wide in shock, then fell backward and tumbled into the river. Gloriana screamed again.

The door to the inn opened and a small crowd rushed into the street, gaping at the scene before them. But

Gloriana's thoughts were only on the monster who still lay on the pavement before her. As though she were holding her gladiator's sword, she lifted Thorne's weapon with two hands above her head and plunged it into Royster's black heart. He gurgled for a moment, then was still.

A bystander called out. "Murder most foul! Send for the Watch!"

Gloriana rushed to the river bank and pointed. "Bring torches! There's a man…" She choked on her words. He *couldn't* be dead. Her heart would never survive the loss.

More and more people had poured into the street, alerted by the shouts and cries. Though others joined Gloriana in scanning the dark waters, there was no movement, no sound from the blackness except the soft lapping of the waves against the pilings. Gloriana sank to her knees, weeping bitterly.

She was roused at last by a firm hand on her shoulder. She glanced up, tears still streaming from her eyes. She recognized the man by his badge of office. A constable.

"Get up, girl," he growled. "You be comin' wi' me."

"But you must search the river," she said in panic. "There's a man—"

"Ain't no one there, leastwise as I can tell." He nodded toward Royster's corpse, still impaled with Thorne's sword. "But you be comin' to Newgate wi' me. To be tried for murder. And hanged for it, God willin'." He hauled her to her feet and passed her on to two of his men. "What be your name?"

About to answer him, she stopped. She could tell him she was the Lady Gloriana Baniard. Notify the Ridleys. Grey and Allegra would surely see that she had the best lawyer to plead her case before the courts. Even bribe someone, if it was necessary.

No! To add to Billy's shame as he grew, knowing that his mother was a murderess? She wasn't worthy to take her place among their kind. She never had been. Stupid, uncultured, ignorant. 'Twould be better to be hanged at Tyburn than disgrace the family further. And with Thorne dead, what did she have to live for? She stared the constable full in the face. "My name is Molly Sharpe," she lied.

• • •

The next few weeks were filled with numbness, as though she had already been condemned and put to death. She still had enough of her wits left to remember that she had her purse, filled with a goodly number of coins, tucked into her bodice. She was able to pay for her own dirty little apartment in the press-room in Newgate prison, away from the general population. A few more coins bought her a shifty lawyer, a stout man with shrewd, pig-like eyes.

He listened carefully to her account of that night, truthful as far as she wished to go. She had met the gentleman on the street, she said. They had arranged an assignation. Then Royster had appeared and attacked them.

After hearing her story, her lawyer had returned to the inn near the river and found several of the patrons who had seen her kill Royster. With a handsome bribe, they had gone with her and her lawyer before the magistrate at the Old Bailey, and sworn an oath that they had seen Royster kill the gentleman, and that Gloriana's attack had only been an attempt to protect herself from further harm.

To her lawyer's satisfaction, the court had accepted her plea of self-defense, without the need of a jury trial. It was a reprieve, of course, not a pardon. A man was still dead on her account. But instead of prison or the gallows, she was offered the option of being transported to America.

She ignored her lawyer's apology for not getting a full acquittal, and shook her head. "'Tis no matter," she said. "'Twill be a new life for me, a new beginning in America." Once in the Colonies, she could pay her way out of bond servitude and try to build a new life. Resigned to whatever the future might hold, she settled into her dingy little room in the prison, until she should be transported. Gnawed by guilt over her part in Thorne's sad fate, she was willing to accept a lonely life of exile from England—all she deserved.

Overcome with despair, she sank onto her small cot. What did any of it matter? Thorne was dead. And so was she.

• • •

Wrapping his morning gown more tightly around his chest, Thorne stepped outside onto the terrace of his country house in Surrey and glanced up at the November sky. Sunny and clear, with a few white clouds drifting across the vivid blue horizon. And still mild enough so a few roses lingered on the bushes of the formal garden. He breathed deeply of the sweet air—as deeply as his still-healing lung would allow—and walked slowly and carefully along the gravel path toward the glasshouse.

Nearly a month since that fateful night in London. His doctors said he was healing well, and he was getting stronger every day. It still seemed unreal, like a misty, terrifying dream only half-remembered. The fight with Royster. The feel of the cold water on his flesh as he tumbled into the river. He remembered the pain in his back, the water filling his nose, his desperate gasps for air. The rest was a blur. Dobson had told him that he had managed to make it to shore, where he was found at dawn by a dustman, but he recalled nothing of that. They said he'd even contrived to whisper his name before he collapsed completely.

He understood why his mother had quickly arranged for him to be transported out of London to Thorneleigh Hall, near Mayfield, almost in secret, like a highwayman on the run. The damage to his reputation, to his family name, would have created a scandal. A great nobleman, friend to the Duke of Arundel, no less, found gravely injured in a disreputable part of the city. There would have been questions he was not prepared to answer.

The glasshouse was warm, sheltering seedlings and plants that would have long-since withered outside. There would be oranges for Christmastide, he noted, admiring the healthy trees. He nodded to Purdy, the head gardener, then bent to a box of small plants nestled in fragrant loam, and frowned. "These seedlings are too close together. And the box is too shallow. No room for the carrots to grow."

Purdy touched his forehead in salute and crossed to Thorne's side, frowning in his turn. "You be a gardener now, Your Grace?" he asked, clearly struggling to keep a civil tone in the face of his master's intrusion into *his* domain.

"I've had a bit of experience," he said, a sharp edge to his voice. He was the Lord of the Manor, after all. What right did this man have to question him? With an impatient sweep of his fingers, he indicated a cluster of plants in one corner of the box. "Look there. Scarcely room to breathe and spread. And when the carrots begin to grow down, where can they go?"

"Beggin' your pardon, milord, but when they gets bigger, they gets a bigger box." Purdy's tone was that of an exasperated parent explaining things to a difficult child.

Thorne smiled ruefully, aware that he must have sounded like an arrogant prig. "A point well taken, my good man. But if I may, I'd like to help you replant them when they're ready. I'd welcome the feel of dirt under my nails again."

Purdy raised a questioning eyebrow, then nodded. "Aye, milord. If you wish it. I'll leave you to your tour around the glasshouse now. Them tulips in the corner be needin' my care." He saluted once again, his wrinkled face relaxing into a grin. "Truth be told, Your Grace, 'tis grand to see you up and about at last."

The gardener moved away and left Thorne to his examination of the various shrubs and plants. He found the strong scent of the greenery and the rich earth almost painful, reminding him once again of his garden at Whitby, the unexpected joy he'd found in being useful.

And, of course, thoughts of Whitby always reminded him of Gloriana. He wanted her. He needed her. Dear God, he *loved* her. It no longer mattered that she'd been a whore, that she might betray him some day. Why should he feel jealousy, that she'd had other lovers? Even that villain, Royster. He himself had scarcely been faithful to a woman for any length of time.

The past was dead and buried. He only knew that his future was meaningless without her by his side. She was a free spirit who had brought joy to his constrained life. And his days were empty unless he could find her again.

But where was she? As soon as he'd recovered his senses, he'd sent Rogers to London to search for her, to enquire of the lowest denizens of the city and scour the meanest streets. He'd even had Rogers ask about Jeremy Royster, with little success. The man had disappeared, though some rumors had it that he had been killed in a fight.

And with each fresh report, his heart sank and a dreadful notion added to his despair: She didn't want him to find her. Why should she, after the terrible things he'd said and done? He suspected that Dobson guessed the truth about his feelings for Gloriana, and had probably shared the Whitby adventure with his mother. Her tenderness in the past few weeks had seemed to go far beyond her concern for his health.

"Merciful heaven! What are you doing out—and in your condition?" Thorne turned at the sound of Lady Penelope Crawford's voice. Her face was a mask of concern.

"'Tis not as though I had asked for a horse to ride!" he snapped, feeling like a child caught snatching a forbidden sweet. The injured look on her delicate face, the soft blue eyes filling with tears, made him instantly regret his harsh reply. He gave her an apologetic smile. "Forgive me. That was cruel."

She crossed the glasshouse floor and placed a tender hand on his arm. "Dearest Thorne. To see you out of your sickbed, after we nearly lost you, is reason enough to rejoice. I can forgive your impatience with your slow recovery."

"Too slow," he grumbled. "I shall go mad with boredom."

"Would you like me to read to you? I mark that my voice brought you comfort in the early days."

That was certainly true enough. As soon as news of his mysterious illness had spread in his London circles, Penelope had appeared in Surrey, settling herself into his household and declaring that she would be his nurse. In some perverse way, it pleased him that his mother had been supplanted as his caretaker.

And Penelope had shown a sweet side to her nature that he had never suspected. She had sat by his bedside for hours, mopping his fevered brow and directing his diet of milk-pottage and weak tea as he slowly recovered.

He smiled at her and shook his head. "No. I'm too restless to concentrate on a book."

"Cards? Though I vow you allow me to win, you scoundrel." Penelope pursed her lips in a mock pout and wagged her finger at him.

He shrugged ruefully. She was right, of course. But she always looked so crestfallen when she lost, and so filled with girlish joy when she won, that he hadn't the heart to best her very often. "Cards it is. And I promise to challenge you severely."

She slipped her arm through his. "Come into the house now. I'm sure all this walking and standing is not good for your recovery." She guided him into a small parlor, helped him into a chair in front of the card table, and fetched a footstool to put under his feet.

"Thank you, Penelope. It's been many years since I've been so pampered." If he admitted it to himself, he rather enjoyed being cosseted. He had rebuffed his mother's attempts to indulge his needs for so long that she had simply given up trying.

Penelope sat opposite him and took his hands in hers. "I

wish I could do more," she said softly. "Your eyes are filled with pain. And not from your wound, I think. Will you tell me, at last, what happened in London?"

He wasn't about to tell the whole sordid tale to anyone, and certainly not to this fragile creature. He repeated the story he'd told to Dobson. "There's little to tell. I left the theatre and was confronted by a ruffian. I should never have turned my back on him."

"That's all? I would have expected anger from you. A desire to see justice done. Not the sadness that you've seemed to carry around like a heavy burden."

He fidgeted in his chair, uneasy with the direction of their conversation, and determined to change the subject. He pasted a bright smile on his face. "Why, then," he said, "you must bring me cheer."

She guided one of his hands to her mouth, turned it palm-upward, and planted a soft kiss on his flesh. Then she looked away, seeming embarrassed. "As to that... when you have quite recovered your strength, there is much more than cheer that I should like to offer you."

He stared in surprise. The last favors—without the need for his impassioned entreaties? "But surely..." he began.

Her smile was soft and tender, almost virginal. "You are so dear to me, Thorne. Why should I not give you what I know you have so eagerly sought, though you've never spoken the words?"

He cleared his throat, unsure of how to proceed. "Time enough to discuss the matter when I'm better." He frowned. That seemed such an inadequate response, after the woman had just offered him her body. He had a sudden thought. "In the meantime, I'm touched by your loyalty and devotion. I shall ask Dobson to bring round a jeweler from Mayfield. A sapphire or two to go with your eyes would not be amiss."

"Oh!" She clapped her hands, her eyes lighting up with joy. "You mustn't!"

He gave her a lopsided grin. "Well, then, perhaps I shan't," he teased.

"No!" she cried, an unseemly eagerness in her voice. He suddenly recalled her ill-disguised envy at the sight of other women's jewels, then shook off his ungentlemanly thoughts. He'd known other women who were hungry for his wealth, but none of them would have been a devoted nurse for weeks, as Penelope had been.

As though she had read the momentary doubt on his face, Penelope smiled shyly. "Of course, my dear, you may do as you wish. It matters not to me. But I should prefer something more personal from you."

"Indeed?"

"I've noted that you often wear a signet ring on your little finger. I should very much like to have that."

That alarmed him at once. A ring with his crest? "Not as a covenant, surely!"

"Of course not, my dear. I would never take advantage of your weakened state to force you into a marriage agreement. 'Twould simply be something to remind me of you when we're apart. Something that has touched you as intimately as... as I would like to."

He scratched his head. Would he ever understand the mind of a female? "Foolish request. 'Tis old and worn, a base metal, with little value. I wear it out of habit. But I shall give it." He grinned. "And a sapphire too, I think."

She jumped from her chair, came around the table, leaned down and kissed him. Her mouth was hot and eager; he was surprised that he felt no answering response. She lifted her head and giggled. "I knew it was not madcap of me to abandon London for all these weeks."

"Pardon. I did not mean to intrude." Thorne turned. His mother stood in the doorway, a letter in her hand.

Penelope curtsied. "Your Grace. 'Tis always a pleasure to see you. You have merely interrupted an innocent kiss. Your splendid son has just promised me a lovely gift for my weeks of service. I thought only to thank him."

Lady Sarah smiled, a tight grimace that seemed to Thorne to be forced. "Of course, my dear. You have been positively selfless all this time. A paragon of virtue." She crossed the room and nodded graciously to Penelope. "It has always been clear to me what brought you here," she added dryly.

Thorne frowned. Was that sarcasm in his mother's voice? He cursed to himself. Where the devil was Dobson? No one, outside of his households, suspected his animosity toward his mother. But with Dobson absent, he would have to speak directly to her, unless he was clever. He gave her a warm smile, then turned to Penelope. "It would seem my lady mother has brought me a letter." He held out his hand in silence.

"From your friend, DeWitt," she said, placing the letter in his palm.

He looked hopefully behind her toward the doorway. "I have not seen my valet for half the afternoon. Have you, Penelope?" He was quite pleased with himself for managing to avoid speaking directly to his mother for any length of time.

She was clearly aware of his slight, as well. She sighed and rolled her eyes. "While you were resting, John, I allowed him to go into Mayfield. He's quite musical, you know. And there's a violinist in the village who has expressed interest in a musical afternoon one of these days. I thought that perhaps their duets would please you."

Thorne twisted his lips in a mocking smile. "We cannot deny my mother her indulgences, can we, Penelope? But I should like Dobson here when I need him. Henceforth," he added. He broke the seal and tore open the letter. "Now what does Felix have to say?"

Defeated, his mother turned to the door and beat a hasty retreat.

Thorne quickly perused Felix's note. "He wants me to come to London. The gambling is boring without me, he says."

Penelope looked horrified. "Oh, but you can't!"

He was flattered by her seeming concern for his health. "Perhaps in another week or so…"

She stamped her dainty foot. "And then I'll have to share you with others," she pouted.

So much for being flattered, he thought ruefully. She hadn't been thinking of *him*. He felt suddenly weary of her company, her clinging helplessness. He missed Gloriana's strength, her independence. "Perhaps it would be best if you return to the city in a day or so. Your presence here must surely have caused some unkind gossip. I shall join you within the fortnight, or sooner. I'll wager the excitement of the city will do more for my health than many more tedious days here."

She sighed, clearly reading the resolve in his eyes. "If

I must go," she said, "'twill be done. I shall miss you, my dear." She flounced toward the door, then whirled about, her skirts billowing. "But you will remember my ring and my sapphire before I go, won't you?"

Chapter Thirteen

Felix settled himself comfortably into an armchair in Thorne's drawing room, took the serving maid's proffered cordial, and gave the girl's ample bottom a vicious pinch as she turned toward Thorne. She squeaked in pain, hastily set down her master's glass before him, and scurried from the room.

Thorne frowned. "I will thank you not to molest my servants, Felix," he growled.

Felix shook his head. "I don't know what's happened to you, friend Thorne. You've changed so, since your injury. You've turned down every gaming afternoon I've arranged since you've returned to London and Havilland House. Not dice, not cards. Not even the opportunity to wager on the new wrestler who's come to town. And now to scold me about my behavior toward the lower orders? You've always been soft toward your servants, but this is absurd. A harmless pinch? The girl expects it."

"Not in my house," Thorne said in a tight voice. "Not

now." He felt comfortable saying the words, comfortable with the man he had become since his days in Whitby. He was no longer the distant aristocrat, seeing the people beneath him as faceless ciphers but as flesh and blood men and women, with the same hopes and dreams as he had. And he was doubly appreciative of their toil, almost envying them, remembering his own satisfaction after a long, tiring day at the forge.

Felix shrugged. "As you wish." He sipped at his cordial. "But you must begin to get out again, even if you reject the amusements I offer you. Or the whole town will begin to think that you've become a monk!"

"Let them think what they wish. I can use my recuperation as an excuse for a time. After that, I shall deal with the gossips."

"And Lady Penelope Crawford? I must tell you that she has confided in me, with a deal of self-pity, that she has not been invited here since your return."

That was true enough. He had avoided sending around an invitation to the lady, had even had Dobson tell her that he'd gone for a stroll on the one day she had come to call. He feared she would be more aggressive in her offer of sexual favors, and he didn't want her. Not after he had known Gloriana. "I'll have a small musical evening here when I'm feeling stronger. That should satisfy the lady."

Felix leered. "An enticing singer, perhaps?"

"No. My valet, Cleve Dobson. He has an extraordinary talent for the flute. I've even allowed him to take in a few pupils since we've returned." It had pleased him to allow the man a modest life of his own, apart from his duties, seeing his valet with fresh eyes since their time in Whitby. A man of character and strength, a calming presence who accepted his lower position in life without ever becoming servile.

Felix snorted. "Humph! You're getting quite democratic in your ways, friend Thorne. I do not like it. As for Lady Penelope, I fear a large gathering is not what she desires. You should know that she has been displaying your signet ring on her finger at every assembly she attends. She never speaks of it, but she allows the gossips to assume it's a prelude to a betrothal."

Thorne scowled. "I never meant it as such! I shall have to disabuse her of the notion when next we meet."

"She's a headstrong young woman. If you do marry her, I would suggest you take a firm hand to her bare bottom with some regularity. I know I would." He smacked his hands together to emphasize his words.

Thorne pursed his lips in disapproval. "Really, Felix, I—" He was interrupted by a soft tap on the open door. He looked up and smiled. "Ah, Dobson. We were just speaking of you. How is your new pupil, that rather charming silk merchant's daughter?"

To Thorne's surprise, Dobson blushed to the roots of his blond hair. "Very apt, Your Grace," he murmured. "I... that is... she..." He cleared his throat. "I've only come to tell you that the tailor is here to fit your new coat," he said in his proper valet's voice.

Thorne suppressed a smile. He'd caught a glimpse of the young woman this morning—a raven-haired beauty with bright eyes—and had almost laughed aloud at Dobson's loss of his usual composure. He suspected that, in a short time, more than music would bind them together. "I shall come soon enough, Dobson. Thank you." He rose from his chair.

"But first, let us see Lord DeWitt out."

They walked Felix to the door. Dobson helped the man into his warm cloak and handed him his hat. About to go out to the street, Felix turned. "At least, can I interest you in a visit to Bedlam, friend Thorne? They say the madmen are great sport to watch. They babble and tear their hair, and even strip naked when asked. Or even Newgate. I've heard there's a condemned highwayman there who is most amusing. He can go on for hours about how bravely he intends to die."

Thorne resisted the sudden urge to push Felix into the street. How had he ever enjoyed the company of this depraved voluptuary? "I've never been to either place," he said in a tight voice. "Nor do I plan to go. I scarce can see amusement in the misfortunes of others."

After the door had closed, Thorne turned to Dobson. "I will not be home to that man again. *Ever.*" He headed toward the staircase and the waiting tailor, Dobson following close behind him. "Prisons. Madhouses. I would never set foot in such places. Would you?" He looked back at his valet. To his surprise, the man had stopped, his face turning red. "What is it, man?" he asked.

"In truth, Your Grace," Dobson said softly, "I was once a prisoner in a gaol."

Thorne gaped in surprise. "Gads, man! How did that come to be? Where?"

Dobson looked away. "Debtor's prison."

Thorne turned about on the staircase and headed back to the drawing room. "I should like to know your story, if it doesn't offend you to tell it. Come. Sit with me." Though Dobson protested that it was unseemly for a servant to sit with his master, Thorne insisted that he take a chair opposite him. When they were comfortably settled, Thorne raised a quizzical eyebrow. "What was your background? I've always assumed a respectable education." It shamed him now to remember that he had never cared enough to wonder how this clearly talented man had become a valet.

Dobson sighed. "My father was a merchant of spices. I had a comfortable upbringing. Music, as you have learned, was my true passion."

"And then your father died and left you destitute?"

Dobson's face darkened. Thorne could hear the crunch of his jaw. "Not at all. My esteemed parent is very much alive. My late mother was Dutch. In consequence, my father was able, some years ago, to join with one of my mother's distant relatives to buy into a cinnamon plantation in Ceylon. In the Dutch East Indies, where he lives to this day."

"And you didn't join him? Surely it would have ensured a comfortable life."

"I was young and headstrong. And I wished to pursue my musical talents." Dobson shrugged. "And so he disowned me and sailed away."

"Leaving you to fend for yourself." He had to admire Dobson's courage. He wasn't sure that he himself would ever have had the strength to renounce his own secure future.

"I managed well enough at first. A small group of musicians. Here in London Town. We played at assembly balls. But there were quarrels. After we had drifted apart, I piped on the streets."

Thorne managed a smile. "Much as you did in Whitby, under quite different circumstances."

"Yes. But my debts for lessons, a new flute, became

more than I could bear. And I found it increasingly difficult to find work."

"And so you were sent to prison. But how did you effect your release?"

"A very kind gentlewoman, who visits prisons regularly, paid my debts and hired me as a valet. For her son."

"And who was that remarkable creature?" Thorne couldn't imagine anyone in his circle being that benevolent.

"The Dowager Duchess, the Lady Sarah Havilland."

"Good God!" Thorne took a moment to digest this news. He had never wondered how his mother spent her days, still seeing her with the bitterness of his youth. But clearly she had a more refined sensibility than he, sympathetic to the misfortunes of others. He stirred uncomfortably and cleared his throat. "Isn't my tailor waiting?"

Dobson rose from his chair. "Yes, Your Grace." He shook his head. "I fear all of your coats will have to be replaced. Your tailor has complained that the sleeves seem too tight now. Your arms have grown quite muscular."

"Another reason not to regret the time in Whitby."

"Do you miss it, milord?"

He sighed. "Oddly enough, I do. I never knew there could be such pleasure in work."

Dobson laughed. "Forgive me, Your Grace, but 'tis said that to be rich and idle is the hallmark of a gentleman. But to be poor and unemployed is contemptible."

"Wisely put. I shall have to find something useful that doesn't disgrace my family name." He chuckled. "Perhaps I shall open a blacksmith shop in Mayfield, and work in secret, as Gloriana did."

Dobson gave him a searching look, his clear blue eyes

filled with warmth and understanding. "Do you miss her?" he said at last.

Thorne groaned and covered his eyes with his hand. "More than I can express. How could I have been so vile, with that absurd wager?"

"Begging your pardon, milord, but the man who set out for Whitby last summer has long since vanished. I am proud to call you my master." He grinned. "Even if you open a blacksmith shop, and toil beneath your station."

Thorne slapped at his forehead. A blacksmith shop! How had he forgotten? What was the name Gloriana had told him? *Old Diggory.* "Dobson!" he cried. "Have Rogers look in the city for a blacksmith named Diggory Dyer. I must speak to him."

His valet looked bemused. "Of course, Your Grace."

Thorne started up the stairs, feeling more hopeful than he had in weeks. If the man could be found, he surely would have news of Gloriana.

• • •

The old man smiled, a toothless grin that lit up his wizened face. "'Course I remembers the wench, your worship. Best 'prentice I ever had in all me days."

Thorne sighed his relief. "When did you see her last?"

Diggory Dyer scratched his balding head. "She come to me end o' summer. Wi' a heavy purse o' gold coins." He frowned at Thorne. "And don't be thinkin' they was stolen. Her Charlie had give her a heap o' jewels, and she sold 'em. But, says she, she was goin' back to the ring, and didn't want to keep all that gold for Royster to find. I has her money locked up in a safe place, never you fear."

End of summer. When she'd run away from Whitby. "And you haven't seen her since?"

"She sent around a note wi' a fat little man. Eyes like black buttons. Mebbe a month ago. Wanted a hundred bob, no questions asked. I give it. And not a word since then."

"And you still have the rest?"

"Safe and sound. And a pretty little fan, all lace and pictures and such. She wept when she give it me."

Thorne closed his eyes for a moment. She'd kept his fan as a keepsake. A sweet reminder of their dance in the garden, perhaps. Maybe, if he found her, there was hope for them both. He said a silent prayer. He pressed a coin into Old Diggory's hand. "Thank you, my good man. If you hear from her again, send word around to Havilland House." He eyed the old man's forge, half tempted to pick up a hammer and see if he still retained his skill with the iron. Then he suddenly realized what Diggory had said about Royster. "She wanted you to keep her money. Didn't she trust Royster?"

The old man laughed, sucking in air as he did so; scarcely a sound came from his open mouth. "That villain? She hated 'im. He were always tryin' to have his way wi' her, but he were afraid o' her Da. And Charlie be so jealous he would have run 'im through."

He felt a surge of relief. She had only flirted with Royster to hurt him. He frowned. He hated himself for his next ugly thought, but he had to ask. "And her other men?"

"Be ye daft? Weren't no other men. Not ever. She were too good a girl for that."

Thorne groaned. And he had called her a whore, and

thought it so. There would be much to atone for, when he found her again.

• • •

Thorne looked around the crowded space in Newgate and shook his head. The noise and the filth and the stench of the prisoners were almost unbearable. Men and women huddled in corners, laughing and shouting at one another, or sitting in quiet grief. A few small fires burned in braziers, but did little to dispel the cold December air that seeped in at the barred windows. He turned to his valet. "By the cross of St. George, Dobson, how could you have endured such misery?"

Dobson averted his gaze from a ragged couple who were copulating in a corner of the room. "I had my flute. I let my music soothe me."

"God forgive me for not knowing or caring about such unfortunates as these."

"Don't reproach yourself, Your Grace. They're not all innocent. There's many a thief and footpad and highwayman amongst this lot." He indicated a corridor leading to what seemed like small rooms. "And the ones with money can pay for an apartment in the press-yard, where they have a bit of privacy, at the least."

Thorne sighed. "Well, let's get to business. Surely there are a few wretches here who are worth redeeming. The housekeeper can use a new scullery maid, she says, and my horses would profit from a groom or two."

They enlisted the aid of a prison-keeper and toured the large room, asking questions of the keeper, speaking to the prisoners, and discussing the merits of the various prisoners they came across. At last they settled on a healthy-looking female who had been arrested on suspicion of prostitution and two scrawny young boys who had been accused of stealing a loaf of bread.

Thorne handed a few gold coins to his valet. "Take their names and particulars, Dobson, and see what you can do to effect their release. I'll stay for a bit and see if I can find any more promising candidates."

"Very good, Your Grace. I'll have them put to work as soon as we reach Havilland House."

When Dobson had gone, shepherding the new servants before him, the prison-keeper turned to Thorne. "Will you see the coves in the apartments now, m'lud? They be the real beauties. Murderers and villains what be waitin' on their executions and such. A real rum crew." He led Thorne down the long corridor, shouting curses at the prisoners as they passed. He glanced in at one man, a well-dressed fellow in a room that seemed supplied with all manner of comforts. "Hey, Gilbert," he cried. "Will you let me have your goods when they hauls you to Tyburn Tree?" He was answered by a tin cup hurled at his head. Laughing, he ducked the missile and grinned at Thorne. "I likes to twit 'em, I does, m'lud."

"How very amusing," Thorne said with a sneer.

The keeper looked in at another room, where a woman sat crouched in a corner, her head buried in her arms, her greasy hair lank around her shoulders. She was a picture of abject despair. "Hey, Molly," he called. "Come look at the nob what's come to visit."

"Bugger off, pig!" she shrilled in an ugly voice. Then she lifted her head and glared toward the doorway.

Thorne gasped. *"Gloriana?"* he whispered.

She rose slowly to her feet, her face turning white, her mouth opening wide in disbelief. "But... but you're dead! Dear God, am I dreaming?" She moved unsteadily toward Thorne, her hand at her breast. Her eyes rolled in her head, her limbs shaking; after a few tottering steps, she collapsed with a sigh into Thorne's arms.

• • •

Gloriana stirred, dimly aware that she was on her cot, and that a gentle hand was stroking her cheek. She opened her eyes and let out a soft cry. It wasn't a dream. The prison-keeper had vanished, but John, her beloved John, was bending low, his eyes dark with concern. "I... I thought you were dead. The river... Royster with his knife..."

He gave a gentle laugh. "I'm more hardy than you would suppose. I made it to shore. And was found."

She reached up a trembling hand and caressed his face. "But so thin, so pale." She couldn't keep the tears from welling in her eyes.

"I'm strong enough to kiss you," he murmured. He threw off his cloak and bent to her. His mouth was gentle at first, taking her lips, then gliding across her face to do honor to her cheeks, her closed eyes. But when he returned to her mouth and she threw her arms around his neck, his kiss deepened, demanding her own impassioned response.

She clung to him, thrilling at the fire that burned through her and consumed every part of her eager body. His frenzied hands clasped her breasts, tugged at her shift to expose them. And when he curled his mouth around her nipples, she moaned in pleasure. She reached for her skirts and pulled them above her thighs, then groped at his breeches. He was hard and firm, his own fingers searching for the buttons and tearing them open.

He poised himself above her, placed his hands beneath her hips to lift her to his erect manhood, and plunged wildly into her. She cried out in ecstasy, thrusting her core against his throbbing entrance, reveling in his strength and power. Her head swam and she seemed to lose all sense of her body except for the pulsing thrusts that slammed into her again and again, with an ever increasing tempo that made her ache with anticipation, awaiting the moment of glorious release.

They climaxed together with a mutual roar, a dazzling explosion that left them both panting and spent, entwined in each other's arms.

At last, Thorne sighed and sat up. He smoothed down Gloriana's skirts and straightened her bodice, then lifted her onto his lap. She closed her eyes and leaned against his chest, soothed by the pounding of his heart, the warmth of his encircling arms.

He chuckled softly above her. "You see, I wasn't so gravely injured that I've lost all my strength."

She felt the tears springing to her eyes again. "But Royster could have killed you. And it was all my fault."

"Nonsense. I was the impulsive one, thinking to get you out of that place." He clicked his tongue in disbelief. "A gladiator! I thought you were an Amazon the first time I saw you. Clearly, you are."

"The best of the lot," she said defiantly. "I never lost a match."

"I don't give a tinker's dam what you were," he said.

"What the devil are you doing here? I've been looking for you for months. Till I thought I'd go mad with worry."

"I killed Royster," she said simply. "After you went into the river."

"Dear God, are you condemned?" He lifted her chin to his searching gaze, his eyes dark with sudden fear.

"No. Only transported to the Colonies. My lawyer was able to find witnesses who swore I'd killed the rogue in self-defense."

He pulled away from her and scowled. "You thought I was dead. But why didn't you send a message to Ridley? To your family? They would have seen to your release. Ridley has powerful friends at Court. And you're still a Baniard, with a name that could open doors."

"Not here," she said softly. "I told them my name was Molly Sharpe."

"That's absurd! Why didn't you tell them who you were?"

"And who am I?" she said bitterly. "A bastard from the streets who never knew her mother? A common, worthless thing, destined only to bring disgrace to a fine family? 'Twere better that the Lady Gloriana Baniard vanish from their lives. From her..." she choked back a sob, "from her son's life."

"Worthless? You proved your worth in Whitby. A successful tradeswoman. And as for common... at the Cholmley ball, you were more elegant and magnificent than any ten aristocrats there. You should be proud to call yourself the Lady Gloriana Baniard."

She smiled for the first time in weeks. This man, this high-born duke, found her worthy. Then she shook her head. "Nevertheless, I shall remain Molly Sharpe here, and no other."

He nodded. "Perhaps it's the wisest course. I shall arrange with my secretary, Rogers, to effect your release on the grounds that you were defending me. A stranger you'd met on the street."

"Can you do it?" Her heart stopped for a moment. "Why would you do it?" she added softly, praying for an answer she had no right to expect.

"Firstly, because it's true. And then…" He clutched her tightly to his breast. "Oh, sweet woman, because I love you. That's what I wanted to tell you that night in the garden. And to confess my shameless wager. And beg you to forgive me." He held her away and looked deeply into her eyes. "You should know that I paid off the wager and swore I had never found you. Your shame was no worse than mine, for the wrong I did you."

He *loved* her! She stroked the side of his face, her heart swelling with love and gratitude. "I think I forgave you a long time ago."

"We must talk about our future together. I don't intend to lose you ever again."

"If you think—"

She was interrupted by the prison-keeper at the door. "Be you done here, m'lud?"

"Another moment, sirrah," Thorne growled. He turned back to Gloriana. "We were talking of our future, my love," he said gently.

She shook her head, suddenly aware of her shabby room, the coarse keeper at the door. "This is scarcely the place for tender sentiments." If he intended to propose marriage, she would be ashamed to receive his offer in such ugly surroundings.

"Of course. I'll see to your pardon, and then come back for you."

"No!" She plucked at her filthy garments, her stringy hair. "I don't want you to see me in this place again. And looking like this."

"It matters not to me, my sweet. But if it will please you… there's an inn nearby. The Golden Crown. I'll send the pardon along and arrange for a room at the inn. Meet me there." He groped for his purse. "Do you need money in the meantime?"

She clutched at her pocket, where her purse was hidden. "No. I have enough." She looked up at him, unsure of her next request. "But you were so good at choosing a gown for me in Whitby. Could you…?"

He grinned. "I'll see that a splendid gown is waiting for you at the inn. And I'll send you a few books in the meantime. You must keep up your lessons, you know. Your tutor expects it."

"Now that I know you're safe, I'll have the composure to read again." She bit her lip. "One more thing. The Ridleys must never know what happened here. When I reclaim my name, it will be time enough to…"

"Reconcile?"

"A fine word. Yes. Reconcile with the family."

He rose from the cot, bent low, and kissed her once more. "You haven't said it, you know."

She returned his kiss, throwing her arms around his neck. "Oh, John. You know I love you. Rogue that you might have been, when you kissed me at the forge that first day, I think I was lost."

Chapter Fourteen

"Dobson!" Thorne threw his cloak at the waiting footman and bellowed up the staircase. "Where the devil are you, man?"

In a second, his valet came clattering down the stairs into the vestibule, hastily pulling on his coat. "What is it, Your Grace?"

Thorne rushed forward and pummeled the man on the shoulders. He knew he was grinning like an idiot, but he didn't care. "I've *found* her!"

Dobson's face lit up with joy. "Praise be to God! Where?"

"In Newgate Prison. After you left." He rubbed at his forehead. "I still can't believe it myself. But she's safe and well. I'll give you the details later. Rogers should hear it all. I'll need him to arrange her release."

"I'll do whatever I can to help. Oh, Your Grace, such excellent news. Let me fetch Rogers at once." He turned back to the staircase.

"Wait! She's using a different name. No one is to know otherwise, not even Rogers. She's calling herself Molly Sharpe. We can reestablish her proper name once she's free."

"I understand. Perhaps we can return to the prison to see to her comfort before Rogers' work is done."

"No. She doesn't wish to be seen in such mean circumstances. We'll meet at the inn nearby after she's released."

"The Golden Crown?"

"Yes. That's the one. Oh, Dobson, there's so much to do! You must arrange the finest room there for her. And we'll need to find a mantua-maker to see that she's properly dressed. The best we can find. And books to pass the time. It's the least I owe her."

"Of course." Dobson grinned broadly. "But to find her again, after all this time…'tis scarce to be believed!" he cried. "I share your joy, Your—"

"What is all this noise?" Lady Sarah Havilland sailed into the vestibule from the drawing room, Penelope Crawford close on her heels.

Deflated by their sudden appearance, Thorne shrugged at Dobson. "It would seem we disturbed my mother's tête-à-tête," he said dryly.

His mother gave him a tight smile. "So loudly that we seem to have heard every word." The smile expanded into a grin of genuine pleasure. "But did I hear aright? The woman is safe and well?" At Dobson's nod, she sighed happily. "Ah! My prayers have been answered. 'Tis a blessed day for you, John."

Lady Penelope put her hands on her hips. "I should like to know, who *is* this woman? This… Molly Sharpe?" She fairly spat the name.

Thorne squirmed. How the devil was he to explain Gloriana to Penelope? "Merely someone who… who has gone missing for several months," he stammered at last.

"Humph! My rival, I should guess, from your ill-disguised joy."

He tried to be as gentle as he could. "You must understand, Penelope," he began. "I value your friendship, but—"

"Oh, I understand very well! All these weeks you've been courting me while harboring a secret passion for some trollop in prison."

"Courting you?" His eyes narrowed. "I never gave you leave to presume any serious affection on my part, madam, beyond a warm friendship. 'Tis you who pursued *me*."

She glared at him. Then her face crumpled, tears springing to her eyes. "You can't jilt me like this, after I nursed you back to health," she whined. "I was depending on your good offices…" She bit her lip and turned away.

Though her words were clearly designed to make Thorne feel guilty, something in her manner sparked an unexpected suspicion in him. "My good offices? And my fortune?" he added sharply. "Was that the only reason for your solicitude these many weeks?"

She stamped her foot. "Of course not! You're very dear to me."

Dobson leaned forward and whispered in Thorne's ear. "You should know, milord, that the lady's brother is deeply in debt. It's been the talk of London for months."

Thorne turned to Penelope, his lip curling in scorn. "And were my 'good offices,' as you put it, expected to save your brother's reputation?"

Penelope drew herself up. "I'll not stay in this house to be insulted for another moment." She waved an imperious hand toward the footman, who still stood at attention near the door. "Sirrah! My cloak." She stormed to the door, snatched the garment from the footman, and stomped into the chilly afternoon, her back stiff with righteous indignation.

Lady Sarah grunted. "Good riddance. She was nothing but a fortune hunter. I saw it at once, though she seems to have cozened you for a time, John."

That hurt. He'd always prided himself on being in control of all his affairs; the thought of Penelope playing him for a fool was a blow to his pride. Perhaps, without his knowing it, other women in his past had duped him. Certainly his wondrous experience with Gloriana had upset his normal way of thinking about the fairer sex.

He turned to Dobson. "Kindly ask my mother why the witch was therefore welcomed here, since my mother's vision seems to have been far less clouded than mine," he said coldly.

His mother's reply was equally cold. "If you want an answer, you shall have to address me directly, John."

He looked down, reluctant to meet her eyes. "Very well," he said at last. "Why was Lady Penelope here? Did you invite her?"

She rolled her eyes. "Of course not! She feared she was losing you. She wanted me to intercede on her behalf. To push you into marriage."

"And would you have been her ally in the matter?"

Lady Sarah shook her head. "You may not appreciate it, John, but I'm your mother and I love you. I would have done everything possible to keep you from being trapped by that conniving shrew. Not least because I guessed, long before Dobson told me, that you had lost your heart to someone else whilst you were gone this summer." She smiled tenderly. "And now you've found her again. I'm so happy for you." She reached out and clasped his hand, her fingers soft on his.

At that moment, still rethinking his many unsatisfying conquests, Thorne suddenly realized that his warped view of women was all the fault of the creature before him. He jerked his hand away. "Dobson, please thank my mother for her kind wishes."

Lady Sarah drew in a sharp breath at his rebuff and turned to the staircase. "Dobson," she murmured, "please tell my son that he is a stiff-necked ass, whose pride will do him in some day. I pity the woman he claims to love."

Head held high, she sailed up the staircase, leaving Thorne to wonder if she had spoken the truth.

· · ·

"Be there anything more you need, ma'am?" The innkeeper's daughter, busily directing a manservant to carry out Gloriana's bathing tub, turned and smiled. "Shall I comb your hair for you?"

Gloriana leaned toward the warmth of the fireplace, toweling dry her long hair. It felt wonderful to be clean again, to sit in comfort in a gown that didn't crawl with fleas, to smooth her skin with the fragrant oils that had been included in the packet that Dobson had sent along. She nodded her thanks to the girl. "You are kind to offer, but I can do for myself," she said.

"As you wish, ma'am. I'll be comin' back for the dishes

when you finishes your meal."

"No. They can wait. Only show my visitor up the moment he arrives."

"Of course, ma'am." The maid glanced out the window and clicked her tongue. "Rain again. What a bother."

Gloriana smiled. "'Tis only rain." It could scarcely dampen her happiness. She pressed a coin into the girl's hand. "Now run along."

"Thank you, ma'am." The maid curtsied and left the room.

Gloriana sighed in contentment. She could scarcely believe all that had happened. And all in less than a week. She had been visited by her lawyer, summoned before the magistrate, and issued her pardon, along with that worthy's apologies for her wrongful imprisonment. Then it was back to the prison to gather her meager belongings. She had been met outside Newgate by a coachman, who had been instructed to carry her here to The Golden Crown. And in the coach she had found Dobson's large bundle and a note from the man instructing her to request anything she wished from the innkeeper, if he had forgotten anything she might need.

And now, all she had to do was wait for Thorne. The coachman had been directed to return to Havilland House and tell the master that she was settled comfortably at the inn. She had added the instruction that His Grace was to allow her several hours before he arrived, that she might make herself fit to greet him.

She finished drying her hair and pinned it loosely, disregarding the small lace cap Dobson had sent along. Thorne had always admired the brilliant color of her uncovered hair.

"And then," she murmured to the empty room, smiling as she looked toward the comfortable bed, "'twill be tousled soon enough." The thought of seeing him again, of making love, his hard body pressed to hers, made her heart race.

She gulped down the rest of her simple meal, then paced the room, her impatient steps echoed by the ticking of the clock on the mantel, the tap of the cold raindrops on the windowpane. She smoothed her skirts, adjusted the lace neckerchief at her bodice, tucked up a stray curl. She knew she looked beautiful; Dobson had sent a superb outfit—a gown of deep purple damask, with all the accessories she might need, including a magnificent quilted cloak that matched the gown. But where was Thorne? Her joy in her splendid garments could only be complete by seeing herself mirrored in her lover's eyes.

She jumped at the gentle tap on her door; then she turned, a smile of welcome on her face. "Enter," she said.

The woman who glided gracefully into the room took her by surprise. A fragile blond with clear blue eyes, and a modest pink gown and hooded cloak that made her appear even more delicate.

Conscious of her own elegant garments, Gloriana resisted the urge to curtsy, though this was surely a high-born lady. Clearly she had mistaken Gloriana's room for her own. "I fear you have the wrong chamber, madam," she said.

The woman pulled off her damp cloak and draped it across a chair. "No," she said in a sweet voice. "You are... Molly?"

Gloriana frowned. Who else would have known she was here? "Yes," she admitted. "And you are...?"

"Lady Penelope Crawford. I've come from Havilland House."

"Merciful heaven! Has something happened to John?" Her fevered mind imagined him ambushed in some dark alley.

Lady Penelope stepped forward and patted Gloriana's hand. "Not at all. Thorne will be here anon. But I thought I'd come and greet you first." She scanned Gloriana from the top of her hair to the tips of her shoes. "And you're as beautiful as he said you were."

Gloriana managed a tight smile. The last thing she wanted at this moment was a visit from one of John's friends, clearly sent to take her measure and report back to Thorne's circle. Then she thought better of it. His friends would likely become *her* friends. Best to make a good impression. She gestured toward a chair in front of the fireplace. "Won't you be seated, milady? You can dry your shoes before the fire." She turned toward the table. "Will you have some wine?"

"No. I am quite content." Lady Penelope sat gracefully in the chair and patted the small footstool in front her. "Sit here, my dear. Let me examine you more carefully." When Gloriana had seated herself, Lady Penelope took Gloriana's chin in her hand, turning her face from side to side. "Lovely bones. I can see what he sees in you."

Gloriana pulled her chin away. "You'll make me blush, milady."

Penelope gave a tinkling laugh. "Oh, my dear, a woman should never be embarrassed by her beauty. Nor by the envy she arouses in other women. 'Twill be amusing to see the faces of our female friends at our next assembly ball."

Gloriana returned the woman's smile and allowed herself to relax a bit. With Thorne—and Lady Penelope—at her side, she might find it easier to fit into her new life than she had hoped. "You are too kind, milady," she murmured.

"Only concerned with your welfare, my dear. And I know how Thorne values you. He has spoken of you often. You met this summer, I understand?"

She smiled, recalling the wonder of their weeks together, the work and the laughter and the sweet love-making. "In Whitby," she said softly.

"I see by your smile that you will have years of happy memories." Penelope stroked Gloriana's hand, her fingers like a gentle caress. "Now, let us speak of arrangements," she said, her voice taking on a businesslike tone.

"Arrangements?" Was this gentle lady offering to help her with marriage preparations? She felt doubly blessed.

Penelope cleared her throat. "I've made a few inquiries. There's a lovely house on Great Russell Street that might serve you well. Close enough to Havilland House to be convenient."

Gloriana stared in perplexity. "I... I don't understand," she stammered.

"I know it must seem surprising to you. But, unlike so many other women, I'm tolerant of a husband's straying. It will leave me free to seek my own diversions."

"Husband?" The word was like a knife to Gloriana's heart. Was Thorne more dishonest than she had supposed? She jumped up and glared down at the woman in disbelief. "Are you married to him?"

"Not yet, my dear. But soon." Penelope held up her hand, displaying a small ring on her finger. Gloriana recognized Thorne's crest.

"Bloody hell," she whispered. "And I?"

"You're to be his mistress, as I told you. And live in splendor in your very own house."

Gloriana shook her head. She couldn't believe what she was hearing. "But he loves me!" she cried.

"Of course he does. I understand that. But he doesn't marry someone like you. The Thorneleighs have a name that goes back for generations. He would scarcely shame his ancestors by..." Penelope shrugged apologetically. "You understand, I'm sure."

"The poxy villain!" Gloriana clenched her fists, wishing that Thorne was before her at this very moment. She wanted to beat his face into the ground, to tear at his eyes until he begged for mercy. In Newgate, he had spoken of their future together. This is what he had meant for her—the sordid life of a concubine. Clearly he still thought of her as a common whore. "He can go to hell," she spat.

Penelope rose from her chair, her eyes warm with concern. "Oh, my dear, I didn't mean to upset you. I thought surely that Thorne had explained it all to you." She stroked Gloriana's arm with a motherly hand. "Do consider how well you'd be cared for."

Gloriana turned away, her eyes filling with tears. "I'd rather die than live that life," she choked.

"But what will you do? I would suggest you leave London, of course. Thorne will be in a fury when he learns how his comfortable plans have been upset."

Leave London. Yes, of course. She took a deep breath, swallowing her grief. There was only one way for her to begin life anew. "I think I shall to go to the Colonies. I've heard Virginia is quite a pleasant place."

"That sounds splendid. You're a very strong and determined woman. I admire you for that." Penelope frowned. "Do you need money? I think I can arrange—"

"No. I'm quite able to care for myself." She'd go to Old Diggory, reclaim her purse of gold and book passage on the next ship leaving for America. She felt her pain rising in her breast, ready to choke her. She needed to cry for a few moments, to vent her anger and grief. But not in front of this woman, who seemed so genuinely concerned for her welfare. "If you please, milady," she said, "I should like to be alone now."

"I quite understand." Penelope picked up her cloak and turned to the door. Then she stopped. "But what will Thorne think when he comes here and finds you gone?"

"I don't give a tinker's dam what the rogue thinks."

"No, no. He'll search for you again, as he's done in the past. And if he finds you, who knows what will happen, given his wounded pride?" Her face brightened. "Why don't you leave him a note?"

What did it matter? She shrugged. "If you think it's best." At Penelope's nod, she found pen and ink and paper. With the woman's help, she wrote a brief letter, telling Thorne that it was over between them. She never wanted to see him again. She was going far away, and he was not to look for her. She intended to forget him as soon as possible. She hated him too much to even sign her full name; she simply wrote "G." She sealed the note, then handed it to Penelope, begging her to leave it with the innkeeper.

"How brave you are," said Penelope. "To reject Thorne's unworthy offer. I should never have the strength." She sighed unhappily. "I shall miss your sweet company in London." She gave Gloriana a sisterly hug and swept from the room, casting a final sad look in Gloriana's direction.

When she had gone, closing the door softly behind her,

Gloriana sank to the bed and gave way to the sobs that burst from her. Miserable Gypsy's spawn that she was, she would never be worthy of a nobly-born man. *Any* man of rank. Charlie had only made her his Lady because, as a wanted highwayman, he had sunk to her level. Not because she deserved the honor.

As for Thorne, she would curse his name for the rest of her life.

• • •

Thorne heard the crash of wheels outside his coach a second before the collision jerked him forward, sending his hat to the floor. "What the devil is going on?" he cried to his coachman.

He heard the panicked whinnying of horses, then the sound of his coachman scrambling from his box. The door flew open. The man gaped in at him, looking bewildered and breathless. Rain dripped from his hat. "Forgive me, Your Grace," he panted. "Some bloody fool swerved in front of the coach. I couldn't stop in time."

Thorne moved toward the open door. "Is anyone hurt?" He stepped out into the road, hunching his shoulders against the downpour, and frowned at the curious onlookers who had begun to crowd near. He was already late to meet Gloriana at The Golden Crown. He had foolishly waited for a jeweler to bring around the ring he had picked out for her, and the man had been late. Thorne had paced his drawing room, bursting with impatience. And now this unfortunate interruption.

He surveyed the scene of the accident. A small

coach rested just beyond Thorne's snorting team; it tilted precariously on one axle, its dislodged wheel lazily spinning on the rain-slicked cobblestones. Clearly the other coachman had attempted to make a turn without seeing if the way was clear. The man sat lopsidedly on his box, looking dazed.

As Thorne watched, a young gentleman staggered from the damaged vehicle, one hand to his forehead. His small periwig was askew, and a few blond strands of hair had escaped from beneath the powdered curls and now hung limply around his face. "Your pardon, sir," he said in a hoarse voice. "My great looby of a coachman should never have taken the turn at such speed. And in this weather." He glared up at the man. "Come down here, sirrah, that I may box your ears!"

"That's hardly necessary," said Thorne. He patted his watch pocket in annoyance. Gloriana would have to wait. He could scarcely drive off and leave the young man in such helpless circumstances. He was young, of slight build, almost fragile-looking. There was no way he could take a hand in righting the coach.

Thorne waved the man's coachman from his box and turned to his own servant. "Do you think the two of you can attach the wheel again?"

"Aye, milord. If we can find the pin, me and him can set things to rights." The coachman frowned. "But we be needin' a few strong arms to lift the coach while we puts back the wheel."

Thorne took off his coat and rolled up his sleeves, grateful for his newly expanded muscles. "I can do it." He pointed to a robust man in the gathering crowd. A carpenter, he guessed, from the small axe slung over one shoulder. "You, there. Give me a hand, man." When the worker hesitated, Thorne fished in his pocket and threw him a silver coin. The carpenter smiled, tossed down his axe and stepped forward.

The two of them bent to the coach, struggling against its weight to lift it to the proper height. Thorne gritted his teeth with the effort, cursing the passage of time as the two coachmen righted the wheel and tried to slip it back onto its axle. Half a dozen attempts, while the rain beat down on their heads, their hands, the wheel, making the chore twice as difficult.

It took many precious minutes, and much tugging and straining before the wheel was restored to its proper place and pinned securely. And more long minutes as the young man clung to Thorne's arm and refused to release him without many expressions of thanks and gratitude.

At last Thorne was able to break away. "Get me to the bloody inn," he growled to his coachman, and leaped into his carriage, discarding his wet coat and shirt in favor of the warm cloak he'd left behind. Gloriana must be frantic with worry by now. He drummed the seat with impatient fingers as the coach splashed through puddles on the wet streets and finally arrived at the Golden Crown. He dashed into the inn and shouted at the innkeeper. "The Duke of Thorneleigh's room!"

"Top o' the stairs, milord." The man shook his head. "But you won't be findin' the lady there."

"What the devil do you mean?"

"Why, your worship, she left near to a quarter of an hour ago."

He staggered back, stunned by the man's words. "Left? Did she not say where she was going?"

"She were cryin', milord. Didn't seem proper to ask." He fished in the pocket of his apron. "But there be a note…"

Thorne snatched it from his hand and tore it open. He read Gloriana's words in disbelief, his heart thudding with dread. She never wanted to see him again? What the deuce had happened? His coachman had assured him that the lady was smiling and happy when he'd delivered her to the inn several hours ago. He looked plaintively at the innkeeper. "Did she say nothing when she gave you this note?"

"Oh, no, your worship. 'Twasn't her that give it me. 'Twas t'other one."

"Another woman?"

"A little thing, she were. With yellow hair."

"Christ's blood! And blue eyes?" At the man's nod, he gnashed his teeth. That witch, Penelope! What could she have said to Gloriana to produce the hatred that seeped out of every word on the page?

He raced back to his carriage, shouting Penelope's address at his coachman. Then he stopped. "No. Wait." He'd have to pass Havilland House on the way. It might be wise to stop and get Dobson to accompany him. He needed a cool head to keep himself from possibly strangling Penelope. And he needed a dry shirt and coat. He was grateful, at least, that the rain had finally stopped.

As he dressed in the carriage on the ride to the Crawford house, he briefly explained the situation to his valet, his words alternately expressing outrage at Penelope and bewilderment at Gloriana's leaving without allowing him to speak to her. "And that blasted accident," he muttered, carelessly tying his cravat. "I would have been there on time, save for a reckless coachman."

He slammed his fist against the Crawford door until it opened, and brushed past the footman, gesturing toward a small parlor. "Is the lady there?" At the man's nod, he stormed to the door. "I'll announce myself," he growled.

Dobson said a few conciliatory words to the stunned footman, then followed Thorne into the parlor.

At sight of Thorne, Penelope rose from her chair in a flurry of skirts. Her eyes opened wide in alarm. "Thorne, my dear! What brings you here? And looking so distraught."

He tried with limited success to keep his voice calm. "Were you at The Golden Crown this afternoon?"

She moved closer to him, managing a gentle smile. "Merciful heaven, an inn? Why should I want to go there? In point of fact, I haven't been out all day." She waved a dainty hand toward the window. "And in this weather? My constitution is far too delicate to take pleasure in a winter rainstorm."

Thorne glanced back at Dobson, a frown of doubt creasing his brow. "Then who the devil—"

Penelope pressed her fingers against his mouth, silencing him. "Not another word, my dear Thorne. You come bursting into my parlor, unannounced, and clearly beside yourself. Come and sit. I'll ring for a cordial, and then you can tell me what has disturbed you so."

He plopped into a chair, feeling as helpless as a child. If it hadn't been Penelope, then... *who*? And what was he to do now? He accepted the offered cordial, drank it in a daze, and sighed in weariness. All the while, Penelope watched him with sympathetic eyes, concern etched deep on her face. "'Tis only..." he began at last, his voice deep and muffled, "...'tis only that Glo—*Molly* has gone. And I don't know where."

Penelope knelt in front of him. "And you never had a chance to see her? Oh, my dearest Thorne. My heart bleeds for you."

He shook his head. "I don't even know why. I only—" He glanced across the room toward Dobson. From the moment they had come into the parlor, his valet had been casually circling the room, picking up an occasional trinket, riffling the pages of an open book. Now he had suddenly stopped. He glanced at Thorne, then dropped his gaze to a settee in the corner. Thorne followed his glance. A pink cloak, companion to the gown that Penelope was wearing. And even from here he could see the wet stains on the shoulders and hood.

He jumped to his feet and roughly pulled up Penelope to stand before him. He gave a savage tug to her skirt, exposing the damp and muddy hem. "You bitch," he growled. "It *was* you."

Her face turned white. "I... I was only trying to be helpful," she whispered.

"And what did you tell her?"

"Nothing!" Penelope rubbed her hands together, then covered one hand with the other, a surreptitious gesture that seemed to be more deliberate than casual.

Thorne cursed aloud. His ring! "Did you tell her we were betrothed?"

"I... I might have... suggested that... some day... I didn't mean any harm."

He clenched his fists at his sides. It was all he could do to keep himself from smacking her to the floor. "And where has she gone?"

"I know not," she whined. "Truly I don't. You must believe me. And forgive my thoughtlessness. I meant only to greet her as your dear friend. I deeply regret that she misread my words." She bit her lip, tears trembling on her lashes.

He stared at her for a moment, feeling like a fool. How often had she used her tears, her seemingly helpless manner to get her way with him? His lip curled in scorn. "What a damnable liar you are. And I never saw it before." He towered over her, all angry menace. "I have no doubt you know where she is. I shouldn't be surprised if you had helped her with her plans. I've never struck a woman, but, by the horn of Satan, if you don't tell me where she has gone..."

Dobson hurried to his side. "Your Grace!" he cried in alarm.

Thorne took a steadying breath. "You're right, man. There are other ways to get the truth from the lady. Her brother, I believe you mentioned, is somewhat profligate at the gaming tables?"

"I believe ivory cubes are his weakness."

"'Twould be a simple matter to speak to the right people at Court. Have his creditors call in their debts."

Penelope sucked in a horrified breath. "But we would be ruined!"

"Then I want the truth. Where did she go?"

"She said she would go to the Colonies. On the first ship that leaves the port."

"And that's all?"

"She might have mentioned Virginia. That's all I know. Truly, Thorne. I beg you to spare my brother." She choked on a sob. "With our parents gone, we only have each other," she wailed.

"Your story has touched my heart," he said, his voice dripping with sarcasm. "Come, Dobson. We must—"

He was interrupted by the sound of the door bursting open and the voice of a man behind him. "Well, Penny, I did my part. Did you?"

Thorne whirled about, his eyes widening in surprise. The young man gasped. His periwig was gone, but his lank blond hair and delicate features made him all too familiar to Thorne. "Christ's blood!" he exclaimed. "You! The accident with the coaches."

The young man gave a tepid smile. "An unfortunate coincidence, Your Grace. Imagine my astonishment—"

"Not another word, Nick!" snapped Penelope. "His lordship seems to think he can storm in here and accuse us of all manner of foul deeds. We Crawfords should not tolerate such slander."

Thorne spun to her. "I wouldn't strike you, madam, but I'm not above bloodying his nose. Who is this man?"

Dobson stepped forward. "Nick Crawford, sir. Her brother."

Thorne grabbed Nick Crawford by his shirt front and held his fist before the man's face. "How did you manage it? Your 'coincidence.'"

Crawford began to blubber, cringing away from the expected blow. "I told you it was a stupid plan, Penny. Now we shall be ruined."

Thorne glared at Penelope. It had all been her doing. "Do you fancy your brother without his teeth, madam?" he growled.

Penelope sighed and sank into a chair. "You remember I overheard your conversation with Dobson the other day.

Nick paid a prison-keeper to tell him the day… she would be released."

"You waited at the prison. And saw my coachman deposit her at the inn." Thorne shook his head in disgust. "And you, Crawford? I assume you instructed your coachman to swerve into my carriage. But how did you manage to find me?"

Nick pulled free of Thorne's grasp and scurried behind Penelope's chair, safely out of Thorne's reach. "I… I waited in the lane near Havilland House and followed you." He rubbed mournfully at his forehead. "And only got a hard knock for my pains."

"What a despicable pair you are," Thorne sneered. He turned to his valet. "Come, Dobson, let us leave these two to their fate."

Penelope rose unsteadily from her chair. "You don't mean to ruin Nick, do you?" she asked in a quavering voice.

"I certainly do."

"Oh, but you can't! You… you…" Penelope gasped, blinking her eyes, then collapsed on the floor, shaking violently.

"Penny!" Crawford leaped forward and knelt to his sister. He looked at Thorne, his face dark with accusation. "Now look what you've done."

Thorne stared at the woman. Though she seemed to be having a fit, her complexion was rosy, without the pallid coloring that usually accompanied such an episode. He glanced at Dobson, who had a knowing smirk on his face. He nodded in agreement. Stepping to a small table, Thorne picked up a vase of flowers, tossed the blossoms aside, crossed back to Penelope and dumped the water onto her face.

She sputtered and sat up abruptly, water streaming from her hair. "You villain!" she cried. Then her face crumpled. "I beg you not to call in Nick's debts," she moaned.

He thought about it for a moment. It would be needlessly cruel. And he was scarcely blameless; he had allowed himself to be taken in by her devious ways. He felt nothing but contempt and pity for her. "I shall leave you to your own devices, madam. You're scarcely worth the effort." He marched to the door, then turned back. "You shall have to find another moneybags to entrap."

In the coach, he and Dobson discussed the need to find Gloriana in earnest. Dobson suggested that they send men to Deptford and Gravesend, enquiring about ships heading to the Colonies. It would be a difficult search, since she might not be using the name of Molly Sharpe.

"And have them stay at the ports for a few days and look for her. With that hair, she will be easy to recognize," said Thorne, all the while knowing that Gloriana might have left London outright and planned to sail from another seaport on the coast.

It was only the next morning that he remembered she had left her money with Old Diggory. She'd need it to book passage. Dobson hurried around to Diggory's forge and came back, his face wreathed in disappointment. She had retrieved her money the day before and had wished the old blacksmith a tearful farewell. Dobson reluctantly told Thorne the whole story: She had taken back the fan, broken it into a dozen pieces and stamped on it. Thorne's heart sank.

The days that followed were a misery. No reports from his men on sighting her, no news from any ship's manifest that a redheaded woman had made arrangements to sail.

Thorne wrote letters to planters he knew in Virginia, asking them to notify him should she appear.

He drifted into despair. It was all his fault. The life he had led, the false friends—why should Gloriana have ever believed he could be sincere in his feelings? But with his grief came a new strength. She had made a better man of him.

If, heaven forbid, he had lost her forever, he was resolved to honor her memory, to lead a more decent and useful life.

But what would ever heal his broken heart?

Chapter Fifteen

The world was turned to gray, echoing the desolation in Gloriana's heart. The leaden winter sky, the mist rising over the pewter-hued Thames, the granite stones of Tilbury Fort, the chalky hills that rose behind the coastline. Even the merchant ship that rode in the harbor swarmed with gray-coated customs' agents, making their final inspection before the ship set sail.

Gloriana was glad she'd hired a coach to take her to Tilbury. If Thorne had learned of her plans, he might be searching for her at landings closer to London. She shivered. It was cold. Madness to take a dangerous voyage to Virginia in the dead of winter. But at least she'd be comfortable. She'd had a couple of days to see to her needs on the long trip: a fine cabin, a soft mattress for her bunk, a table and chair, and several books to keep her occupied. Her sea chest, already stowed aboard, held warm clothing as well as several jugs of rum, a tin of tea, and a canister of biscuits. She'd paid a pretty penny to dine with the ship's captain every night, but she could afford it. She had enough left over from Charlie's gifts to rent a decent house in Williamsburg and perhaps even open a blacksmith shop.

It was said that the colonists were a bit more democratic in their thinking and would not frown on a lady blacksmith. She prayed it was so. She had little desire to hire another front for her shop—not after her disastrous adventure with Thorne.

She looked up. The customs' agents had finished their tour and were leaving the ship. The first mate was striding down the gangway, motioning to Gloriana to come aboard. Just then, a small coach clattered up to the quay, thudding to a halt. The door opened and a young man came out, followed by a woman carrying a baby. Three more children, of varying ages, burst from the interior, laughing and pointing to the ship.

The man waved his hand at the children. "Come along, my pets. The start of our great adventure. The tide waits for no man."

Gloriana's heart sank. Children on the voyage? How could she endure it? Every moment would remind her of Billy, and of all she was missing. It was his birthday in a fortnight. One year. She clutched at her belly, as though she could still feel his vigorous kicks within her. He might be walking by now, tottering along on those solid little legs.

Still laughing, the family had mounted the gangway and was now being escorted to their cabin. And still Gloriana lingered, lost in thought, fighting the pain that seared her soul. She was startled by the voice of the mate, just in front of her. "Be ye comin' aboard, milady?"

Milady, he had called her, though she had booked

passage as plain Mary Smith. Clearly he assumed she was a noblewoman, traveling as a commoner. But wasn't she? The Lady Gloriana Baniard. And her clothes, her manner, her soft tones bespoke a gracious upbringing. *Tis not an accident of birth that gives a woman true nobility,* Thorne had said. And perhaps it was so. She had fled Baniard Hall because she had felt unworthy, crude, and unlettered. But now she behaved like a lady, had learned to read, to speak in civil tones, to show respect in order to receive respect. Why should she fear to take her place with the Ridleys, to turn aside the mocking of the servants? And Billy would be hers again.

She felt a great weight lifting from her shoulders. She smiled at the mate. "I've changed my mind," she said. "I shall not sail. Please have my sea chest brought ashore."

He frowned. "But your furnishings, milady. There be no time to unload 'em, if we're to catch the tide."

She shrugged. "See that that lovely family gets them. My farewell gift for a successful voyage and a happy life together." For better or worse, she had her own path to follow.

It was nearly a week before her hired coach pulled up to the gates of Baniard Hall. Gloriana had spent the trip in wild anticipation, pacing the floors of the various inns she had stayed at, grumbling when a sudden winter storm had delayed the trip for a day, forcing herself to stay focused on seeing Billy again, not on the difficulties she might face in explaining herself to Allegra and Grey.

Humphrey, the Ridley gatekeeper, opened the coach door and glanced inside. With Gloriana's hood draped over her bright hair, the man didn't seem to recognize her, but he was clearly impressed by her fine clothes. With a deferential nod, he waved her coachman down the long gravel drive that led to the hall.

It was as beautiful as Gloriana remembered it—honey-colored stones and gray pediments, modest yet elegant. *My home*, she thought in sudden wonder. And Billy's legacy. Perhaps, even without Thorne, she could find happiness here.

She waited for the coachman to scramble down from his box and open the door, giving him a gold sovereign and her thanks for a successful trip. He touched his cap in salute, then ran forward and banged the knocker on the front door. When the door opened, he tapped his cap again and hurried back to his coach.

Gloriana was momentarily dismayed to see her old maid, Barbara, standing before her. The girl gasped, her eyes opening wide. Then she frowned. "So you've decided to come back," she said with a sneer.

You can catch more flies with honey than with vinegar, Thorne had said. Gloriana smiled graciously. "Yes," she murmured. "Thank you for your greeting. I shan't forget it. A pity you haven't decided to be more civil. I should appreciate a kindlier tone the next time you speak to me, if you would be so good." She swept past a dumbstruck Barbara into the vestibule. "If Lady Allegra is at home, I should like to be received by her. Please announce me. May I wait in the parlor?"

Barbara bobbed a curtsy, clearly flustered. "Of... of course, milady," she stammered.

Gloriana was warming her hands by the parlor fire when Allegra rushed into the room, her arms held wide. "Gloriana! I couldn't believe it when Barbara told me." She clutched Gloriana to her breast, her voice choking. "Sister. I thought we'd never see you again in this life." She scanned Gloriana quickly. "You look splendid. What brings you here?"

Gloriana gulped. "I… I want…" She looked at Allegra, all her old uncertainties overwhelming her for a moment. "If you can forgive me for… running away, may I… come home?" she said at last.

"To stay for good?"

"If I may."

Allegra clapped her hands together, her eyes filling with tears. "Oh, thanks be to God. Come home and welcome. As for forgiveness, there's no need. I think Grey and I always understood your desire to leave. It was the reason we scarcely searched for you." She unfastened Gloriana's hood and threw her cloak carelessly on a chair. "Now let me ring for tea. You must be frozen. Have you traveled far?"

Gloriana turned away. Her soul had been on a journey that had taken her to realms far more distant than the trip to Whitby and back. "Farther than you might imagine," she murmured.

Allegra turned her about and stared deeply into her eyes. "I see by your face that 'tis not something you wish to speak of. But surely there is sadness deep within you. And a man, I suspect, who broke your heart."

Gloriana had forgotten how sensitive Allegra was to people's moods. She managed a small laugh. "Perhaps someday I'll tell you about him. But not now."

Allegra shook her head. "And you've changed so. Your manner, your voice, your speech. Everything. A lovely transformation."

Gloriana sighed. "That story, too, must wait for another telling." She stared at Allegra, almost seeing her for the first time since she'd entered the parlor. "But you've changed as well. How stupid of me not to have noticed." She patted Allegra's flat belly. "Happy news, I trust?"

Allegra beamed. "A healthy boy. Josslyn. Near on to six months old now."

"And you're well? And Grey? No winter fevers?"

Allegra took Gloriana's hands in hers and searched her face, her dark eyes warm with understanding. "Oh, my dear sister, why don't you ask the only question that truly matters to you?"

Gloriana bit her lip, fighting her tears. She had come all this way, but now her fears held her back, kept her exchanging only meaningless pleasantries with Allegra. "God forgive me," she whispered. "I'm afraid to ask." She took a steadying breath. "How is... Billy?" she said at last. "Has he forgotten me?"

"Healthy, happy—a treasure in every way. Would you like to see him now?" At Gloriana's nod, she laughed and waved her hand toward the parlor door. "You have only to go through there. The moment Barbara told me of your arrival, I had his nursemaid bring him down from his room."

Trembling in anticipation and dread, Gloriana crossed the threshold into the vestibule. Had she lost too much time to reclaim her son's love? She gasped in wonder at the sight before her and dropped to her knees.

She had parted with an infant, but a little boy stood before her, holding tightly to his nursemaid's hand. He wore a tiny brown velvet suit that intensified the golden brown of his large eyes, and his mass of copper curls was a brilliant halo around his sweet face. Gloriana imagined she could see traces of her beloved Da in his features.

She hesitated, seeing the look of doubt on his face,

then held out her arms. "Will you come to me, Billy?" she murmured.

The nursemaid cleared her throat. "*Sir William* can be shy around strangers," she said sharply.

Gloriana smiled up at the woman, but her chin was thrust forward in determination. "If you please, I should like him to be called Billy henceforth, so that he may become accustomed to the name. Time enough for a lofty title when he's older." She was pleased to see the look of consternation on the woman's face, as though she had just been forced to swallow an unpleasant morsel of food. "Are you agreeable to that?"

The woman bobbed a curtsy, clearly intimidated by her manner. "Of course, milady. Billy it is."

Gloriana turned her attention back to her son, her arms still open wide. She made a clicking sound with her tongue, a sound that had always brought Black Jack to her. Billy smiled tentatively, tiny dimples appearing in his rosy cheeks, and moved toward her, still holding his nursemaid's hand. She resisted the urge to bundle him into her embrace, and tousled his curls instead. The smile deepened into a grin and he gurgled happily. At last, sensing his acceptance, she pulled him away from his nursemaid and swept him into her arms. She smelled the sweetness of his hair, felt his sturdy little body settling comfortably against her breast. "My little boy," she said with a sob. "We shall never be parted again."

The next few weeks were a wonder for Gloriana. Grey and Allegra joyously accepted her return, without questioning where she had been. They celebrated Billy's birthday and Christmastide with quiet country pleasures, with gifts and good wishes. They were a family again, with Gloriana at its heart, rather than as the outsider she had been. At supper, she found herself able to converse intelligently with Grey and Allegra, discussing books she had read, and even feeling confident enough to ask for the meaning of an occasional word that was beyond her comprehension.

As for Billy, he had happily welcomed her after that first day. They played peekaboo together, made funny noises, clapped their hands. And when Billy was able to walk without holding anyone's hand, he'd steer a straight course to Gloriana, ignoring everyone else. And when it snowed, late in February, Gloriana was thrilled that she was the one to introduce him to another wonder that the world was unfolding for his young eyes.

She spent many cozy hours with Allegra, watching their sons play together, delighting in the bonds of motherhood that deepened their mutual affection. She had never had many female friends in her mean and wretched London days, not even among the other gladiators; she gloried in the joy of a woman she could call "sister."

She only thought of Thorne when she was in bed at night, aching for the intimacy of his body next to hers, remembering his sweet words, the look of devotion in his eyes. Then she would remember that that devotion was reserved for her only as his mistress, and she would curse his name as she drifted into a dreamless sleep.

• • •

The bells in the Church of St. Dunstan began to peal softly, wafted on the early March breeze to roll across the village of Mayfield. Thorne laid his hammer across the anvil and wiped the sweat from his brow. He turned to the blacksmith and shook his head. "Vespers, Tom," he said. "A few more horseshoes and then I should be getting back to the Hall. Supper awaits."

Tom smiled, a rather patronizing smirk, it seemed to Thorne. "Whatever amuses you, Your Grace."

Thorne resisted the urge to snap back with a lordly rejoinder. How could Tom, or anyone in the village, understand the joy he took in his work, when any one of them would give a king's ransom to enjoy his easy life of wealth and privilege. But deciding to work alongside Tom, whatever others might think of his motive, had been his salvation. After his summer at Whitby, he had discovered that he needed to work. Hammering away at the forge, turning out horseshoes, nails, and an occasional iron gate, had kept him from going mad these last couple of months.

Somehow, bent over the anvil, he could think more clearly, accept the loss of Gloriana. He had taught her pride in herself, a sense of her own worth. Why should he be surprised that Penelope's lies had wounded her so deeply? Perhaps, if his gambler's luck followed its usual pattern, someone in Virginia would eventually recognize her and send word back to him. He prayed it might be so.

While Tom left the smithy to see to a horse outside, Thorne picked up his tongs, bent over the forge, and pulled out a glowing iron bar from the hot coals, placing it carefully on the anvil. Lifting up his heavy hammer, he began to pound the bar into a graceful curve.

"Your Grace, I've brought the carriage around. Will you return to Thorneleigh Hall now?"

Thorne looked up. Dobson stood in the doorway of

the shop, hat in hand. Behind him, Thorne could see a very attractive young woman, who peered over Dobson's shoulder, her dark eyes bright with curiosity. She looked vaguely familiar.

"A few more minutes, Dobson," he said, pausing in his labors. He smiled at the young woman, noting the fineness of her form, the long ebony curl that sprang from beneath her prim cap to rest on her shoulder. "And this young woman?"

The girl stepped in front of Dobson and gave Thorne a deep curtsy. "Your Grace," she murmured. "Cleve has told me so much about you."

Thorne raised a quizzical eyebrow. "Indeed?"

Dobson cleared his throat, his face reddening to the roots of his blond hair. "This is Mistress Martha Rill, my... my pupil from London."

Thorne suppressed a smirk. "Ah, yes, the silk merchant's daughter. I saw you once at Havilland House, on your way to your... lesson."

It was the girl's turn to blush, her eyes cast down to the floor. "I've learned so much... I mean to say... that is, Cleve...*Master Dobson* is a very skilled tutor."

From the look on both their faces, Thorne was sure that more than music lessons had been involved. Aware of their embarrassment, he took pity on the couple and changed the subject. "And what brings you down here to Surrey, Mistress Rill?" he asked.

The girl's face relaxed in relief. "My father had business in Mayfield. I thought... that is, *he* thought it might make a nice holiday for the whole family. I recalled that Master Dobson was here with you, and determined to keep up with my lessons." She turned a tender gaze to Dobson. "He has

234

been kindly showing me around the village."

Thorne laughed. "Has he told you the legend of St. Dunstan, for whom the church is named?"

"Not yet."

"Well, then, allow me. It seems that the good saint was a fine blacksmith."

"Even as you yourself, milord, from what I saw."

Thorne nodded in silent acknowledgement of her compliment. "Just so. It seems that one day, the Devil, disguised as a beautiful woman, paid the good man a visit, hoping to lead him into sin."

Dobson chuckled. "Even as you yourself, milord?" He grinned.

Thorne gave him a rueful smile. "I've had my share of devils disguised as women. I fear the good saint was more clever than I. At least for a time."

Mistress Rill frowned in bewilderment. "But St. Dunstan?"

"Ah, yes. Of course. It seems that the good man spied the Devil's cloven hoofs beneath the woman's dress and grabbed Satan's nose with his red-hot pincers, thus foiling his evil plan." He looked meaningfully at Dobson. "'Tis astonishing what a wicked woman can hide beneath her hem."

Dobson clapped his hat back on his head and reached for Thorne's coat. "But evil will out, Your Grace. Now, will you return to the Hall before it grows dark?"

Thorne turned back to the anvil. "Only allow me to finish this horseshoe." He hammered away, the sharp blows of his hammer accompanied by Mistress Rill's girlish cries of admiration at his skill. Dobson merely smiled his pleasure, having watched Thorne at the forge many times since he had begun working with Tom.

When Thorne was done, he slipped into his coat and made his way to his carriage, which waited outside the forge. He turned to Dobson. "Will you be escorting Mistress Rill back to her inn?"

"If you don't mind, milord. I can walk back to the Hall. 'Tis not so far."

"No. I'll wait for you here. I'll require your presence at supper."

Dobson shook his head, clearly vexed by this order. Though Thorne's relations with his mother had finally begun to thaw, he still found it difficult to address her directly. His valet was still needed to stand at attention behind Thorne's chair in the dining parlor, silent as always as Thorne directed him to "Tell my mother" this or that.

Thorne wondered when he would ever find it in his heart to forgive her.

• • •

Thorne helped himself to a large slice of cold mutton and plopped a spoonful of mint jelly onto his plate. He murmured his thanks to the footman who had served him, then glanced across the table at his mother. They had scarcely said a word to each other since coming to supper, only nodding politely as they took their seats. But Lady Sarah was looking as smug and satisfied as a cat that had just caught a mouse, her lips curled in a sly smile. Thorne motioned to Dobson behind him. "Kindly ask my mother if there is a reason for her unusual air of merriment this evening."

Lady Sarah put down her fork, carefully wiped her mouth

with her napkin, and took a sip of her wine. "I thought you would never ask." She took another sip from her glass and smiled mysteriously at Thorne.

Thorne clenched his jaw. His mother was clearly enjoying tormenting him. "Dobson," he said in a tight voice, "please ask my mother if she intends to answer my question."

"If you must know, John, I had a letter from London this afternoon. From Lady Singleton. You remember her, don't you? A tedious woman, but a font of gossip. Wasn't her daughter the one who ran off with an officer? The girl who bounced when she walked. Didn't you once liken her to a rabbit? Or was it a grasshopper?"

At this point, Thorne was too impatient to use Dobson as his intermediary. "Enough prattle! What did the woman say in her letter?" he demanded, speaking directly to his mother.

Lady Sarah laughed, a warm chuckle devoid of mockery. "I knew I could get you to speak straightaways to me if I tried. Well then, John, you shall know at once that Lady Singleton passed on the most delicious news. To wit, that Lady Penelope Crawford is married."

"I'll be damned! To whom?"

"To Lord Felix DeWitt."

"Felix? Gads my life! I would have thought him immune to her tricks, her sham helplessness."

"That may be so. But Lady Singleton has impeccable sources. I suspect she has half the servants in London on a stipend just to feed her gossip. According to her, Penelope began her campaign to win Felix as soon as we had left the city, begging for his comfort and companionship to ease her broken heart after you had jilted her." Lady Sarah's smiling face suddenly dissolved into a concerned frown, warm with sympathy. "Someday, you must tell me the whole story. I know, from overhearing your conversations with Dobson, that the witch managed to cause Gloriana to flee to America, but I should like to hear the tale from you."

Thorne was suddenly aware that the conversation had become too intimate for his comfort; he wasn't about to share the pain in his heart with his mother. He motioned to Dobson. "Please tell my mother that I scarcely think Felix would be susceptible to tears and lamentations."

Lady Sarah sighed at her son's rebuff and turned her head aside for a moment. She sighed again and continued her narrative. "He was taken in for a time, and Penelope had even begun to hint at a marriage proposal to their mutual friends. When they announced their betrothal, all of London accepted the news as a natural progression from their courtship."

"'Tis understandable," he said directly to her, suddenly finding his dependence on Dobson a distraction, given the importance of his mother's news.

Lady Sarah smiled, clearly pleased with his change of heart. "Not quite as happily as you might suppose," she said. "Lady Singleton's spies tell a different story. It seems that, when Felix balked at marriage at the last moment, Penelope contrived to get him alone and offer him the last favors. With a certain amount of discreet disrobing, I'm led to believe. At that juncture, her brother burst in upon them and accused Felix of dishonoring his sister. He threatened to blacken DeWitt's name all over London unless he agreed to the marriage."

Thorne shook his head. "My God, the Crawfords must

be desperate for money to pay off Nick's gambling debts. I recall what Felix used to say regarding women who married for money. Matrimonial whoredom, he called it, as though the woman would reap the worst of the bargain. But not in this case. Poor Felix. To be saddled with that conniver for a lifetime."

Lady Sarah snickered. "I should rather pity the lady, not DeWitt. We both know what a cheeseparing miser he is. I fear Lady Penelope will have to choose between rescuing her brother or outfitting herself in a new gown."

"True enough." Thorne had a sudden recollection and laughed aloud. "I'll wager that Penelope will be paying a higher price than a new gown, if Felix is true to his inclinations."

His mother raised a questioning eye brow. "Indeed? What do you mean?"

Thorne cleared his throat delicately. "'Tis too immodest a subject to dwell upon. I'll only say that the lady may have a bit of trouble sitting down after her... encounters with her new husband." Somehow, the thought of Penelope being soundly thrashed by Felix brought Thorne a measure of satisfaction.

Lady Sarah giggled. "A fitting retribution, and one she deserves." She looked beyond Thorne to his valet. "But didn't you get a letter today as well, Dobson? It looked quite thick, with several foreign markings."

Thorne turned about to see Dobson fidgeting uncomfortably. His valet shook his head. "This is scarcely the proper time or place, milady, to discuss my personal business. Not while I'm serving you."

"Nonsense," Thorne growled. "You're practically family, privy to our intimate conversations." He motioned to an empty chair at the table. "Sit. You may discuss your business freely here."

Lady Sarah smiled her approval. While Dobson took his seat, reluctantly sliding into his chair, she poured a glass of wine for him and signaled the footman to bring it to the man.

"It... it was a letter from my father," Dobson began at last, ignoring the wine. "It seems he has had a change of heart after all this time, and sent me a letter of credit to one of his bankers."

"A decent sum, I trust?" asked Thorne.

"Eighty pounds."

Thorne whistled. "A goodly amount. Not enough to live as a gentleman, but..."

"If you please, Your Grace," Dobson blurted out, "I should like to leave your service."

Thorne snorted. "Has your sudden wealth made you dissatisfied with living in this household?"

"Not at all, Your Grace. It has been my pleasure to serve you and Her Ladyship these past four years. But I have missed my music."

Thorne frowned. If he admitted it to himself, he would miss the company of this fine man. "But I've allowed you to give lessons. Isn't that enough?"

"With the money from my father, I thought to open a music shop as well as continuing with the lessons."

Lady Sarah beamed across the table at him. "A splendid idea. I'm sure there are shops in London where you could rent a space." The smile deepened. "And court Mistress Rill more freely, I have no doubt."

Thorne felt torn. On the one hand, he was pleased that Dobson could make an independent life for himself. But he was losing a friend, a man with whom he had shared the most meaningful experiences in his life. "See here," he said impulsively, "eighty pounds is scarcely enough to start your new venture. I propose a gift of a thousand pounds. That should get you started."

Dobson's blue eyes narrowed. "I couldn't accept it, Your Grace," he said in a tight voice. "I may be your inferior, but I have my pride."

Thorne dropped his gaze. "Forgive me, *Cleve*. I offered as a friend. For I should like to maintain our association once you're settled in London. Will you accept my money as an investment?"

Dobson relaxed. "To be paid back when I have established myself, milord."

"Of course. And you must call me Thorne."

"No." Dobson shook his head, though Thorne could see that he was pleased their relationship would change. "Not until I've left your service. I have my standards. I will, of course, find you another valet before I go." He looked meaningfully at Thorne, and then at Lady Sarah. "And must I train him as a go-between?"

Lady Sarah stared at her son. "What do you think, John? We've done quite well this evening, speaking directly to one another."

Thorne hesitated. A sudden vision of his father, lying cold and dead in his coffin, flashed before his eyes. "Yes, Dobson, I think the new man should be properly trained."

His mother rose from her chair, tears welling in her eyes. She stumbled to the door, then stopped. "Will you not be satisfied until you've quite broken my heart?" With a sob, she fled the room.

Cleve stood up, frowning, and bowed formally to Thorne. "By your leave, Your Grace," he said coldly. "Allow me to go and comfort your mother." At the door he turned. "Circumstances have broken your heart. But the unhappiness in this household is of your doing alone. I find that unfortunate in a man who wishes to call me friend."

He was out the door before Thorne could find an angry response, leaving him sputtering in outrage at his servant's effrontery.

But a small finger of self-doubt scratched at his gut, wondering what Gloriana would have thought of his cruelty to his mother.

Chapter Sixteen

The March wind whistled around the stone corners of Baniard Hall, rattling the windowpanes and shaking the trees outside, but within the snug parlor a blazing fire from the hearth warmed the room. A large round table, pulled close to the fireplace, was comfortable enough to seat Grey and Allegra and their guests.

Gloriana carefully poured out a cup of tea and handed it to the elderly woman who sat across from her. "Your tea, Lady Mary. Just a touch of cream, as you requested." She acknowledged Allegra's smile of pleasure with a nod of her head; they had spent several busy hours together this week, as Allegra patiently and kindly instructed Gloriana on the niceties of presiding over the tea table. Lord and Lady Sewell, Shropshire neighbors, were the first guests invited to the Hall since Gloriana had returned home.

Lady Mary took the proffered cup and saucer. "Thank you, my dear," she said. "How nice to be cozy on such a blustery day." She sighed. "I fear spring will never come."

Gloriana shook her head. "Oh, but I saw a few crocuses popping up next to the garden wall on my walk this morning. And the lilacs have begun to bud. You mustn't be…" She searched for one of her newly learned words, "… melancholy. Spring will soon be here."

Lord Sewell reached over and patted Gloriana's hand. His aging fingers were dry and wrinkled, but his touch was warm with sincerity. "I like your spirit, young woman. For my part, the chill weather makes me sleepy."

Allegra laughed. "It seems to affect my dear sister-in-law the same way. After her walk, we had to rouse her to come to the dinner table."

"Indeed." Gloriana hoped that the smile she had pasted on her face wouldn't betray her. "All I wanted to do after my walk was curl up with a warm coverlet and sleep. I felt chilled to the bone." In truth, she knew exactly why she had become so sleepy these past three months. She was clearly pregnant with Thorne's child. It had been difficult to hide her condition from Allegra, to pretend she was simply not hungry when her stomach grew queasy; she was grateful at least that she'd been able to vomit in private on her morning walks.

Lady Mary clicked her tongue and wagged a reproachful finger at Allegra. "For shame, Lady Ridley. Your brother's widow is surely the most charming and lovely woman I've met in many an age. To keep her to yourself all this time. How could you?"

Lord Sewell harrumphed. "Now, now, my turtledove…"

She glared at her husband. "Do you deny she is beautiful? Gracious?"

"N-no, of course not," he stuttered.

"Then why should she be hidden away, like a precious flower under a rock?" She gave Gloriana a motherly smile. "How old are you, my dear?"

That caught Gloriana by surprise. "I'll be twenty-one in April."

"Humph! 'Tis time to find you a new husband. You and your lovely little boy need someone to take care of you."

Lord Sewell wrinkled his nose in distaste. "Really, my nightingale, you go too far."

Lady Mary pursed her lips and shook her head, the lappets of her cap bouncing against her rosy cheeks. "I *will* play matchmaker, husband. I can think of any number of fine young men who would be suitable. Our own grandson, perhaps." She stared pointedly at Grey and Allegra. "I think I shall have a small assembly in April to celebrate Lady Gloriana's birthday. Do you have any objections?"

Grey frowned. "'Twould only be fitting for Allegra and me, as Gloriana's kin, to hold an assembly for such an important milestone in her life. Though I appreciate your generous offer—and I know my lady wife shares my opinion—Baniard Hall should properly be the site of the festivities." He turned to Gloriana. "What is the date of your birth?"

Gloriana's head was spinning from the sudden shift in the conversation. They had been speaking about the weather, the London season—sharing simple pleasantries, topics that were safe and non-threatening. Suddenly they were discussing her future as though she were invisible and had no say in the matter. "The... the fourteenth," she stammered.

Grey tapped the table. "Then it's settled. Nearly a month

to make arrangements." He raised a questioning eyebrow to Allegra. "That is, if you're agreed, madam."

She gazed tenderly at him. "With all my heart," she murmured.

Lady Sewell smiled bravely, clearly trying to hide her disappointment at the usurpation of her own plans. "As you wish, milord. But will you allow me to help you with the guest list, at least? Edwin and I spend far more time in the city than you do. I can think of any number of eligible bachelors."

"Just a moment." Allegra raised her hand in protest. "We're being quite thoughtless. 'Tis all well and good to make plans, but we haven't even asked the lady herself if she would like to celebrate her birthday in such a public manner." She turned to Gloriana. "What do you say, Sister?"

Gloriana closed her eyes for a moment. Did she feel ready to preside over a hall full of strangers, to smile and laugh and pretend that any other man would suit her after Thorne? Surely, after such an official introduction to society, she would be expected to go to London, to allow a host of men to court her, to choose one for a husband. Despite her newly acquired social skills, she wasn't sure she could endure such a rigorous routine, so different from the gentle life she had been leading since coming back to Baniard Hall.

And yet... sooner or later, she would want Billy to have a father. And, more importantly, she would need a father for the child she was carrying. How long before her flat belly began to grow, betraying her, exposing her and her beloved family to scorn? The sooner she found another man and married, the better it would be for all of them. "I think a party for my birthday would be lovely. Thank you, Grey. As for you, Lady Mary, I dub you my official matchmaker. Find me a suitable man and you will be invited to the christening of our first child." She lifted the plate of sweet cakes in front of her and held them out to the older woman. "Now, will you have another biscuit?"

She had married Charlie to give her son a name. She was strong enough to marry another man to give her unborn child a heritage. As for love, she was done with it. Thorne had taught her that it was a dangerous emotion, like a poisonous serpent eating away at her soul.

• • •

The heady aroma of April lilacs massed in large vases against the wall of Lady Cooper's large drawing room was almost overpowering. Thorne frowned in vexation and fidgeted in his chair. He didn't want to be here, didn't want to be back in London. He missed his forge, and the sight of the assembled guests, so many of whom had been his false friends during his years of riotous living, now merely annoyed him. He nodded mechanically toward several former comrades, then turned to his mother with a tight smile.

"If it weren't for Cleve," he said in a low voice, "I'm damned if I'd sit here for another minute."

"Oh, don't be an old crosspatch, John," she said with a gentle laugh. "You know you're as proud of him as I am."

"True enough," he confessed. He wasn't happy to be in the city, but at least he'd had the chance to see Cleve Dobson again and cement their growing friendship. The man had been a whirlwind of activity since the night they'd discussed his future in Surrey. In less than a month, he'd come to London and found a suitable shop for his music business as well as his lessons, a compact space with living accommodations on the floor above. With the loan from Thorne, he'd purchased a goodly number of instruments, tastefully arranged on the shelves, and hung a discreet sign over the door: *Music Shop, C. Dobson, prop.*

He had interviewed half a dozen candidates for the position of valet to Thorne, finally settling on Rowland, an older man who had served several London gentlemen of note. Thorne found the man pleasant enough, and properly deferential, though somewhat set in his ways. He still couldn't quite manage the business of intermediary between Thorne and his mother, which had produced a few tense moments in their recent encounters. By mutual consent, they had agreed to a truce this evening, leaving Rowland back at Havilland House, and had managed to converse in a civil manner since arriving at Lady Cooper's home.

In London, Dobson had sought out his old musician friends, and held a few concerts in his shop, which had brought him to the attention of the gentry. Lady Cooper's assembly this evening was the happy result.

Thorne looked around the drawing room, noting that people were beginning to fill more and more of the chairs lined up in rows to face the small platform on one side of the room, which held a harpsichord and three chairs, each with a musical instrument waiting on its seat. He turned to his mother. "It shouldn't be long now."

"I never asked you. Did you spend a pleasant afternoon with Cleve today?"

Thorne chuckled. "We had a jolly time. The food in the tavern was good, and we had many memories to laugh about. I hope to see a great deal of him while we're in London.

I think I shall value his friendship more and more as the years roll by."

"I'm of the same mind. True friendship rests on the ability to share the deepest secrets of your heart. And I suspect your months with him in Whitby were some of the most meaningful times of your life. I think... Oh!"

Thorne frowned at his mother's startled cry. "What is it?"

Lady Sarah fanned herself with agitated fingers. "Lord and Lady DeWitt just came in," she whispered.

"Felix and Penelope? Gads! I'm not sure I want to see them."

"Too late. Felix has seen us and is coming over here." She gave her son a motherly scowl. "Do try to be pleasant, John."

"I have no quarrel with the man. As to the harpy he married..." Thorne rose from his chair as Felix approached them. He nodded a greeting, and even managed to hold out his hand. "Felix," he said. "You and your... wife are well?"

Felix bowed to Thorne's mother. "Lady Sarah. Thorne," he murmured, accepting the proffered handshake. Then he sighed deeply. "As well as can be, under the circumstances." He leaned in close to Thorne's ear. "I don't much like the woman," he muttered softly.

Thorne glanced briefly at Penelope, who had found chairs next to a young couple, and was chatting gaily with them. "She seems to be happy enough, and glad to be here."

Felix snorted. "In truth, she didn't want to come. But I... persuaded her."

Thorne suppressed a smile as he saw Penelope settle into her chair, wincing slightly as she did so. "I'm sure you did. In your own inimitable manner." He nodded again and regained his seat. "You must rejoin your wife. I'll wager the music is about to start."

"Hah! I'll wager that that's the first bet you've made in months." Felix shook his head. "I miss you, friend Thorne. The gaming at Belsize simply isn't the same without you."

"I regret, for your sake, that I've turned over a new leaf. But..." He shrugged. "Now go to your wife. It might be awkward if she comes here to fetch you."

When Felix had gone, grumbling as he crossed the room, Lady Sarah giggled. "Never have two people more deserved each other." She pointed with her fan to a door that had opened near the platform. "But it looks as though the musicians will be coming out in a moment. And see! There's Cleve. And he's with Mistress Rill."

Thorne frowned. "But they seem to be quarreling." In truth, he had never seen Martha Rill look so miserable. She pouted and wiped at her cheeks as Cleve spoke to her, his brow furrowed in anxiety. "She's usually as sunny as a spring day."

"Indeed. We shall have to ask him when the concert is over."

The guests grew quiet as the musicians filed into the hall and took their seats, Cleve at the last, plodding to his place as though the world rested heavily on his shoulders. Mistress Rill turned about and flounced to the door that led to the vestibule and the street beyond. *A very serious quarrel*, thought Thorne sadly. He had never seen Cleve looking so dejected.

The concert was pleasant enough, but Thorne was distracted by his concern over Cleve. The man lacked his usual enthusiasm, even during his flute solos. Thorne burst with impatience, waiting to question him about the direction of a growing courtship that had, up until now, seemed to be going smoothly.

But when the small orchestra began to play a delicate minuet, Thorne's thoughts turned unexpectedly to the night he had danced in the garden with Gloriana. They had been one person in two bodies in those moments, joined with a strong thread that seemed to connect his heart to hers. He felt an odd twinge of anger that surprised him. After that night, and their joyous reunion in Newgate, how could she have been so unfeeling as to believe Penelope? How could she have doubted his love for a moment? And to leave for America without even speaking to him, allowing him to explain...

His mother tapped him on the wrist with her fan. "Are you so displeased with the music that you must frown so, John?" she whispered.

He forced himself to smile weakly and shook his head. But he had to acknowledge his anger at Gloriana. If he admitted it to himself, he couldn't quite forgive her for her lack of faith in him.

The concert was over. The assembled guests applauded politely, then began to rise and move toward an adjoining room, where supper had been laid out. Thorne gestured toward Dobson and patted the empty chair next to him. "A fine performance, Cleve," he said with enthusiasm, when Dobson had joined them.

"Thank you, Your... *Thorne*," Dobson said in a lackluster voice.

Thorne eyed him with sympathy. "I can see that this evening didn't bring you as much pleasure as you gave to this company. May I credit the disappearance of Mistress Rill for your unhappiness?"

Dobson sighed. "You may. If you must know, I've heard from my father again. With another large bank draft from which I shall be able to pay back your generous loan."

"And that makes you unhappy?"

"Alas. His generosity is not without intrigue. He complains again about his failing health. And his need for someone to help him manage the plantation."

Thorne shook his head. "Perhaps he should have been the musician. Playing upon the strings of your conscience."

"Yes. I fear his next missive will be a direct plea for me to join him in Ceylon."

"And Mistress Rill is not amenable to that."

"I fear not." Dobson rose from his chair. "Well, allow me to leave you and find her if I can. I've scarcely made up my own mind on the matter, but she is so unalterably opposed that it's difficult for me to make a reasoned decision."

Thorne watched him go, then turned to Lady Sarah. "The poor man. In the years I've known him, I've never seen a woman turn his head the way Mistress Rill has. Ah, well." He held out his arm. "Supper, madam?"

The moment they entered the tea room for supper, Thorne knew that something was wrong. He had heard the buzz of conversation as they approached the door, but the whole room seemed to fall silent as he led his mother toward a table. And he distinctly heard a snicker from Felix, sitting in a corner with several mutual friends.

Lady Sarah frowned. "Something is amiss."

"Indeed. Is my periwig askew?"

"Of course not, John. You look fine." She waved to a couple sitting to one side. "Look. There are Lord and Lady Latham. Shall we sit with them?"

They crossed the room to the table. Thorne was aware that many eyes followed their progress. He smiled at the Lathams. "May we join you?" he asked, scarcely waiting for their reply to hold out a chair for his mother.

Lord Latham stood and bowed in deference to Thorne's rank, then regained his chair as Thorne and his mother sat down. "You are well, Your Grace?" he asked.

Thorne quirked a smile in his direction. "Unless I've suddenly grown horns." He indicated the guests, who had begun to buzz amongst themselves again. "Have we missed the latest gossip? I see Lady Singleton has come in."

Lady Latham blushed, while Lord Latham suddenly found a speck of lint on his impeccable velvet sleeve.

"Well?" demanded Thorne.

Lord Latham cleared his throat. "Well," he began reluctantly, "we are all wondering if Your Grace, so noted for your wild wagers, intends to make another bet."

"Concerning what?"

"The... the Lady Gloriana Baniard."

Thorne nearly choked on his anger. Was he never to live down that shameful episode? "'Twas a foolish wager," he snapped. "An insult to an honorable lady. I was only too happy to concede my defeat. Why should it matter now, after all these months?"

"Because the lady has come home. She is even now at Baniard Hall in Shropshire, with her kin."

Thorne struggled to hide his shocked surprise, though he kept his hands in his lap to keep them from shaking. She was *here*? In England? He said nothing, fearful that his voice would betray his roiling emotions.

His mother rescued him. "Why shouldn't she return

home?" she asked with an airy laugh. "She owed it to her family, to ease their fears. What is so extraordinary about that?"

Lord Latham snorted. "If I were her kin, I'd be filled with recriminations for burdening them with months of scandal and grief. Instead, Lord and Lady Ridley are celebrating her return—and her birthday, if I understand the gossip—by holding a large assembly at their country home."

Lady Latham gave Thorne a waspish smile, twisted with malice. "And Lady Mary Sewell has agreed to serve as matchmaker, inviting a dozen eligible London bachelors to come to Shropshire and pay court to the lady." The smile deepened to a grin of pure vindictiveness. "Have you received your invitation yet, Your Grace?" Thorne clenched his jaw, stifling the string of curses he ached to hurl at these vile creatures.

Lord Latham, all smug confidence, was clearly enjoying Thorne's discomfort. "The company this evening has been speculating on whether Your Grace intends to make another wager. 'Tis too late to *find* the lady, but..." He shrugged. "I shan't continue, out of respect for the ladies."

Thorne jumped to his feet and held out his hand to his mother. "Come, madam," he growled. "It would seem that this evening's company is too low-minded for our taste." A proud smile on his face, he guided his mother to the door, accepted his cocked hat from the footman, and waved to his waiting carriage on the street. But once settled onto the plush seat, he sagged in misery.

Damn her to hell, he thought. She had stayed in England, and still had not found the generosity of heart to send him a message. And to accept suitors with such haste, as though their months together had meant nothing to her?

He would need a great deal of Madeira tonight to wash away the bitterness he could almost taste at her complete betrayal.

• • •

Thorne drained the wine from his glass and hastily poured himself another. No matter how much he drank, he couldn't ease the pain and anger in his heart. He had taught her to be a lady, to be self-sufficient and confident—and she had repaid him by accepting Penelope's lies without question. He hated her.

He glared at the nearly empty decanter and hurled it toward the hearth, where it smashed into a dozen pieces and sent up a tongue of flame from the last few drops of liquid. That made him feel better. He glanced around his sitting room, his eyes lighting on a collection of antique China vases on a side table. With one sweep of his arm, he cast them to the floor, grimacing in pleasure at the loud crash.

The door flew open. Lady Sarah and his valet Rowland burst into the room. "Dear God, John, what is it?" exclaimed his mother.

He hated her. He hated Rowland. He hated the whole damned world. He turned to Rowland with frosty eyes. "Kindly tell my mother I wish to be alone."

Rowland smiled uneasily. "Milady, His Grace wishes to be alone."

Lady Sarah shook her head. "To wallow in self-pity?"

"Tell my mother 'tis none of her concern," said Thorne, his eyes narrowing.

Rowland sighed. "His lordship says 'tis none of—"

Lady Sarah stamped her foot to silence him and pointed to the door. "Rowland. Out!"

"But milady…"

"Out, I say!" When the valet had slunk from the room, she slammed the door viciously behind him and whirled on her son. "Now, John, you may be too foolish, or addled with wine, to answer me, but you *will* hear what I have to say."

He sneered at her. "And should I believe you? I might have learned by now. Women are liars, deceivers."

"But surely not your Gloriana."

"Why not?" he said bitterly. "Was her faith in me so shallow that she could not come to me with Penelope's story? She said she loved me, and now she looks for suitors. How am I to reconcile that? I have my pride."

Lady Sarah snorted. "Indeed you have. And what of *her* pride? You made a vile wager against her honor, deceived her into trusting you. And then Penelope did her worst. Can you fault Gloriana for thinking that you view her with contempt? When you made your wager, you thought she was a whore. A common creature, beneath your station."

That shamed him. "I… I learned differently," he stammered.

"And if she *had* been a whore? It would have been out of necessity, to put food on the table. Was your whoring more virtuous? Yes, you're a man. Society views your *amours* with an understanding eye. But you took pleasure in casting aside your women through the years. Did you ever wonder how those ladies you jilted felt about your betrayal?"

"Now, madam," he growled. "You go too far."

"I only wanted to remind you that you're scarcely a

creature of virtue. And filled with overweening pride. Oh, John," she said, patting his arm with a tender hand. "'Tis your infernal pride that keeps you from going to her. That woman is the best thing that has ever happened to you. I've watched you change and grow these past months. My heart has burst with gratitude for a woman I've never even met. She has turned you into a man of strength and compassion. Is she not worth swallowing your pride?"

"I can never forgive her."

Lady Sarah bit her lip and closed her eyes for a moment. "Does it never end?" she whispered. "Will your father cast his shadow eternally over you?"

"You dare to speak of him?" he shouted. "*You?* Who betrayed him?"

She sighed. "You are much like him. A good man. But equally blind. Unforgiving. And self-righteous in your pride."

"Get out," he said ominously.

"No. You will hear me out. Once and for all." She pointed to a chair. "Sit you down."

Something in her steely manner touched a chord within him, reminding him of the mother he had known and revered for years—until the day he had found his father's body. He sat as she directed.

"Now," she said, taking a seat near him, "I don't ask you for understanding. Only to listen." She reached out and took his hand in hers. "To begin... though our marriage was arranged by our families, I loved your father."

His mouth curled in a sneer and he pulled his hand away. "You had a wonderful way of showing that love."

Her brow furrowed in anger. "'Twill be time enough for your usual rude comments when I'm done."

He turned his head aside, unwilling to look her in the eyes. In all the years that he had treated her cruelly, he suddenly realized that she had seldom spoken an unkind word to him. "Your pardon, madam," he said quietly. "Please continue your story."

"I think your father loved me, in his way. Though not enough to be faithful."

He jerked up his head in surprise, but said nothing. He remembered the many times his father had gone to London alone, leaving them in the country. His mother would mope and sigh until her husband returned. He had always supposed that her sadness was due to loneliness. Not grief at his father's infidelities. "Why did you never complain? Rail against him?" he said at last.

She shrugged. "I had a good life. I had you. And friends aplenty. And he was good to me. Kind and thoughtful and generous. He did love me, even if that love had to be shared with others. I persuaded myself that it was enough." She gave a heavy sigh. "But as the years went on, our life together became empty and stale. We were like two automatons, going through the motions of a marriage, acting our parts with no more passion than mechanical creatures."

"I never saw any of that," he murmured.

"You were not meant to. We played the part for you as well as for the world at large. But love had died in this house. I felt as cold and empty as though I were in my grave." She stood up and glanced around the room. "Do you have more wine, my dear? This is difficult for me."

He jumped from his chair and hurried to a sideboard, pouring two glasses of sherry and handing one to her. "Please go on."

"It was then that I encountered a childhood sweetheart. He swept me off my feet. Made me feel loved and needed again."

"And so you ran off with him." Thorne was surprised that he had uttered the words with no anger or condemnation, suddenly aware of the unhappiness that must have driven her to her rash decision.

"It was a disappointing affair, but it made me realize I could love again. I knew with a certainty that what I'd had with your father was more real and precious to me than the illusion of happiness I'd shared with a man I scarcely knew. I came home and begged your father to forgive me. I fell on my knees and pleaded for his understanding, for the opportunity for us to start afresh." She took a large swallow of her sherry, placing a hand on her breast as the liquid burned into her.

"I remember his anger when you were gone. But why did he take you back?"

"Because of his pride. His fear of society's scorn, should the truth be known. But that same pride couldn't unbend. Couldn't accept my contrition. He nursed his bitterness like a wound, a wound a child displays with mixed sorrow and joy."

"Joy?" Thorne was incredulous at the word.

"Indeed. He reveled in his misery. Willingly embraced his dark moods. I was devastated by his refusal to reconcile. And then when he..." She fought back her tears. "I've lived with regret since the moment you found him in his bedchamber."

Thorne took a moment to digest her story, seeing his long-held notions vanish like the morning mist. Then he clasped his mother's hand in his and raised it to his lips. "And

I've lived with anger, casting you always as the villainess. Forgive me."

"My dear boy, I thank you for that. More than words can express. But as for you, don't make your father's mistake. False pride is cold comfort. The woman may hurt you. But you're a gambler. Isn't love worth the risk?"

He hesitated, dreading to see scorn in Gloriana's eyes.

His mother puffed in annoyance. "In the name of all that's holy, have I raised a fool for a son? Swallow your pride and go to her!"

He ran his hands through his hair, torn with indecision. In the silence, his mother strode to the mantel and rang for a servant.

In a moment, Rowland appeared at the door. "Your Grace?" He glanced at Thorne and then at Lady Sarah. She raised a questioning eyebrow to her son.

Thorne squared his shoulders. "Pack my bags," he ordered. "And alert the coachman. We travel to Shropshire on the morrow."

Rowland bowed politely and left the room.

Thorne turned to Lady Sarah, his heart filled with the sharp pang of regret. "I have wronged you for years, Mother. I beg you to forgive me."

She sighed. "I should have told you long since, I suppose. We might have been better friends all this time. But perhaps my years of loneliness were my penance for the pain I gave your father. And you."

He looked at her with fresh eyes, seeing—as though for the first time—that she was still a handsome woman, trim and elegant. She could have found another man to love. To marry. Instead, she had lived a solitary life, with only a carping son for company. "Why did you never re-marry?" he asked impulsively.

"My conscience never gave me a moment's peace."

"And why did you never tell me the whole story?"

She gave him a rueful smile. "Shame, I suppose. I too have a bit of the Havilland pride."

He pulled her up from her chair and wrapped his arms around her. She sighed and nestled into his embrace, then drew back and took his face in her hands. Her eyes were filled with tears. "My dearest boy," she whispered, then kissed him softly on both cheeks.

"Gads," he muttered. "I think I've been a fool for half my life. To have kept you at a distance for so many years."

She gave a tremulous laugh. "I scarce have my son back, and now I'm losing him to another woman."

"If God wills it," he said fervently.

"Go, my foolish, lovesick boy. And Godspeed."

Chapter Seventeen

"Milady, you look beautiful." Verity pinned the amethyst brooch to the bosom of Gloriana's lavender gown, patted it into place and stepped back to admire her handiwork. "And such a lovely gift from Their Lordships for your birthday."

Gloriana glanced down at the pin in pleasure, then smoothed the folds of her figured silk mantua. "Thank you," she murmured. "They have been so kind to me." She gave her maid a smile, filled with sincerity. "As have you all."

"Oh, milady, we are so glad to have you home again. I'm sure that little Sir Wil... *Billy* missed you terribly." She handed Gloriana her fan. "Will you go down now?"

Gloriana turned at the sound of a sharp rap from outside her bedchamber. Verity crossed the room and opened the door. Barbara stood on the threshold, a sour grimace on her face. She gave Gloriana a half-hearted curtsy, then turned to Verity with a frown. "Are you quite finished with your fussing and primping? The guests are growing impatient."

Honey, not vinegar, thought Gloriana. Despite the girl's

insolence, she smiled graciously at her. "If you please, Barbara, can you not contrive to be more cheerful as you go about your duties? You mar your lovely face with your constant scowls. And it brings no honor to this household when you show your displeasure to all."

Barbara stared in surprise, clearly not sure if she was being complimented or scolded. She gulped in confusion, then sank into a deep, respectful curtsy. "I shall try, milady," she murmured.

"Thank you. Please inform Lady Ridley that I shall be there directly."

Allegra greeted Gloriana as she swept down the broad staircase that led to the formal drawing room. She held out her arms. "You look beautiful, Sister." They embraced warmly, then Allegra giggled and pointed to the drawing room door, beyond which came the sounds of a happy, laughing crowd. "Are you prepared to meet your adoring public? And the eager suitors who will, no doubt, swoon at the sight of you?"

Gloriana gave her a stiff smile. "Of course." After her success at the Whitby assembly ball, she no longer feared the disapproval of a large company, even one with titles and manners far beyond the experiences of her humble upbringing. But the thought of meeting men who wished to marry her, to smile at them, encourage them... It still brought a lingering pain to her heart, a wound that never seemed to want to heal.

Allegra lifted her chin with soft fingers. "You're still thinking about him, aren't you," she said in the knowing tone that always surprised Gloriana. "Will you ever tell me who he was?"

She sighed. "It scarce matters now. He taught me to be a lady. And then he broke my heart." She squared her shoulders and moved toward the door. "I'm ready now."

A footman nodded as she entered the room, and pounded the floor with the large staff in his hand. "The Lady Gloriana Baniard," he announced solemnly. His words were greeted with applause and scattered calls of congratulations on her birthday. Grey moved forward to take her by the arm, and he and Allegra escorted her around the room, introducing her to the guests as they encountered them. Gloriana noted the scores of young gentlemen as they passed, each one eager to bow to her, to compliment her beauty, to kiss her hand. Lady Sewell had clearly been up to her task of matchmaker.

Since Baniard Hall was too small for a large assembly room, one side of the drawing room had been given over to dancing and another portion set aside for a clump of small tables and chairs. Gloriana was besieged with invitations to dance from the gentlemen, and she accepted with grace, even managing to flirt with the ones she found promising. Grey and Allegra smiled from their seats, clearly pleased with the success of their carefully planned event.

The evening was going well. Gloriana thanked the young baron who had just danced a lively reel with her, declined an invitation to the next dance that had begun, and moved toward Allegra and Grey, fanning herself vigorously. She took the empty chair next to them and smiled. "'Tis a lovely party. I thank you," she breathed, still winded from the dance.

Grey acknowledged her thanks with a contented nod. "'Twas our pleasure. To see you so happy, enjoying—"

He was interrupted by the thump of the footman's staff

at the door. "John Edward Michael, His Grace the Right Honorable Duke of Thorneleigh," he intoned. At his words, the music died, all conversation stopped, and every eye turned to the door.

Gloriana gasped, feeling the blood drain from her face. It couldn't be! Yet there was Thorne at the entrance to the drawing room, standing proud and elegant.

"I'm damned," Grey muttered. "What the devil is that man doing here?"

Allegra put a gentle hand on his arm. "Hush, Grey. The gentleman is a guest in our house. And a personage of rank and stature. We must greet him properly."

Grey rose from his chair and impatiently signaled the musicians to play again. Then he and Allegra moved toward Thorne, almost dragging a reluctant Gloriana with them. Thorne bowed in greeting and received an icy nod from Grey and a more gracious curtsy from Allegra. Gloriana refused to bend her knee and merely glared at Thorne, her jaw clenched in fury.

"Your Grace," said Grey in a frosty tone.

"Lord Ridley. Lady Ridley. Forgive my intrusion. An uninvited guest."

"You are most welcome, milord," said Grey, though his eyes were cold. "What brings you to Baniard Hall?"

Thorne gave Gloriana a hopeful smile, as though nothing unpleasant had ever passed between them. "I had heard of the happy return of your sister-in-law. And many stories of her charm and beauty. I wished to see for myself."

Grey's voice was colder still. "Ah, yes," he said. "I recall a rumor. Something to do with your reputation as a gambling man. And a wager involving Lady Baniard. I give you my word, milord, if I had been able to confirm the rumor, I would have sought you out and left my glove in your face."

"Grey, please!" whispered Allegra.

Thorne shook his head. "No, Lady Ridley. His Lordship has a perfect right to be angry. 'Twas a foolish and cruel wager. I regretted it the moment it passed my lips. I was happy to concede the contest and pay off my opponents. An insult to such a lovely creature. If I can be forgiven, I should like a formal introduction to the lady. For she surely does not disappoint my expectations."

Grey nodded. "I accept your apologies, Your Grace, in the generous spirit in which they've been extended. Now, may I present to you the Lady Gloriana Baniard? Sister, this is John Havilland, Duke of Thorneleigh."

Thorne bowed deeply to Gloriana, his grey eyes searching her face, his mouth curved in a tentative smile. "Your Ladyship. I can scarce express my pleasure in seeing you here." He held out his hand, which Gloriana ignored. Only when Allegra prodded her with an elbow did she manage to curtsy to him.

How did the rogue have the effrontery to appear here? "Your Grace," she muttered sourly.

"I've longed for this moment," he said, his voice deep with sincerity. "To see you face-to-face. You're a pearl among women, to be treasured." His eyes held a silent plea.

"But milord, from what I've heard, you collect women on a string," she said in a scornful tone. "You have pearls aplenty. What need you for more?"

"Perhaps I've found fidelity to be more satisfactory. I only need one woman in my life now."

Curse the villain, she thought. One woman to marry. And

one for a mistress. She gave a mocking laugh. "Of course. And how is your lady wife?"

He snorted. "If you refer to the Lady Penelope Crawford, she is not my wife, nor ever shall be. She has proven herself to be a creature of deception. And lies," he added firmly.

"But you yourself are scarcely a stranger to lies and deceptions. Or so I've heard."

Grey cleared his throat, clearly disconcerted at the ugly tone of their conversation. "Come, come. This is not the time nor place for such serious discourse. We celebrate the Lady Gloriana's birth tonight. Will you take a turn around the room with me, milord? It would be my honor to introduce you to our guests."

Thorne shook his head, his earnest gaze turned to Gloriana. "No. I should prefer to dance with the lady. They've begun a minuet." He held out his hand. "Will you favor me, milady?"

Not bloody likely, she thought. "Alas, milord," she snapped. "I should prefer not."

Allegra clasped Gloriana's wrist tightly and pulled her away from the two men. She had been oddly silent throughout their hostile exchange, her searching eyes darting from Thorne's face to Gloriana's. She stared pointedly at Gloriana, her voice soft yet firm with resolve. "Don't be a fool," she whispered. "You *must* dance with him. Or regret it for the rest of your life."

Gloriana sucked in a sharp breath. *She knows*, she thought. In that magical way that still astounded her, Allegra could read into people's hearts, see the secrets buried there. "Do you really think so?" she asked softly.

"I do. The evening may end joyously for you. Or bring

you grief. But I think there's a door waiting for you that must either be opened or closed once and for all, if you're ever to find peace." She led Gloriana back to Thorne and placed her hand in his. "Your Grace, I give you my dear sister. I charge you with her happiness this evening."

Thorne's smile was filled with relief as he guided Gloriana to the other dancers. They bowed and began the minuet. They danced in silence for a few awkward minutes, avoiding each other's eyes as they pointed and turned. Then Thorne looked her full in the face. "You have to know that Penelope lied," he burst out. "I never intended to marry her."

"A pox on you. She had your ring."

He puffed in exasperation. "A keepsake. Merely given in friendship and thanks. She nursed me back to health after my encounter with Royster."

"I'm sure you welcomed her at your bedside for all those weeks," she sniffed, turning her back on him in the pattern of the dance.

"Sweet Jesus," he muttered, swinging her back to face him. "Gloriana, I came to the inn with a ring that day. I intended to ask you to marry me. To be my duchess. How could you have gone without waiting to speak to me? How could you have believed her lies?"

"Your duchess? You want to marry me, now that I can pass as a lady? The whore you always thought I was?"

"N-no," he stammered, clearly abashed. "Not after..." He stopped and took a deep breath. "I wanted to ask you to marry me the night of the assembly ball in Whitby."

"You can say that now, milord. But your presence in Whitby was founded on a pack of lies. How can I believe you now?"

He gritted his teeth. "You impossible woman! I came here in all humility to beg your forgiveness, and I'm greeted by the harridan I first encountered in Yorkshire."

She stopped in mid-step and drew herself up. "I will not tolerate such impertinence, even from such an exalted personage as Your Grace."

He bowed stiffly. "Thankfully for us both, the dance has ended."

Gloriana shot him one last lingering glance of scorn and began to move away. Just then, the young baron who had danced with her before sidled up to Thorne, smirking as he came near.

"Too late, Thorneleigh," he crowed. "You've long-since forfeited the right to court the lady, having tried to besmirch her reputation with your cowardly, vulgar bet. Unless you intend to wager with me on whom she will favor this evening."

Gloriana gasped. She knew Thorne well enough to be horrified. Surely his pride would never allow such an insult.

Thorne whirled to the baron, his eyes burning with rage. "You craven excuse for a man," he said in a loud voice. "I'll wager I can knock you out of your shoes with one blow!" He held up his fists. "Would you care to take up my challenge?" He turned to the guests who had begun to crowd around, drawn by the quarrel. "Would anyone care to give odds on my making short work of this milksop?"

Grey rushed forward, followed by an alarmed Allegra. "See here, Your Grace, this is not Belsize. We do not wager in this house."

Thorne hesitated, then took a steadying breath and lowered his hands. He bowed deeply to Grey. "Forgive me,

Lord Ridley." Then he smiled wickedly, as though an odd thought had suddenly flashed into his mind, and turned to Gloriana.

Bloody hell, she thought, remembering how impulsive he could be. *What is he up to now?*

"If you'll permit me, milord. One simple wager tonight. With the Lady Gloriana, if she'll accept my challenge."

Gloriana gave a proud toss of her head. "Which is… what, Your Grace?"

"I shall best you at arm-wrestling."

Ignoring the shocked looks on the faces of the guests, Gloriana snickered. The man was mad. She had always bested him. His few months of work at the forge were scarcely a match for her years in the ring. "Not bloody likely," she muttered.

"I'll chance it," he said. "'Tis worth the risk."

"You go too far!" Grey cried. "To overpower a woman with your greater strength… I'll not countenance it here."

"I'm left-handed. I intend to use my right arm. That should make us more equal."

"I shall not permit it! I—"

"A moment, husband," said Allegra softly. She gave Gloriana a knowing smile. "What say you, Sister?"

Gloriana didn't want to refuse until she could learn what Thorne was thinking. "I should like to know what the stakes are."

"If I win, you must agree to marry me. Posthaste."

She laughed sharply. "Truly the most peculiar courtship in the history of the sexes. And if you lose? I am not compelled to marry you? I see no benefit for me in the wager, since I don't wish to marry you in the first place.

There must be a forfeit. If I risk losing my independence to you, there should be some sacrifice for *you*, if I win."

His smile dissolved into a somber frown. "If you win, I shall sign over to you my title and my fortune, only keeping out enough to maintain my mother whilst she lives. And I shall become a country blacksmith."

At his words, the cluster of guests gasped in surprise or turned to one another in shock. "Surely you jest, Your Grace!" said Grey in alarm. "Are you prepared to lose all?"

Thorne's eyes never left Gloriana's face. "If I must." He waved his hand in Grey's direction. "I give you my oath on that."

Grey moved toward Thorne, clearly prepared to stop him. But Allegra clutched her husband's arm and whispered frantically in his ear. Grey's angry expression softened into a smile. "I leave the decision up to you, Sister."

"Then it's settled." Gloriana nodded and moved toward a table. "Let us begin."

Thorne peeled off his coat and tossed it on the back of a chair, then rolled up his sleeve. He held out a chair for Gloriana and took the seat opposite her. The guests tried to crowd around the table, but Grey motioned them back.

Gloriana planted her elbow firmly on the table and scowled at Thorne. "You're a fool," she said softly. "You had best resign yourself to a life of poverty, milord."

His eyes were dark and troubled. "Without you at my side, I shall live in poverty, whatever my circumstances."

They clasped hands and began to strain against one another. As Gloriana had surmised, her hard-toned arm muscles were still stronger than Thorne's. He grunted with the effort, struggling to force her arm onto the table, but she could feel her superior skill wearing him down.

He looked up at her, his eyes soft and pleading. "I love you, Gloriana," he panted through clenched teeth. "More than life itself. I shall die if I can't have you."

I'm the fool, she thought, hearing the sincerity in his voice. She had never stopped loving him, and he had risked humiliation to come here, to challenge her in a manner that would earn him scorn and mockery from society for the rest of his life, if he should lose.

Tears sprang to her eyes. With a sigh, she relaxed her pressure against his hand and allowed him to force her arm to the table. He stared in surprise, then grinned broadly.

"But you've lost on purpose," cried a nearby gentleman.

"No," she said, smiling up at him. "I've won."

Thorne jumped from his chair and pulled her to her feet, wrapping her in his embrace. He turned to Grey and Allegra, who had begun to clap happily. They were soon joined by the other guests. "In the name of pity, Lord Ridley," he said over Gloriana's head, "find us a place where we can be alone."

Grey handed Thorne his coat and swiftly ushered them to a door. "Beyond this door and the next, there's a small sitting room." He laughed. "Thanks to my lady wife's intuition, I think I can guess where—or at least with whom—our dear sister spent last summer and autumn."

Thorne could scarcely wait to close the door behind them before he pulled her into his arms. His mouth sought hers in a burning kiss that reawakened all her old passions. She wrapped her arms around his neck, glorying in the thrill that ran through her body. At last he broke away and led her to a large divan. He lifted her and laid her across the cushions, tossing her heavy skirts above her hips. He tore at the buttons of his breeches, exposing his manhood, poised and waiting.

"Sweet Jesus," he muttered. "How I've ached for you." He bent to her and planted soft kisses on her neck, pulling down her shift to expose her breasts. She moaned in pleasure as he suckled at her nipples. Then, impatient to feel him within her, she clutched at his member and guided it to her burning core. But instead of the hot, passionate lovemaking that was their usual fashion, he entered her gently, gliding softly in and out in a manner that made her feel loved and cherished as well as desired. Only at the last did his thrusts increase in intensity. They climaxed together, crying out in the rapture of their union.

He gathered her into his arms. "My sweet," he murmured. "I love you so much I could barely exist for the wanting of you."

"And I love you," she whispered, her voice choked with emotion.

He raised his head, a quizzical expression on his face. "Then why, in the name of all that's holy, were you so difficult tonight?"

"You taught me to be proud," she replied. "To value myself. And when… that woman told me you wanted me for your mistress, while she would become your wife, I hated you. 'Twas difficult to let that hatred go tonight."

"Forgive me again for Penelope. I was a fool to trust her."

"And I was a fool for not trusting you more. To accept her lies without question." She sighed. "I wish her well. But I can never forgive her."

He chuckled. "Alas. She is already reaping the rewards of her perfidy in an unfortunate marriage."

She sat up and began to straighten her tousled clothing and smooth her hair. "I must look a fright."

Thorne buttoned his breeches and rolled down his sleeve. "You look adorable. Every man will envy me when we return to the drawing room." He stood up, shrugged into his coat, and put his hands on his hips. "And speaking of other men, is it true what I've heard? That you were planning to choose a husband from amongst the suitors tonight?"

She turned away. She hadn't wanted to tell him like this, but she had no choice. "I saw no other way," she said. "I'm carrying your child."

He cried out in joy and lifted her in his arms. "Oh! You wondrous woman. I knew you were meant for me from the first moment I saw you."

She snorted. "All covered in sweat, a hammer in hand that first day in Whitby?"

He chuckled, then took her face in his hands and kissed her gently on the mouth. "No. I was here in Shropshire last spring. Visiting a friend. I went for a midnight stroll and thought to take a swim. But a vision on horseback surprised me. So I climbed a tree."

She gasped. "Burn and blister me. You were the bloody Peeping Tom!"

He smiled ruefully. "Guilty as charged. That's why I made the wager. Went off to find you. I couldn't forget you after that night. I think I loved you from that moment forward." He reached out and straightened a curl on her shoulder. "I think we look presentable enough." He patted his pocket. "No. Wait." He hooked a finger into the pocket and brought forth a large emerald ring. "I almost didn't bring it. I was so fearful you'd reject me. But my mother was more optimistic, and insisted. You'll like her, by the way. And she'll adore you." He kissed her softly. "As I do."

That warmed her heart. She'd never had a mother.

Thorne dropped to one knee before her and held out the ring. "Gloriana Cook, will you marry me? And be the mother of many children?"

She laughed. "We'll start with two. My Billy and…" She patted her belly. "And yes, of course I'll marry you." She allowed him to slip the ring on her finger, then raised a quizzical eyebrow. "Did you mean what you said? That you'd give up everything if I refused? And become a blacksmith?"

"I did indeed. As for smithery, I've been working in a forge in the country. You'll be surprised at how far I've advanced." He stood up, buttoned his coat, and smoothed his breeches. "We should be getting back. They'll be wondering where we are." He held out his arm. "Milady?"

She slipped her hand through the crook of his arm, being careful to hold her fingers so that the guests would see the ring the moment they entered. Thorne opened the door to the drawing room and ushered her through. At once, the assembled guests began to clap, the gentlemen bowing deeply and their women dropping into respectful curtsies.

"Bloody hell," whispered Gloriana. "I'm not your duchess yet."

He slipped his arm around her waist and smiled down at her, his eyes warm with love and devotion. "With or without a title, you are what you've always been in your heart. A lady." Then he shot her a lopsided grin, filled with pride. "*My* lady."

Dreams so Fleeting

Born the illegitimate daughter of a great French nobleman, Ninon knew only a harsh life of cruelty and hardship. It wasn't until the dashing Count of Froissart, Philippe, whisked her off to a different world did she begin to have hope for a better future.

But she soon learns her new life isn't void of misfortune. A slave to both his powerful title and an unbreakable marriage vow, Philippe's love remains just beyond Ninon's reach. Could she dare give her heart to the handsome and cunning rogue, Valentin, instead?

Gold as the Morning Sun

Seeking to ease her ailing father's mind as his body fails him in his final days, Callie Southgate agrees to marry the mail-order groom sent to her from back east. When she meets her husband, she is timid around the handsome but mysterious man. But when they marry, she finds passion she never knew in his embrace.

Jace Greer, a con-man and bank robber, is given the perfect opportunity to start over when the stagecoach carrying a mail-order groom is ambushed, leaving Callie's future husband dead. Taking on the deceased man's identity as his own, Jace continues to Callie's home in Colorado with the hope of leaving his murderous past behind him.

But as true love blooms between Jace and Callie, secrets Jace tried to keep buried begin to surface, threatening their futures—and their lives.

The Ring

Prudence Allbright believes Lord Jamie's declarations of love—so much so that she vows to follow him to the Colonies. It is onboard the ship that will take her to him that she meets the honorable Dr. Ross Manning, and a flame of passion ignites.

Ross is determined not to defile the memory of his late wife, but night after night he longs to hold Prudence in his arms. When Prudence discovers Jamie has already gone back to England without her, Ross knows he may have only one last chance to claim Prudence as his own. But can love stand against the secrets of Prudence's past?

Summer Darkness, Winter Light

Allegra Baniard is an independent young woman who lives for only one thing—revenge. Her family had been branded traitors and banished from Shropshire. After eight years, she returns incognito to the ancestral home of her once-noble family, vowing to avenge her family. But when she meets Greyston Morgan, the new owner of Baniard Hall, he ignites desires inside of her that burn as hot as her fiery rage.

Caught between her own love and hatred, Allegra must decide whether to destroy Grey, or surrender to the flame of passion between them.

The French Maiden Series

Marielle

Armed with only a disguise and her wavering courage, Marielle Saint-Juste goes on a perilous mission to free her brother from unjust captivity. But when she enters the prison of Louis XIII, it isn't her wounded brother she finds, but a mysterious stranger—and her destiny.

In this French dungeon, a love illuminates the darkest shadows in two hearts. Marielle will not only face her deepest fears, but change her life forever.

Lysette

Lysette, the Marquise de Ferrance, is left penniless after her husband dies. With nowhere else to turn, she ventures across the turbulent French countryside to the safety of her brother's home. But when she meets Andre, Comte du Crillon, her plans change. She cares not that he's married; using her beauty as her weapon, she sets out to seduce him.

But little does she know, there's another man in her midst, waiting for the perfect time to take her for himself. It is in his arms that Lysette is destined to find that true love and sanctuary she seeks.

Delphine

Unable to deny the attraction that simmers between them, Delphine and Andre fell willingly into one another's arms on their long journey from Canada to France. But after an impassioned night, come morning, the ship has docked, Delphine wakes alone, and Andre has fled.

Scorned, Delphine soon finds herself determined to avenge her broken heart. But a love that will not be denied soon gets in the way of her journey to vengeance.

Printed in the United States
by Baker & Taylor Publisher Services